TEA LEAVES

A SHORT STORY COLLECTION

BY
JACOB BUDENZ

Amble Press
2023

Print ISBN: 978-1-61294-275-9

Amble Press First Edition: September 2023

Printed in the United States of America on acid-free paper.

Cover design: TreeHouse Studio

Amble Press
PO Box 3671
Ann Arbor MI 48106-3671

www.amblepressbooks.com

Several of the stories in this collection have been published previously in slightly different formats.

"Under Her White Stars," *Broken Metropolis*, Mason Jar Press, 2018.
"Seen," *I Did Not Break the Lamp*, Mad Scientist Journal, 2019.
"Houseguest," *Gllitterwolf Magazine: Halloween Special*, *Glitterwolf Magazine*, 2015.
"And Then Again to the Next," *Issue 06*, *Wizards in Space*, 2021.
"Deadbeat," *Baffling Magazine*, 2020.
"The Girl the Crows Followed," *Corvid Queen*, 2019.
"Ah, Well," *Mirror Dance*, 2019.
"Tea Leaves," *Gingerbread House*, 2019.
"Trial," forthcoming by Lycan Valley Publications, 2023.
"A Theory on Lampposts," *Potluck Magazine*, 2014.

TABLE OF CONTENTS

For all the queers and mystics and fairies and witches who only ever wanted to be seen.

SEEN

When I opened my eyes a little wider and tilted my head just so—to see, really *see*—I noticed the fairies dancing between the floorboards of my bedroom. Have you ever passed by a painting every day without actually looking at it, and then just once, by chance, you take it in and realize all this time you've been walking past something shocking, like a painting of an angel sodomizing an alien, all along? You feel intrigued, but also kind of violated, when you think of how long the image has been slipping itself into your subconscious. Seeing the fairies felt like that, like maybe I'd been glancing at them out of the corner of my eye for my whole life. I watched the tiny glowing bodies dance in the ridges of the teal-painted hardwood, little naked, winged creatures all colorful and aglow like Christmas lights. I could've stared at them all morning if I hadn't had to go to work.

Once I saw them I couldn't stop seeing them, of course. They were everywhere, from a family of four in the orchid on my coworker's desk (her cubicle always overflowed with over-the-top gestures from her fiancé) to three little blue men playing in the urinal like it was a goddamned water park.

When I mentioned my groundbreaking revelation about the fairies to Janet, the receptionist at work, she rolled her eyes and said (of all things), "Where the fuck have you been, Ronnie?"

But when I shrugged and walked off (I think she liked to

call me "Ronnie" instead of "Ron" just to get under my skin), I glanced behind me to see her squinting at my back like I'd sprouted bat wings, and I didn't buy her shtick for a second. No, sir. She'd been acting all snarky and too-cool ever since she'd tried to set me up with her "gay best friend" Enrique. Oh, yeah, she'd given me the whole line, *He's just so sassy and funny like you,* and I'd said, *You know not all us fags are a perfect match by virtue of the fact that you know them, Janet. Anyway, some of us are happier being alone.* It was a petty thing to say, sure, and I was lying through my teeth about preferring to be alone. Still, I had my pride. Anyway, if this Enrique had helped her pick out even *one* of her tacky, ill-fitting skirt suits, then he was as tasteless as she was, and I wanted no part. Honestly, I don't even know why I mentioned the fairies to Janet in the first place. I'd just sort of blurted it, eager to share the knowledge with someone, to share something new and exciting with another human as I had so little occasion to do. Obviously the wrong move.

I typically preferred to take my lunch break off-site, alone, lest I got stuck talking about marketing data during the hour we got to eat. Today, though, I brought lunch in a sad plastic bag to eat in the undersized kitchen on the fifth floor, to see if any of my coworkers talked about the fairies. It would finally give me *something* to talk about with *someone,* for once. I was getting lonelier and lonelier, less and less able to form relationships with the people around me, when the fairies showed up. When I brought my sad, soggy ham sandwich to the lunchroom (another reason I prefer to buy lunch off-site), I thought that if other people saw the tiny glowing creatures, maybe the universe was giving me a way to burst through my bubble of isolation, to soothe my quiet, aching loneliness. I waited until Janet left the lunchroom, because who knew what kind of passive-aggressive humiliation she'd try to subject me to if the topic came up?

I was cautious this time, waiting to see if the topic of fairies came up organically. After forty-five minutes nobody said a word about them, nor did anyone seem to notice the wild antics of the little pink lady dancing lewdly around the rim of Jerry's bowl of tomato soup. Nope. Instead, spreadsheet horror stories consumed the majority of the conversation—precisely why I don't eat lunch with these people. Even Leslie from HR, with her funky hair colors and ayahuasca retreats and transformative experiences at "regional burn" festivals, acted oblivious. I didn't have a chance to bring it up, since after halfhearted mumbles of greeting nobody so much as looked my way the entire time.

By the time I had to clock back in, I felt too embarrassed at how diligently my coworkers ignored me to speak up. Was seeing the tiny glowing bodies so common an experience that nobody cared to talk about it? Had Janet whispered my revelation to the others and brought them in on some sick vengeful joke? Were they fucking with me? Either way, I was no closer to finding out what the fairies really were and whether they might have any real impact on our lives, and I was *certainly* no closer to figuring out how to find common ground with anyone vis-à-vis these weird creatures. Evidently, after all my working up the nerve to sit with these half-strangers I worked with, I was too bland for even my fellow marketing analysts to notice whether I ate with them, or not too bland to make them pause and listen to the sparkling world I'd grown so eager to share.

That night, my kitchen was so packed with little purple ladies dancing rave-style over the black-and-white linoleum that I had to tiptoe ever so slowly across the floor. The purple tide dodged my footfalls effortlessly, without disrupting the ecstatic convulsions of their tiny limbs. Of course they did. They'd been dodging my feet for years, surely, without my oblivious ass of a self having the first clue that they were there.

I poured myself a shot of honey whiskey, slugged it back. Poured myself a half-full glass and bent over so I was eye-level with the black granite counter, upon which several fairies (mostly green or yellow) were having an orgy. "Here's to you,"

I said. I raised the glass like we were all having a toast, like we were all friends. Of course I already knew they weren't listening. I knocked that one back pretty quick as well, practically in one gulp. Poured another glass over ice.

Hazy, I plopped down on the foamy couch in the living room and sprawled out, laptop on my belly. I typed "people who can see fairies what does it mean" into Google, because why the hell not? I scrolled for a while through various fairy enthusiast forums and a site called Witch Vox, but it was all fables or superstitious mumbo-jumbo or hippy spiritual shit. I scanned through legends about the dangers of entering into fairy rings (apparently this is just Not a Thing to Do), others about how to leave gifts out for the "fair folk" so they'd leave you alone or bring fortune on your household or bring back your changeling child or whatever (like, what kind of a fucked-up parent tries to write off their child's developmental issues as their kid being an actual, real changeling?). I wasn't finding anyone who'd actually *seen* the fuckers.

"What the hell are you?" I shouted at the pink man and green lady languishing on the coffee table like they were sunbathing. Figures in profile, the fairies didn't even turn their heads. Even the damned *fairies* ignored me! I might have been the only person on the face of the planet who could see the goddamn things, and they wouldn't give me the time of day. It figured. What else was new?

About an hour (and two more honey whiskies) later—in that sweet spot of drunken exhaustion where I was too tired to get up and drag myself to bed—I stumbled across a thread on the r/Fairy "subreddit" titled, "DOES ANYONE ELSE SEE THOSE TINY GLOWING FAIRY PEOPLE EVERYWHERE? I FEEL LIKE I'M GOING CRAZY." Yes, as it turned out. There were others of us, *many* of us even! My sleepiness melted away. My heart thudded, though I still felt thick with sweet liquor. I read the original post, by a user named

Julianax89, clung to every word and didn't even balk at the awful grammar:

"OK this is going to sound CRAZY and im probably gonna DELETE this but has ANYONE ELSE been seeing like these fairy people all over the place like just doing their thing??? idk how to explain it, i feel like last week something like kinda clicked in my brain and now i just cant stop seeing them ALL OVER THE PLACE, and my girlfriend doesnt see them and she thinks im just tripping, like i use to microdose acid for my anxiety but i even STOPPED bc of the fairies, i havent REALLY gone on like an acid trip or anything in forever. thoughts?"

The time stamp was three years ago. My chest felt like it was expanding, like I was on one of those massive tower rides and it was about to drop. With the exception of one heavily downvoted comment from a user named [[chaosmagick666]]—"Yeah, you probably just took too much acid. It's too late for you now."—scores of users were replying in earnest. The first, catLover900: "Mother of two here. I started seeing them when my second boy was born. Seems like he sees them too, never thought of them as fairies but I guess that makes sense."

I scrolled through, eating everything up. Theories were made: aliens (of course), ghosts, demons, travelers from another dimension. Nothing conclusive, or all that convincing, and after the third theory (evidently inspired by X-Men) about how we must all share some evolved genetics and how we ought to band together to use our power for good but we had to be careful about exposing it to the world lest people fear our mutant gifts and persecute us (like . . .?), I began to get bored with these theories. No, what interested me more was people meeting and talking about it. Reddit users sounded off in various cities. Something like fairy support groups formed. People planned to get together, one-on-one or in groups, depending on the number of fairy-aware individuals in their area.

Common ground! It seemed like a surprising number

of people identified somewhere on the queer spectrum, felt the need to insert their queer identities or queer relationships into their comments somewhere. It was like those guys at the "LGBT-friendly" group therapy (read: all white gay men) who feel the need to slip something in about "how hard it is being a single gay man," and you think, oh my god, you're cruising this group therapy session, aren't you? On Reddit, though? Blame it on the Tumblr millennials, I guess—identity's gotta be a part of everything. In my whiskey-swirled state I thought, god, all this on a Reddit thread, this tiny public pocket hiding out in the open on the internet, untouched by anyone who wasn't looking for it. What else out there was I missing? Elves? Sea monsters? God, as if taking my shirt off at the beach wasn't stressful enough already.

I was getting tired again—slipping away. I hit Control + F and searched the page for the word *Seattle,* just to see if anyone was in my area so I could call it a night. One match, in a comment by a user named mitchthepainter: "Anyone here from Seattle want to meet up? This has been driving me crazy. Glad to know there are others though."

Time stamp: two years ago. Nobody had replied to him.

My hands shook when I went to comment, which signaled to me that I hadn't had enough to drink: I was still that nervous to reply semi-anonymously to someone's comment on a Reddit thread. Was I really that pathetic? Even if the username indicated that person was a guy, and the trend of the thread seemed to imply he might be queer. Anyway, I slugged back a shot of Evan Williams—this was a practical shot, an anxiety-dulling shot, so I didn't bother with the honey whiskey—and the mostly green fairies, still having their orgy on my kitchen counter, god bless 'em, stared up at me in unison. Did they understand? All that alcohol, all that time on my computer, just to type a two-sentence reply, still a little nervous: "I live in Seattle. Just started seeing the fairies, if you're still interested in meeting up?"

God, looking back on it now, I was already setting myself up for rejection: *If you're still interested in meeting up?* With a goddamned question mark. But what if he didn't use Reddit anymore? What if he didn't want to meet up to talk about the fairies anymore? Couldn't see them anymore? Had a boyfriend (or worse, a girlfriend)? Was dead? But that last shot of Evan Williams was hitting me, and I decided that the comment wasn't enough. I clicked on his username, "mitchthepainter," clicked the "send message" link, titled my message "Fairies in Seattle." What ensued was a message I'd rather not repeat in its entirety. A brief preamble about my recent discovery of the fairies. My name, phone number, and (just in case) my rough schedule. I puzzled over a way to convey that I was also a single gay man without coming on too strong, or presuming that that would matter to him and/or had anything to do with why I was messaging him, or whatever. I settled on (and I don't know why the hell I thought this made any sense at the time), "With PRIDE, Ron." What did I tell you? That wasn't even the worst of it.

I fell asleep on the couch, with my clothes on.

Aside from some fairies sitting in a campfire-esque circle next to my keyboard at work, as well as a dreadful honey-whiskey hangover, it was as if the previous night had been a dream. The waking up in my rumpled clothes, on my couch. The dead phone, its alarm failing to wake me up in time for work. The text to my boss when I recharged it—"Running behind, family crisis kept me up really late, so so so sorry"—and that sluggish scramble to get ready for work as quickly as possible without upsetting my mammoth of a headache. I'd stayed up until god knows when because I thought my life might change, what with this fairy nonsense, this discovery that there actually *was* something special and different about me *and* that there were others out there, others who understood and who were therefore connected with me, inextricably, by this shared fact. But when I woke up that morning, everything was still the same—I was still alone, and I was no closer to being any less so, except that I'd messaged somebody on Reddit who'd probably never read my message to him, and if he did, who cared? It wouldn't change anything.

I got to work two hours late and avoided Janet's eyes when I walked past her desk.

"All work and no play, huh?" she shot at my back like a poisoned dart. "Blame it on the fairies, Ronnie?"

I droned through data all morning. Chugged bottle after bottle of water and excused myself to the bathroom every twenty minutes and watched my acid yellow piss progress to clearer and clearer shades. I tried to convince myself that my headache was improving, that I was feeling better.

My phone buzzed while I ate lunch at the tavern down the street. It happened just as I bit into one of those "hangover cure" burgers with the over-easy egg on top, and all I thought was, *What now?* Then, the unfamiliar area code, the text: "Hey, this is Mitchell from Reddit." I froze, phone in one hand, burger in the other. Egg yolk dripped onto the plate and made a yellow puddle. Promptly, two red fairies hopped onto my plate and began to roll around in the fallen yolk.

It took me the entirety of lunch to respond. I took bites of my messy burger, alternating between ravenous hunger, hangover nausea, and of course anxiety over what to say to Mitchell. Yesterday, un-hungover, I would've marveled at the fairies glowing inside the bottles of liquor that lined the shelves behind the bar, some twirling and flipping like showy little mermaids, some still and placid, floating in the alcohol like embryos. Now, I was glaring at them—they were far less charming after drinking heavily on a weeknight. How to reply to Mitchell? Cutting straight to "let's meet up" might read a little desperate (we were meeting via the r/Fairy subreddit, not OKCupid, after all), but I was the worst at perpetuating text message small talk, always allowing conversations to fizzle out before getting to the big "when are you free?" moment. I felt sick. Was it the burger? It was probably the burger.

When I shuffled out of the tavern toward my office, the sun's harsh whiteness mocked my headache. "Hi Mitchell," I typed. "Ron here. How did you first notice them? What was it like? I feel like I have so many questions for you."

That felt right. It implied "I have so many questions for you that it might require a date." A date? *I* didn't say it. Out loud.

When I sat back down at my desk, I read his infuriatingly noncommittal reply: "Ask away." Okay, fair enough. So we were doing the dance. Did I detect a little coyness?

But then, he surprised me by sending *another* message, a long text:

"To answer your question, I was working on my master's thesis, spending a lot of time in the studio and whatnot. Probably sleep deprived, not eating enough . . . But it was way different than any experiences with psychedelics . . . I felt really clear. I didn't feel delirious or anything. But honestly, I had to keep painting in that moment. Art school fucks with you, you get so busy. Bombs could be going off and you'd basically take your canvas to the bomb shelter . . . You know? So then until I finished my thesis, they just faded into the background. It was only after I graduated that I really started to process it."

If I wasn't stunned by the double message, I was floored when he sent a *third* text after that one: "That was a lot, huh? Sorry, I've just never talked to anyone about this."

I distracted myself from my Mitchell-anxiety by doing my actual work, and then I distracted myself from my work by entering his phone number into Facebook to find his profile (you used to be able to do that, you know, and in case you were wondering, he had one of those inscrutable profiles where all you can see is the profile pictures, and they're all stills from obscure cartoons, close-ups of bugs, Karl Marx's face covered in the rainbow flag, etc. But the rainbow flag was promising?). Myriad fairies sat watching me from atop my desk, the rim of my cubicle, the edge of my computer monitor, my keyboard. They just sat, staring, like they were at a movie theater, minus tiny fairy popcorn. They all sat still except the ones on my computer keyboard, who dove out of the way when I went to type something but reclaimed their spots as soon as I lifted my hands.

I went for it. After sending my next two texts (and receiving five responses in return), I told him that we should probably really get together in person—that we had so much to talk about.

Mitchell was short, with clipped dark curls and a thick, well-kept beard that featured the occasional white hair. He was the only customer in the tiny "pop-up" coffee shop (a white-walled, minimally decorated affair), sitting at one of the only two white Ikea tables. He must've known it was me looking nervously about, because he said my name, jumped up, and hugged me. At six feet, four inches, I tower over most people as it is, but Mitchell's cheek pressed just under my left nipple when he hugged me, which suggested he was definitely below average height. It was an odd choice on his part, hugging me, but his body was warm and his embrace was enthusiastic and it was an overcast, cold March day outside, and goddammit, wasn't it true that I hadn't been touched in . . . how long? He pulled away. He sported a blue flannel shirt and genuinely worn-looking jeans (not those "distressed" jeans you pay a lot of money for). And, yes, when he turned to take his seat I *did* notice that the jeans, though loose-fitting, hugged a surprisingly meaty ass. God, how thirsty was I? I mean, it wasn't even clear whether he was actually gay. Anyway, we weren't on a date. We were just two guys meeting up to discuss the fact that we could see these tiny glowing fairies that the majority of the population couldn't see.

I got a cappuccino. Why not?

"I'm so excited to finally meet you," Mitchell said when I sat down. His voice was deceptively deep for his height, and his eyes darted around the room as if he was in awe of everything around him, just taking it all in, overwhelmed by the curvy silicone lampshade on the ceiling, titillated by the bare white walls. There weren't a whole lot of fairies at this joint for him to be looking at either, so I assumed he was just bad at the whole eye contact thing.

Mitchell told me he was a visual artist—a painter, mostly, though he dabbled in some "sculptural work" and "installation."

"So you make sculptures, too?" I said. "That's really cool."

"Not exactly," he said with the patient tone of someone who's answered this question a hundred times. "Not like you'd think, anyway, not like marble sculptures of really toned men with small penises. They're more like, I guess, you know, abstract experiences with light and various materials, usually a lot of steel wool and I guess I've been really into breaking mirrors and coating them in colored resin and making these, you know, it's almost like this sort of gesture toward stained glass, but not so representational; I mean more influenced by postmodernism and, sort of like, futurist movements. You know?"

I did not know, but I nodded emphatically as if I did. Resisted the urge to make a "that's a lot of bad luck" joke about the mirrors. Instead, I said, "Do you ever paint the fairies?"

"God, no. That would be kind of . . ." He gave me a look of sympathy, softened his tone. "I don't know, I always felt like that would be sort of pedestrian, you know? Painting fairies. You know, something so obvious."

"Oh, right." I said. "Of course."

"I mean, I do love the *Pressed Fairy Book,* you know that one? Totally genius. I have the twentieth anniversary edition. I'll show you sometime. They look nothing like the real thing, of course. But the fairies do show up in my pieces occasionally, though. I mean sometimes I make really subtle references, you know, little specks of pink and green light on a landscape instead of fireflies—not that I paint like *landscape* landscapes, but I have some shape studies in, like, I don't know, I'm really interested in marshland and sort of portraying the bog in this minimal but kind of fantastical sort of way sometimes."

"Right."

We both took awkward whose-turn-is-it-to-speak? sips from our respective mugs.

"So what is it you said you do, though?" he said. "Ron." Like he was trying to remind himself of my name so he wouldn't forget it.

"I didn't," I said. "I didn't say. I'm, uh, I'm a marketing analyst."

"No shit!" Mitchell let out a single, low bark of laughter. There was a little blue fairy on the rim of his mug. He put his short, calloused index finger against the rim, and the fairy danced onto it, shocking me. He touched his finger to the table, and the little creature walked daintily onto the white surface. It began to twirl.

I must've been staring, and maybe my mouth was open (can neither confirm nor deny), because Mitchell said, "Oh man, you didn't know you could do that?"

"No!" I said. "Other than avoiding me when I walk through their dance parties, it seems like they don't even notice me. Like they see right through me until I'm in their way."

"They definitely notice you," he said, and he looked up directly into my face—for the first time since we'd sat down—like he knew everything about me, like he was talking about something other than fairies. "You just have to interact with them like you believe they'll respond. You won't get their attention if you don't."

I gulped, froze, didn't know what to say. He'd said it like he saw straight into me all of a sudden, like he knew my problem wasn't getting just the fairies to notice me.

"I guess even the fairies want to be seen, huh?" I managed, weakly, feeling naked.

He smiled on an exhale, with teeth, and shook his head, but it was like the affirmative I-can't-believe-this kind of head shake and not the well-actually-not-quite kind of head shake, and he relieved me of the pressure to speak any further about it. "Oh, there's all sorts of cool things about them. Man, this is so exciting. You have so much to learn, you know? You're like a, I don't know, I don't want to say 'a blank canvas' because that's a little on the nose, but we have *so much* to talk about, you know? I've been paying so much attention to them, writing observations in a journal and whatnot." He repeated, "We have so much to talk about."

I nodded and forced a smile, but I wasn't so sure at this point. I was starting to feel like he'd been without a captive audience as long as I'd been without a steady boyfriend (read: the entirety of my adult life), and now that his floodgates were opening, there wasn't a whole lot of room for anything else. Guys like Mitchell, once they ran out of things to say, they realized guys like me weren't all that interesting, or hip, or arty. God, fairies or not, why had I thought meeting this guy would change anything? He might as well have been straight (and his sexuality still wasn't completely clear to me)—we were light-years from having anything in common.

"Marketing analyst," he went on. "That's cool, though . . ." He pointed his head down, then up at me again (at least he was trying). "Hey, look, there's one on your shoulder."

I twisted my head, and he was right, my god! The white mug I'd been holding clattered against the little plate it came with. Foam sloshed over the rim, but no real damage was done. The uninterested barista glared at me for just a second before returning to whatever it was she was doing on her phone.

I dabbed at the foam on the table with a napkin and swallowed a sigh.

"You know," Mitchell said. "You're actually really pretty cute."

I was so taken aback that I *almost* didn't notice his awkward-as-ever phrasing, and I tried to squash down the suspicion that he was being backhanded as opposed to not knowing how to deliver a genuine compliment. I hated myself a little bit for the way my stomach pitched and my chest fluttered. Was that really all it took? To go from *uncertain-he's-even-gay* to *he's-gay-and-thinks-I'm-cute-so-maybe-there's-a-chance*? God, I was pathetic.

"Thanks," I said weakly. I didn't look up from the foam spill I was still blotting up, even though I'd already sopped up all the rogue cappuccino.

"I mean it," he said. "But I mean, you knew that already, huh?"

I wouldn't meet his gaze, which was probably darting all over the room anyway. I was too afraid I would see sympathy. "I guess, I don't know. I don't really fit into any of the traditional gay . . . types, you know? I don't really fit in with the whole *scene.*"

He perked up at that. "Really? Me neither. I have a really hard time with most gay men. Too, I don't know, vanilla, I guess? Or maybe I'm just, you know, too weird. I wonder if anyone really does? You know, fit in with them?"

"Oh, I could think of plenty who do off the top of my head. Not that I'd remember their names. Or anything else about them. I mean, not much to remember, am I right?"

And then he was laughing. And, goddammit, it felt good to make him laugh. Okay? It did. He had a satisfying belly laugh, a real guffaw, the kind that was a little too loud, maybe a little irritating to anyone that wasn't in on the joke. And I was mugging a little bit. Sure, it was true I didn't fit in with most gay people. But it was less that I found them boring or forgettable and more that I had enough trouble fitting in with most people, and gay men—with their cliques, and their laundry lists of "preferences" boiling down to whiteness and/or physical fitness, and their need to put a label on every kind of homosexual—could be the toughest cookies to crack. Still, it's a well-known fact that all gays like to talk shit on "the scene," even those who are, as it were, totally immersed in it. Everyone seemed to agree: the gay scene was too shallow, too "normative," too judgy, too *whatever,* and guys like Mitchell, cooler-than-thou art guys, straight-passing guys, they always turned out to be, secretly, the judgiest of them all on this topic.

Incredibly, though, he didn't take the bait.

"Yeah," he said. "I mostly keep to myself these days, you know? I don't really date anymore. It just sort of got to be a deal breaker when someone couldn't see the fairies, you know? It's really, I don't know, it gets to be kind of alienating after a while. I guess you'd think it was all of us, you know, you'd think it was just maybe a gay thing in general, but I feel like maybe it's not really that many of us that can see them. But I guess you wouldn't know about any of that yet." He touched my wrist from across the table. "Since you're new to this, and all."

So, the sex with Mitchell. It was kind of awkward and not great, but we both really tried, *you know?* For one thing, I'm not so much beefy as I am freakishly tall and a little out of shape, but the thing about having even the hint of a gut if you're gay, in my experience, is that people want you to be a hairy, roughhousing, hyper-masculine "bear" type, or an emasculated "total bottom." I was neither. I had skinny arms, and all the hair I had on my abdomen and chest was a light dusting of wispy blond, and despite my generally large presence I wasn't gonna shove some guy around and ravage him like he was Helen of fucking Troy—in other words, definitely not the bear anyone's looking for. I'm kind of a soft touch. So I think Mitchell got sort of *bottom* vibes from me right off the bat, which is also not generally the case if I've just met somebody. I mean, I'm not going to let a veritable stranger put his dick inside of me, especially if that stranger hardly comes up to my chest standing on his tiptoes. So when he was going down on me he kept doing that thing where he'd try to coax my thighs apart with his free hand and get a couple of fingers up in there, but I was shut like Fort Knox, thank you very much. Neither of us had a particularly energetic touch, two gay guys in their late twenties who had fallen out of a fitness routine and were maybe not *super* wowed by each other's bodies, but I don't know, I still feel like we were both pretty into it?

I will admit, I was relieved to find that Mitchell, despite his petite stature, had a little bit of a paunch himself, that his torso looked a little slimmer in well-fitted flannel than out of it. And he gave pretty good head. I don't know. And when he finally came, he was polite enough to warn me, polite enough not to do so in my mouth without asking, and that was kind of cool. Whatever, I guess it was really nice to be touched after all this time, okay?

When we'd both finished, Mitchell was resting his scratchy beard on the softness of my left pectoral (this was the postcoital ritual I hated most—two men, covered in rapidly drying semen, pretending that the small amount of heart-fluttery satisfaction that cuddling provided had the *potential* to outweigh the ickiness of sweat and sperm drying on the flesh). It was then I noticed for the first time that *they* were in the room with us. They stood perfectly still in a circle surrounding us (Mitchell had a king-sized bed, of course, despite his size). Just looked on, expressionless. I was generally used to seeing the fairies in a state of perpetual motion, merriment, lewdness, mischief. Heart smacking against my ribs, I sat straight up, and Mitchell recoiled with one of those startled *uh* sounds. I'd spiraled far enough down the search engine rabbit hole the other night to know a thing or two about fairy rings, about falling asleep inside them, getting trapped in their world and kidnapped for god knew how long. I leapt off the bed.

"Are you okay? What just happened?" he said. He sounded vaguely irritated, but his brow was pinched in what could have been genuine concern.

"Don't you see them? Mitchell, get out of there! That's a fairy ring. Oh my god, oh my god." I leaned over and grabbed his arm, trying to pull him off the bed to safety. I thought this to be a heroic gesture, risking falling into the fairy ring and being trapped there forever with him.

But Mitchell didn't budge. Instead, he let out an actual, real belly laugh.

"Fairy rings aren't really a thing." He waved his hand around the room. "They're just a bunch of perverts is all. Far as I can tell, at least." He sat up and kissed me on the cheek.

It was Saturday, the following day, and I was lying in my bed watching reruns of *Twin Peaks* thinking how glad I was that we'd gone to Mitchell's place and I'd seen he was at least as messy as I was. Honestly, I didn't really expect him to reach out to me after that. Heady art queers like him didn't usually get excited about guys they might perceive to be mainstream, guys with nine-to-fives that fed into the "horror of modern capitalism," guys that were guilty of an even worse sin—being boring. And if he did reach out to me (I felt like Mitchell was the kind of guy who'd want to text first, though the lines were always blurry with gay men on who should reach out to whom), I wasn't sure how likely I was to respond. Sure, he seemed more or less normal, and surprisingly sweet, especially for an art queer, and wasn't there a certain charm to the way he seemed to start his sentences with no obvious plan for how they would end? But at the end of the day, he was an artist, likely hiding layers of emotional instability which he'd tout as the wellspring of his creativity. Or he'd be one of those "monogamy is a hegemonic tool that upholds the systemic oppression of queer people" types. Either way, a headache. Right? It wasn't worth it, right?

He waited an acceptable amount of time to reach out to me (around three in the afternoon, approximately six hours since I'd left his house). His message: "Hey, hope your Saturday is great! :) I had a really great time with you. I was wondering if you'd want to get together again soon? XO."

I looked up at the fairies perched atop my television set, gossiping to each other in a long row of orange light. I considered what they might be saying, wondered if maybe Mitchell might know how to listen. I vacillated. If he didn't know, wouldn't it be nice to lie around with someone who was equally confused? Did it even matter what they were saying? I looked back at my phone. I had a hard time believing he'd actually had a good time (okay, so it was not the absolute worst as first dates went, I guess, maybe?). A harder time believing I had the upper hand in this moment. The uncertainty implied in his question mark, the overall sweetness of his message—they weren't lost on me.

I regarded the fairies sitting on my TV and thought about what Mitchell had said, about addressing them with the confidence of someone who expects a response. I did my best: "What do you guys think? Is this 'Mitch the Painter' guy all right?"

And, amazingly, the fairies on my TV turned to me in unison, whispered among themselves and, finally, each gave me what looked like a thumbs up.

The cynical part of me wants to say that the fairies put some kind of spell on me. But probably it was merely the presence of another who could see them, who was willing to see me and hear me and respond to me even when I hadn't believed anyone would. If he was right about how to get through to the fairies, maybe he was right about, well, maybe we really *did* have a lot to talk about. Is this what settling looks like? Whatever, I don't know. At any rate, I picked up my phone, made to tell him I was free that very night. Decided that would sound too eager. Waited a whole five minutes so I didn't look desperate.

I responded, "I'm free tomorrow if you are, or evenings during the week."

OF THE AIR AND LAND

Perhaps it was beneath the spirits of the air and the land and the water and the mud to intervene in the lives of Hailey and Ainsley, two white women who co-owned a Southern fusion food truck, but when spirits go on living even after those who see them have been driven away, when the world goes on believing instead in single, all-knowing gods or in the movement of the planets or in the world as a simulation or in nothing at all, such beings begin to grow bored. With little else to do then, they agreed almost unanimously it was for the women's own good.

They'd formed the plan two months before the big day, after a phone call from an anxious bride-to-be who sighed with relief upon finally receiving an answer.

"Hey," came Ainsley's breathy voice, tiny and tinny through the receiver.

"I'm so sorry I've left, like, four voicemails," began the bride-to-be, "and I know things are super up in the air now that you and Hailey . . . well, you know—I mean, I was just calling to say that Zoe and I love your food and, like, of course if one of you wanted to, say, just do it alone, or if it's too painful for both of you, we totally under—"

"We're in," Ainsley said.

The bride-to-be, Lila, blinked. Three mud spirits hung from the unmoving ceiling fan above her by their long, furling tails, so close that their bulbous noses detected the unfamiliar scent of lavender in Lila's brown hair. Humans, they'd discovered long ago, only worried about who or what was behind them and at their feet—axe murderers or palmetto bugs. They rarely looked up.

"Um, both of you?" Lila said. "You really don't—"

"We committed to it," Ainsley said flatly. "Unless you've found another caterer, which I'd understand, since we sort of ghosted."

"No way," Lila lied, her voice going up (the spirits knew she and Zoe had discussed other options but agreed to *hold out a little longer*), then doubled down. "No! We wouldn't even dream of it! Oh, my god, Ainsley, thank you *so* much. Sorry again, you guys—"

"Don't mention it," Ainsley said, and it was unclear whether she referred to the *thank you* or the breakup, but the spirits were not convinced. When Hailey and Ainsley had visited the home of the engaged couple a few months ago, the spirits had sniffed the trouble between them, but they could not come to a consensus about how to interfere before the "lesbian food truck power couple" (as Zoe called them) had left, untouched by supernatural mischief. When the spirits learned through overheard phone calls that the tumultuous pair had agreed to cater the wedding on this land, all had been delighted at the opportunity for some excitement, then subsequently disappointed two weeks later to hear that the women had split up without supernatural interference.

After this fateful afternoon phone call, however, the news that Hailey and Ainsley planned to honor their commitment to work the wedding set the spirit world abuzz. They'd been forced to share their land with humans long enough to know how these things went, how the right sort of circumstance could force two horribly mismatched mates back into one another's arms. They were not about to let that happen, not on their land, land that had been theirs before ever there was a Lafayette, Louisiana. It was not, after all, Hailey and Ainsley's first time breaking up. They still lived together.

That night, the spirits of the air and land all met in what could only be described as a maelstrom high above the field behind Lila and Zoe's house, where the wedding would take place. They seldom met all together like this, as it posed too great a risk of being seen by day or catching an unsuspecting plane in the chaos of their congress by night, both of which would upset the natural order. The human eye would have seen a swirling, sparking cloud of mud and leaves, water and fire, wind and grass, but the spirits sat serenely within an orb of glassy, obsidian-black walls illuminated by eyes of the spirits of the flame, the glittering skin of the spirits of the stars, and the occasional crackling around the ever-shifting bodies of the spirits of the clouds. What follows is an approximation of the debate, as the spirits of the air and land, of course, would not communicate in anything resembling human speech:

We are against all intervention, argued the only voice of dissent: the spirits of the flame. *It would upset the balance.*

The hobgoblin spirits of the mud exchanged meaningful looks with the mutable spirits of the clouds, with whom they often worked in harmony. All present knew that the spirits of the flame opposed the extinguishing of anything resembling fire, even if the flame between such women as Hailey and Ainsley would prove destructive in the end. Perhaps especially in that case.

And yet, said a glimmering purple representative from the spirits of the stars, surprising everyone (the spirits of the stars, keepers of harmony, seldom stepped in except to arbitrate), *it was you who brought them together around a bonfire years ago, even though it was plain to all present they never would have come together.*

And what spirit of the air and land did not remember that

day a year and a half ago? How the spirits of flame, on a dare from the spirits of air, had infiltrated a bonfire in Lila and Zoe's yard to play a new, dangerous game: kindle passion between the unlikeliest of lovers and see how quickly it went up in flames. How incisive, introverted Hailey had glared across the fire at the brash, gregarious, twenty-six-year-old Ainsley, five years Hailey's junior in rainbow platform boots and a bubblegum pink romper who had, according to Lila's whisper earlier, gone "from zero to full lez" after her first hookup with another woman just a few months earlier. How later, as ashes danced from the hypnotic glow of the remaining embers, Ainsley sat with uncharacteristic tranquility and asked Hailey how long she'd been a sous-chef, and she didn't talk over Hailey even once, and Hailey had wondered if she hadn't been wrong about this rainbow-bright punk. How, six months later, when the two first began fighting, they'd opened their food truck in hopes it would bring them closer and build trust between them. How it had accidentally built a cult following, particularly among the burgeoning Lafayette queer scene, but not the closeness or trust the two had intended. How even after their first breakup it kept them in a feedback loop of on-again, off-again, business-partners-and-sometimes-lovers state of limbo. How the aforementioned bride-to-be, Lila, a journalist and aspiring novelist, had remarked to her fiancé Zoe without irony that together the two were a forest on fire that didn't know how to put itself out, but they made a damned good vegan Po'boy.

"Star-crossed," that's what they're calling it, continued the purple spirit of the stars, indignation deepening their dulcet tones. *Do you know how insulting it is to hear humans say this on the land over which we shine each night?*

Do you know what else we heard? What else, what else we heard? Chimed the spirits of the water, who most closely resembled large silver salamanders, all overlapping one another in their pronouncements like the currents of a brook. *Do you know what else we heard? Yes, we did! We heard them say this is blessed land. Blessed land! They said it was blessed land, yes, and Hailey and Ainsley met under some blessing, yes! That's what they're saying, yes, it is! Yes! Yes, they said—*

And so, concluded the radiant purple spirit of the stars, their firm celestial voice acting as a dam to the overflowing proclamations of the spirits of the water, *it is most urgent we undo this damage, lest the humans flood our small domain for blessings. Lest they believe we would bless such an obviously doomed union. It would be a mockery of our power.*

Besides, said a representative of the spirits of the mud, daring to articulate what was on all the spirits' minds, who had been confined to a mere fifty acres of land, at the heart of which sat Zoe and Lila's little property where Hailey and Ainsley would cater their wedding, *When's the last time we had any real fun?*

The spirits of flame yielded without another complaint, leading some spirits to wonder whether these agents of mischief and destruction hadn't set Hailey and Ainsley's ill-fated relationship in motion for exactly this purpose. After all, they'd done nothing to encourage or discourage the union of the brides-to-be, reasoning that the two held a flame true enough they dared not pollute it. However, none bothered to question them too closely, for all agreed the relationship must be stopped—for the good of Hailey and Ainsley, for the restoration of the natural order, for the risk of cheapening the mystical reputation of their land, or simply for the allure of putting their underused talents toward some much-needed entertainment.

Over the weeks leading up to the wedding, the spirits of the water dragged the runoff from heavy rains toward the ditch at the end of the property, a little at a time. They were careful not to make the whole property into a mire, working with the spirits of the mud and the clouds not to ruin the entire wedding. The brides, though less than the indigenous people who once occupied the land, did make some effort to acknowledge the unseen forces around them. The spirits were not especially inclined to ruin *their* relationship.

At the start of the big event, although Hailey and Ainsley had shakily agreed not only to cater the wedding but also to "try things out one last time" (a phrase they'd used the last time they'd gotten back together, according to Lila's most recent sources of gossip), the spirits wondered how much incorporeal assistance Hailey and Ainsley would really need to confirm that any relationship between them, romantic or business or otherwise, would be doomed to fail. It was perfect weather for a Louisiana spring—the spirits of the sunbeams and the air made sure it was neither too hot nor too windy, but instead, pleasant warmth reigned while a mild, consistent breeze blew. However, this was largely where supernatural assistance ceased, at first: in the cultivation of the kind of day that would make any homosexuals in their late twenties to early-thirties seethe with envy.

Lila and Zoe exchanged thoughtful and original vows beneath an enormous and wise-looking oak (in reality, the squat little golem-like spirits that inhabited it were more cunning than wise). The brides walked down the aisle toward the tree to a live, mellow synth-pop cover of Björk's "Hyperballad" (of *course* the spirits knew who Björk was, and knew that the couple, like many other young, anxious queers, considered this to be "their" song). In lieu of a sermon, a friend of the brides gave a brief tribal history of the land upon which they stood ("This was sacred land," the large man began, and the watching spirits bristled at the word "was" coming from this man who, for his apparent cultural awareness, still refused to see them). The reception took place beneath a large tent hung with string lights, just outside of which several rented consignment couches surrounded firepits (in which, later in the night, the spirits of the flame would dance, licking occasionally at the hands of party guests too drunk to notice the blisters forming).

In short, the spirits initially wondered whether, even without their intervention, there was any way Hailey and Ainsley could witness such a majestic confluence of love and think their tense, passive-aggressive exchanges could ever hope to lead them to the same.

Still, needful or not, the spirits intervened. Whereas the air outside Hailey and Ainsley's food truck was crisp and breezy, the spirits of the air ensured no pleasant wind flowed through the open windows of the sweltering vessel; the spirits of the flame roared hot and unwieldy on the grills within; and the spirits of the sunbeams beat silently upon the shiny aluminum roof so that the tiny space felt all the more stifling. When either Hailey or Ainsley left to refill buffet trays, out in the breeze, each could not help but sigh at the relief of getting away from the other. Their food truck became a prison, and the already tense interactions between a broken-up-then-maybe-back-together couple working together in the supreme heat turned downright snappy. Outside, the happily wedded couple danced serenely to the tears and cheers of their loved ones.

"White people dancing," remarked Ainsley with a cruel smirk at the bride, Lila, stumbling momentarily over her own feet on the spongy grass, Zoe catching her gallantly.

"You know criticizing other white people doesn't make you any less white," replied Hailey, though the creases at the grin she tried to hide suggested that she'd been thinking it too. She flipped the fried rice on the griddle and said, almost as an afterthought, "It doesn't make you exempt from examining your own privilege, either."

The spirits of the mud, who clung to the windowsill outside of the food truck with tiny claws one would only see with a discriminating squint, snickered amongst themselves. They, too, had been playing their part clinging to Hailey and Ainsley's shoes. Though the ground was no wetter than usual for April in Lafayette, the wedding guests found their shoes surprisingly unsoiled while the floor of the food truck was splotched with slippery earth. But the spirits of the mud would have their real moment soon.

In the meantime, the spirits of the air delivered one swift, whooshing gust through the window that knocked the half-opened cayenne pepper into the bubbling pot of curried vegetables. The rush of air did not linger long enough to cool the cramped space.

"Really?" Ainsley snapped at Hailey, whose job it was to mix and watch the curry and who had yelped at the spill—and, yes, whom Ainsley clearly hadn't forgiven for criticizing her joke moments before.

"It was the wind!" moaned Hailey helplessly, dumping their last can of coconut milk into the brew to offset the heap of spice that had sunken into the mix of swimming vegetables before it could be scooped out. This remaining can, it was clear, would not be enough to undo the damage.

"And we just leave the lid off our spices now?" said Ainsley, not looking up from her chopping.

Of course, it had been a web-like spirit of the grass that had crept up beside the spirits of the mud and curled one of its tendrils around the lid, twisting, while another spirit of the grass had held the container firmly in place with its own tendril. But since the lid had already fallen to the muddy floor where the spice jar had rolled from the windowsill to join it, the two women would never suspect divine intervention even if they'd known how to look for it.

Thus, the rumblings began, even from the most gastronomically adventurous of the guests, that the curry was too spicy. Some, who knew a thing or two about Hailey and Ainsley's situation, even giggled guiltily to themselves about the over-spiced curry, giving variations on, *That's what you get when you hire a pair of fiery on, again-off-again girlfriends to cater a wedding—they fight, and they over-spice the curry.* One guest turned mock-serious at the giggling and murmured that perhaps

Hailey and Ainsley had over-spiced the curry in a small, bitter gesture of defiance at the newlywed couple's happiness. The married couple continued to dance, feeding one another dinner rolls, apparently unaware of the spice saga unfolding at the edge of their tent.

It is a marvel what the right kind of wind can carry. The spirits of the air, always listening, snatched the juiciest tidbits of these hushed conversations and slithered as fast as striking cottonmouths toward the food truck windows. As the sun sank, doing nothing to mitigate the oppressive heat inside the traveling kitchen, the spirits of the air subjected Hailey and Ainsley to snatches of conversation about their crumbling ("Yet again!") relationship.

"A shame," they eventually heard *Lila,* of all people, replying to some busybody who was filling her in on the miserable state of the fallen-from-grace lesbian food truck power couple in their hot, slippery food truck. *Fucking Lila*, who had paused from dancing in her sweat-soaked wedding dress. But what must have stung most, the spirits agreed, was the sincerity in her voice. "There was a hot minute there where we all thought they might, you know, actually be happy together. They were kind of, like, heroes for me and Zoe, when things got a little tough and we hadn't started therapy together yet. We were like, 'One day we're gonna grow up and be like Hailey and Ainsley.'"

Hailey refused to look up from stirring frosting (to accommodate the last-minute request for vegan cake for the half-dozen guests who'd forgotten to fill out their dietary preferences on the RSVP letter); Hailey and Ainsley both knew the "hot minute" Lila meant, and as it had happened on this land, the spirits did, as well. The grand opening of their food truck had been on this very field, surrounded by what Ainsley had dubbed "big gay love," the two working in perfect tandem, Ainsley's eccentric flavor fusions carried out by Hailey's dexterous hand and chemist's eye for spice proportions. None of Hailey's resentment for Ainsley carrying her "kitchen dom energy" into the bedroom had yet emerged, nor Ainsley's exasperation at Hailey's tendency to stew for weeks on end without saying what was on her mind. The two had executed orders swiftly and flawlessly, pausing to peck one another on the cheek to the admiring eyes of their patrons and the suspicious gazes of the spirits of the air and land. The latter, of course, had recognized a performance when they'd seen one; enough generations of tenants had rotted in front of the television on this land that the spirits had seen their share of sitcoms.

Now, on Zoe and Lila's wedding day, the spirits of the flame could feel Hailey burn with the weight of Ainsley's gaze behind her, both women screaming silently into the void, *What happened to us? How did we fall so far?*

The *pièce de résistance* on the spirits' part, however, came when the growing shadows and dwindling guests indicated to Hailey and Ainsley, who hardly spoke to one another at this point in anything beyond single-word grumbles, that they could collect their buffet trays and bow out.

They had parked their food truck far enough from the tent that they could easily pull out. But heat exhaustion and the gathering dark—thickened immensely by the mouse-like spirits of the shadows—ensured that they missed one important detail. As they backed up to turn their truck toward the gravel road, it began to slide backwards faster, and even when Ainsley realized what was happening and shifted to drive, the spirits of the mud pulled with all their strength, and the spirits of the water added moisture from the readily nearby water table to make the ground all the more slippery, and the truck plopped itself firmly into the ditch, which had deepened over the weeks thanks to the spirits of the water and the mud and the clouds. The soft ground cushioned the impact, of course; the spirits did not aim to *harm* Hailey and Ainsley. Quite the opposite!

Guests gathered. Drunk men explained to Hailey and

Ainsley that if they turned the steering wheel just this far over and hit the gas just so, while John-Mark and Pauly G. pushed just hard enough, they'd be on their way. Nothing worked. The aforementioned distant cousins stripped off their shoes and rolled up their suit pants, pushing and pushing. The shadows turned to total darkness, and the only light came from the tent's string lights and the fire pits, where dancing or lounging guests pretended not to notice the calamity that had befallen the hired help or convinced themselves that the small crowd around the truck "had it covered."

Ainsley called a tow truck. The concerned guests petered off. The drunk men lost interest, but not without each of them offering Hailey his own inconsistently detailed, well-intended, but ultimately unsolicited suggestion for how Hailey—the more butch of the two and so, in their eyes, presumably the more competent—might avoid this sort of predicament in the future. The spirits smiled among themselves.

That is, until Hailey and Ainsley, in spite of it all, found themselves waiting for the tow truck on an empty couch damp with dew, beside a fire pit whose one wavering ember snuffed out the moment they sat before it, and they curled into the familiar warmth of one another's arms more out of habit than affection. They said nothing. They didn't need to. Nobody understood what tribulations each had been through that evening better than the other. No guest occupied any of the other couches around that particular fire pit nor attempted to revive its flame. None dared.

The spirits of the air and the land and the mud and the shadows and the sky and the stars looked sadly at the neighboring fire, where the newlyweds shared whiskey and stories with their inner circle of remaining friends, then back at Hailey and Ainsley, curled together on their lone couch waiting for the tow truck, apparently closer than ever, in spite of all the signs of doom the spirits had worked so hard to orchestrate.

Well, the spirits had hoped not to spoil the newlyweds'

night, but it had to be done. Plump clouds had gathered in case of this very emergency, and perhaps the married couple, at least, would see it as a happy omen. The spirits of the air and the land and the mud and the shadows and the sky and the stars nodded in a symphony of silent agreement, turning their full attention to Hailey and Ainsley.

It began to rain.

UNDER HER WHITE STARS

There were many attempts to take down the witch Amarande in his subtropical convenience store kingdom, though nobody talks about him much these days.

Amarande: unapologetically powerful, unapologetically wicked, in the glamorous sprawl of Miami where winter consisted of three weeks of sixty-degree weather, where stucco houses with terra cotta roofs clashed with the glassy curvature of coastal high-rises, where speculators dredged islands out of the sea itself. Amarande, who lured tourists into dingy shops that offered kitsch towels for the forgetful, slushies for the thirsty, sunscreen for the cautious, eternal life for the poor wretches who didn't know any better—all for the small price of their souls. Healers, sorcerers, druids, magicians, and witches alike tried to take him down, outraged at his boldness, at his wickedness, at his ability to elude detection while drinking the lives of countless adults and children. What tourists broadcast their whereabouts before entering into a convenience store never to be found again, stopping in for an ice cream sandwich and maybe a lighter engraved with an ibis? Many practitioners tried to kill

Amarande, catch him, coerce his secrets from him, become his apprentice, test their power against his. Whispers traveled up the East Coast among magic practitioners, like cocaine from warmer climates barreling up the interstate in a black car with tinted windows. Most every practitioner with a lick of sense objected outwardly to Amarande's legendary Evil behavior, even if some of us nursed an envy at his effortless ability to bottle up other people's lives and lengthen his own. I listened to the rumors, fed them, propagated them for months until I finally told my fiancé I was going after him myself.

"So," I said to him the night before I was set to go. "About this weekend. There's this witch queen down South . . ."

"Amarande?" Lionel said, blowing a puff of pot smoke out through the window fan in our cramped little kitchen so it wouldn't stink up our building. "Sure, babe. I was wondering when you'd bring him up."

"How do *you* know about him?" I asked. Lionel was about as un-witchy as they came. He worked for the National Arts Council, where he'd been that night, in fact, working an event until ten. Despite his feverish interest in the occult—as feverish as his obsession with experimental art, exotic animals, and all the other oddities he pursued with frenzied persistence—he didn't have a drop of magic in him.

"The painter doing a residency with us is a druid," Lionel said. He reclined in the only chair in the kitchen, wearing his wide, goofy smile. "And you practitioners can't keep your mouths shut."

"Oh."

"Are you sure this is a good idea? Babe, I heard he's, like, *really* no joke."

"I guess you could say that," I said. Crossed my arms. Sniffed. "I mean, I'm no joke either, Lionel."

The truth was, I thought taking down Amarande would be *it* for me. At the time, I was feeling stagnated in my career as a witch, working mostly as a healer (a damn good one, mind you), as well as selling spells and amulets for things like magical defense and metamorphosis. It was more of a long game, a "build your business from the ground up" kind of a deal. From time to time I went after lawless witches, capturing them in a flask or executing them, depending on the type of warrant that was out on them. Even in those days, the government wouldn't do much more than offer a reward for someone like Amarande. They wouldn't go after the magic-wielding bad eggs themselves. And it made sense. If you think about it, the establishment has always been afraid of us. Back in the day, for example, New Orleans left diviners alone, making tarot and palmistry the only money-making activities that were untaxed and unregulated. They didn't even ask for permits, like with the other street sellers—the government just didn't want to get involved where magic was concerned. Even today, with the increase of out-and-proud practitioners and the relative acceptance we enjoy—especially in urban centers, neoliberal universities, and . . . you understand, the government drags its feet on any legislation pertaining to magic. The stigma's still there. We've always governed ourselves, and in the case of criminals like Amarande, an understaffed branch of the US Marshals at the time offered untaxed, practically under-the-table freelance rewards for their capture. It was lucrative as hell, and the more guys like Amarande you nabbed, the more likely you were to be contacted directly by the state instead of relying on rumors or trolling their website for jobs.

"Don't get me wrong, you're a powerful witch," Lionel said and looked at me sheepishly, blowing pot from the side of his mouth which the window fan snatched away. "If you weren't brilliant at what you did, I wouldn't . . . well, this would probably never have worked out."

He'd said it before. A curator himself, he'd worked with best-of-the-best artists for years, and with a somewhat snobbish charm he'd told me early on in our relationship that he could sniff out any kind of talent, artistic or otherwise—and I had it.

He continued. "I just don't know why you have to go all over the country chasing bad guys when you're such a brilliant healer. Healing plays to your *strengths* so well. It's really something to be proud of, love."

"Okay, but how can I call myself a healer if I can't purge the world of a sickness every now and again?" I said. "Lionel, he's taking people's souls and using them to stay young forever. It's healing gone wrong. This feels personal. How can I let someone like that exist in the world and not do anything about it? Anyway, couldn't we use the money?" I gestured toward the kitchen door and the rest of our one-bedroom apartment, which was beautiful—all hardwood floors and high ceilings, full of strange treasures worthy of a curio cabinet. Just not big enough for the enormity of our personalities, our penchant for collecting (read: hoarding).

"Okay," he said, and he looked down. "It's just, you know, I worry about you sometimes."

"I'll be fine! Listen," I said. "Guys like Amarande, they're all smoke and mirrors. Defense magic, trickery, elusiveness. I'll be totally safe."

Strictly speaking, I wasn't entirely sure this was true of Amarande. Call it my educated guess? Or perhaps my lie of omission. My first mistake.

He said, "And it has to be tomorrow?"

"It's a Super Moon tomorrow. Plus, Miami is closer to the Moon's path in September, near the equinox, so my energy will be really strong down there this time of year." A water sign, I gathered most of my strength from the Moon, revered Her like a goddess.

Only then, I noticed the gears were turning in his head. "Well, listen," he said. "Sarah's having a party not far from where you're going, some tiny little cove up near Jensen Beach. Callisto, I think. Isn't that a funny name for a cove? Anyway, if this Amarande fellow isn't so dangerous, I'll come along with you for moral support and, well, bait. Then we can go to Sarah's."

"Lionel!" I said.

"What?" he said, and he giggled, crow's feet crinkling behind the square lenses of his glasses. This was a quality in Lionel I always adored: he was a ready laugher and a shameless giggler. "Doesn't he target regular, non-magical people? Don't tell me you were planning on using a tourist as bait. That would've been kind of unethical, huh?"

And just like that, he'd painted me into a corner. I thought about coming clean, telling him I had no idea just how dangerous this "Amarande fellow" was, that he might be an absolute terror with a battle spell. But Lionel was right, of course. I needed bait, and he'd be perfect: slim, not at all athletic, a few early grays in his thin, dark curls. In other words, particularly non-threatening—and, most importantly, willing. "Lionel . . ."

"So, it's settled then," he said, giggling again. "And we can fly over to where Sarah is and join the party when you nab this Amarande character. Plus—" he winked "—you'll have someone you'll need to protect. It'll be better for you when you feel like, well, like a hero."

And it was something about that unwavering support, that "when" not "if," something about his unshakeable faith that made me agree, against my better judgment, to let my very mortal fiancé accompany me on a mission to take down a dangerous sorcerer.

The security desk at the National Arts Council was in a large, round room with a ceiling so high that if you shouted you'd feel like you were standing at the bottom of an empty well. The floor was marble with a massive compass painted on it; in fact, the NAC shared space with other nonprofits in a building that reminded me of a renovated castle, all dramatic oak doors, stony walls, and ivy. I waited for Lionel in the lobby. He had a proposal he needed to drop on his boss's desk before we skipped town. All the doors to this echoey room were open, as well as the windows all the way up the stone walls, letting in almost-chilly September morning air. Normally I'd go up and say hi to Lionel's coworkers—Lionel, the only guy in his office, worked with the warmest people—but that day I wanted to expedite the process of leaving by staying down here. So I stood there tapping my bare foot, having smiled tightly at the gaunt security guard so many times I was worried I'd have to say something in the way of small talk. I exhaled with relief when my fiancé emerged from the large oak door.

"Ready?" I said.

"Sure," he said.

"Shoes," I said. "You'll have to leave them. I'll call them back to you when we get there."

As he took his shoes off, I closed my eyes and breathed in a big gulp of crisp morning, letting invisible roots of power grow from my feet down into the earth below the floor—grounding, which I did every time I performed body-altering magic on other people. I opened my eyes, feeling gusts of wind in my belly as I bloated with power. I looked at Lionel's feet, pictured them curling into the yellow talons of the peregrine falcon; saw the brown feathers sprouting where his thin, salty-black curls always tangled; willed the arms to spread, web, and feather. While he shrank and his stretchy gray shirt sank into his skin, I noticed the glazed-over look of the security guard snap into focus, noticed his jaw clench. Then, he relaxed, walked out from behind the counter, grabbed Lionel's shoes, and smiled.

In a stupor from the intoxicating magic, I slurred, "Seen some bird magic at the NAC, huh?"

With much less effort—metamorphosis is a whole lot easier

on the self—I let the feathers of the peregrine falcon sprout from my own arms, legs, chest, head, and pelvis before the guard had the chance to reply. It was sort of like getting a tooth pulled or a cavity filled. As the bones twisted and snapped and resituated, my brain registered that it hurt excruciatingly while the magic numbed the pain like a lidocaine shot.

I launched myself toward the topmost windows, trusting Lionel to follow me as the air rushed past. We burst into the open sky.

Peregrines—the fastest birds in the world, though fastest when they were diving. With the help of my magic, we could access that breakneck speed flying horizontally. We flew southward. Wind blasting past my ears, I heard Lionel's nasally voice faintly inside my skull, a sensation similar to wearing headphones while riding a bicycle:

"I think I smell a southerly wind above us!"

It always amazed (and, if I'm being honest, frustrated) me what a natural he was at flying. I was the witch, and yet every time we took flight it occurred to me that he'd been a bird in at least one past life. Unlike him, I was a bit clumsy, the feathers and talons never quite feeling natural, unable to give myself wholly to the experience of flight.

We rose.

"Not too high," I shouted with my brain. The last thing I wanted was for one of us to drop clean out of the sky, fainting from the thinness of the atmosphere. This was more a concern for me than for Lionel, who was better at preventing such mishaps.

The southerly wind was just low enough to be breathable, though the air was thin enough that every so often we'd drop a couple hundred feet and gulp in thicker air like dehydrated marathoners glugging water at the nineteenth-mile mark of the race.

—ʌʌ——ʌʌ——ʌʌ—

The journey to Miami is usually five hours by wing, or so I'd heard, but in just four and a half hours we touched down in an alleyway behind tourist-infested Lincoln Road.

I have encountered few transitions in this world as jarring as that of emerging from a Lincoln Road alley onto Lincoln Road itself. We changed back into ourselves and threw on our shoes (which materialized, as promised, with a snap of my fingers) in the alley—the awful stench of dumpsters baking in the sun, the oily puddles of rainwater mixing with the juices leaking from restaurant trash bags, the palmetto bugs skittering past our feet. I can't exactly say why I could never get the shoes to melt into the feet as the clothes did into the body, but I was glad we didn't have to land in this alley in the buff. We startled a chef in a greasy apron enough as it was. We rushed to the street pinching our noses, only to be immersed in the decadent, tacky glamour of the outdoor mall known as Lincoln Road—the designer boutiques and expensive essential oil perfumeries squeezed next to tourist-trap T-shirt shops, the palm trees stuffed into over-gardened mulch beds. In September, the subtropical sun was still hot enough to melt your face off, but not quite hot enough to scorch the bones beneath it. After passing our third silver-painted "living statue" and nearly getting bowled over by a saggy man on roller blades wearing nothing but tiny leather shorts, Lionel and I decided we'd have an easier time stumbling accidentally-on-purpose into one of Amarande's shops if we walked down Alton Road or Ocean Avenue where there were fewer people.

As cars whipped through the palms lining the median strip, I told Lionel, "Okay, so they say Amarande's portals open at the doors to a convenience store when somebody's really desperate for something."

"Great," Lionel said. "I'm fucking starving. I mean, I'd probably sell my soul for a couple taquitos right now."

Suddenly I was uneasy about having brought him with me. What had I been thinking? Though I'd adorned his wrists, ankles, and neck with an abundance of charmed jewelry to protect him from harmful spells, I still felt like I'd made a big mistake bringing him.

"Babe, you know, if this . . . goes well, if I get direct work from the state department or something, they're not gonna like it if you, uh, tag along in the future. It's not gonna be like I'm taking my house-husband on a conference-vacation. It's—this is—Lionel, uh, I'm not so sure about you coming with me. Maybe you should meet me at Lincoln Road, get yourself a drink, wait for me there."

I was being cagey, afraid to tell him outright, *Hey, I'm putting us both at risk, but you especially, right now*. But I couldn't tell him what he was in for, because I didn't quite know myself.

He remained unflappable. "It's little old me or an innocent tourist as bait. Could your conscience take it if some poor tourist died because of you? Hey, look! On the corner, across the street."

He pointed to a particularly sketchy-looking corner store with a pink and green neon sign that said "FLAMINGO," its glow faded and depressing in the bright afternoon sun. Not to mention the "O" wasn't lighting up, so it looked more like it said "FLAMING." Plastered over the windows were the standard beer brand signs and a huge, red-painted poster that said "ICE."

He said, "Let's get some *ice,* babe."

I put my hand on his shoulder and looked at him very seriously. "Okay, we really just need to get in there and get Amarande to show himself. Then, I open this flask and *poof,* he's caught, no fuss, no showdown. Just, babe, don't do anything crazy, okay?"

He rolled his eyes. "Of *course.* Have a little faith!"

As we crossed the street, I pulled in a meditative breath

and whispered a minor spell to shield my aura from Amarande's detection, instructing Lionel to focus on anything in the shop, however trivial, that he might want or need. It didn't have to be his true heart's desire or anything—portal magic wouldn't be attuned to such depth of emotion—but he needed to focus on something he knew Amarande would have: a lighter, a hot dog, a slushie, or even the proudly advertised *ice*.

"Hopefully they have those gross hot dogs on the rolling heat things," Lionel said. "I always get such a kick out of them."

Not exactly a fiercely held wish, but he giggled and opened the door with gusto. It ding-donged with one of those phony electronic doorbells, and then my fiancé entered and promptly vanished.

"SHIT!" I ran in after him. "Lionel! Wait!"

He wasn't in the crammed convenience store. *Shit, shit, shit.* I went back outside. Who cared if I had to blow my cover? The motherfucker could be sipping on my fiancé's soul any second. I focused, closed my eyes, reopened them with a second-sight spell. It revealed that the door was booby-trapped with a *very* sophisticated portal, a transparent silver sheen over the doorway shimmering in the air. It was what we in "the business" call a "selective portal." Subtle, but brilliant. It was all in that fake doorbell, which, when triggered, was wired to open the portal only for non-practitioners like Lionel. Carefully, like pulling a wire from a time bomb, I focused on the *selective* element of the portal magic (which showed up as a gossamer red sigil above the door) and pulled it out. The doorbell rang. I leapt in, seizing the opportunity before it shut behind me.

Lionel was in front of me again, already slurping down a syrupy red slushy, and I rushed over to him, grabbing his shoulders. I heaved a sigh of relief. My spell had worked, and I'd made it through the same portal that had caused my Lionel to disappear. If I hadn't, I'd be in Amarande's dummy storefront while my fiancé traipsed alone through this dimension like a beetle dancing gleefully into the mouth of a pitcher plant.

"What took you so long, babe?" he said. I was so relieved I could weep. He was very much alive. I threw my arms around him. Reminded myself of my plan: get Amarande to show up, open the flask. It seemed we hadn't triggered any of his alarms yet. Good. But we'd have to be more careful.

"You okay?" Lionel asked.

I let go of him and nodded. The convenience store was poorly lit from the one large window that wasn't covered in beer and lotto ads; still, the sunlight didn't quite penetrate the gloom. What we saw through this window, surely, was an illusion—a time loop of cars whizzing by outside that would twitch and repeat if we stayed long enough, with little relationship to what really happened out in the Florida sun.

Not bad, Amarande. This kind of dimensional magic wasn't easy to pull off, but now that we were inside, I was free to focus on bagging him . . . as soon as he decided to show up.

I grabbed a slushy cup and made like I was going to get the sickly-looking off-white "piña colada" flavor and then, with an ounce of will and a flick of the wrist, I killed the slushy machine. There was a crackling sound from behind it, like a moth caught in a bug zapper. The propellers that mixed the slushies in perpetuity slowed to a halt. When I pressed my cup against the piña colada flavor, syrup the color of dehydrated piss oozed out. As if I hadn't noticed the machine was broken—hadn't, in fact, broken it—I tried the red, blue, and purple flavors, which all yielded the same result in various icky hues.

I marched up to the lady at the counter and said, as bitchily as I could manage, "Your slushy machine's busted. I want to talk to the manager."

"And don't you have any hot food?" Lionel demanded from behind me. He slurped the remains of his slushy, having somehow downed most of it already.

"I'd give *anything* for an empanada," I said. "Just anything."

"Anything," Lionel repeated.

We were overdoing it, really laying it on, but what was the point of hunting down ageless witches with your fiancé if it's not even a little bit fun?

I turned to grin at Lionel, from whom I'd expected at least a quiet snicker. But he just stood there, open-mouthed, frozen in place but visibly trembling. His quaking increased, became so violent that the empty cup fell from his grasp as his face sank into itself, grew paler, paler, the cheekbones sharpening, the jaw poking through, thinner, thinner, and he wasted away before I understood what I was witnessing.

His clothes dropped to the floor, kicking up a plume from the pile of ash that had, moments ago, been the love of my life.

I spun around and lunged at the woman behind the counter, smacking right into an invisible wall. Amarande peered at me from inside her. She looked the same, except for the irises, which shined a cold silver light that caught, converted, and reflected what little light was in the tiny store.

"Give him back!" I screamed. "Give me back his soul or I'll burn this store to the ground."

The lady opened her mouth, but it was Amarande's deep, smooth bass humming from her vocal cords.

"I haven't got his soul. It's all filthy with your magic. The souls of witches' lovers give me indigestion. No," he said, sounding bored. "I just poisoned him. What did you expect?"

The puppet-woman raised a sleepy finger and pointed to the empty slushy cup on the floor.

"You little do-gooder witches are so dumb," he said through the cashier's mouth.

God, the worst part was, he wasn't wrong. I'd given Lionel

all that defense against harmful spells, but the idea of a good old-fashioned poison hadn't even occurred to me. Without a sound, I yanked at the air, sending the metal shelf of condoms and cigarettes behind the counter crashing into the cashier. She stumbled forward, and Amarande's silver sheen in her eyes disappeared. She looked around, seeming confused. *His* voice came from all around us:

"Go ahead, little witch. You're only going to hurt her."

I reached for my back pocket, only to find that the flask I used to bottle up bad guys had vanished. So I did what any grieving, angry witch who'd hunted down an infamous life stealer–and had nothing to show for it but a pile of ash where their fiancé used to be would have done: I set out to destroy Amarande's shop. Did he have more shops? Maybe. Would it be easy for him to clean up? Sure. Did that matter right then? No.

Bags of Cheetos and Funyuns exploded in snowstorms of orange and beige; beer bottles flew off refrigerated shelves; the goddamned slushy machine crashed against the wall behind it, obliterated; Skittles like marbles skittered across the ground. Shelves toppled, posters burst into flames. I myself didn't move a muscle. Amarande let me do it without comment. He was probably used to the collateral damage of failed practitioners. It probably didn't bother him. Maybe he even got a kick out of it, although he didn't laugh, didn't try to humiliate me further—I was doing a great job of that on my own.

When I finally turned, covered in sweat and crumbs, the lady behind the counter had disappeared, leaving me face-to-face with the notorious witch himself. Amarande was excessively tall—like, professional-basketball-player tall—thin and lanky as a daddy longlegs, with skin so pale it seemed to glow. Bald head, pale pink lips. He wore a sleeveless, silver-sequined dress tight enough to boast the outline of his absurdly large penis. A white fur stole rested across his bare shoulders. He had one hand on his hip, one perfectly plucked eyebrow raised, in a bratty pose that said, "Are you done yet?" Whether or not he'd enhanced his figure with glamour magic, I could see why this tacky, overly stylized witch bitch had made this Art Deco city his home.

Amarande was, of course, holding my missing witch-catching flask in his right hand. In his left hand, the hand on his hip, he held a white plastic bag that said "THANK YOU THANK YOU THANK YOU" in red letters. He tossed it at me, and it floated to my feet like a dust mote.

"In case you wanted to take your boyfriend with you. No tricks this time."

He let a touch of sincere pity pinch his brow when I bent pathetically to pick up the bag. I told myself over and over that I wouldn't let myself cry in front of him. I stuffed Lionel's clothes in the bag and as many fistfuls of his ashes as I could until it dimly occurred to me that I could collect the ashes with magic. I did so. The remaining soot on the floor swirled into the bag like a dejected, wannabe tornado that couldn't quite form. The soot that stained my hands peeled off and slid into the crinkling plastic. I didn't even process until later that my hands had been covered in the ashes of my dead partner.

"You know, little witch, we're all just doing what we can," he said. "You came to do what you thought you had to, and I did what I had to do. It's the way things work. You'll learn."

I barely squeaked out, "Just shut up!" I tied the bag up and tiptoed toward the door, candy and chips sticking to my shoes.

"Sorry about your boyfriend," he called after me, obviously not meaning it, and I opened the door to the sound of the chintzy electronic doorbell.

"Fiancé," I choked. I turned back to spit on the floor, but the squat, middle-aged lady was behind the counter again, and the corner store was completely immaculate, if dingy as ever. The real corner store. Amarande had receded, taking his phantom store with him. I spat anyway.

Wings tore through my back; feathers shot out from my

pores. It was sloppy magic, and it hurt like hell, but I didn't have any time. I knew what I had to do.

Our friend Sarah came from a long line of diviners, and as I flew to Callisto, it suddenly made sense why she was throwing a destination birthday party there instead of doing something back up north where we lived—the party we'd said we'd make it to after we bagged the bad boy. The cove was a perfect circle of rock with a small opening out to sea. Perfect place to look at the full Moon (Super Moon, no less, when the Moon appears largest in the sky). Sarah had said it was apparently the closest place on earth to the Moon that night. The knowing way she'd shared this information with me, the relative inconvenience of taking a road trip or a wing trip all the way down to Florida for a Super Moon party, suddenly added up. She knew exactly what I would be up to this weekend and exactly what I'd need to do should I fail. Maybe she wasn't having a party there at all. As a falcon with a plastic bag clutched between its teeth, I got there just before she left.

The entrance to the cove was through the locker room of a public pool, and for some arcane reason the wards around the cove prevented practitioners from entering anywhere but through there. I alighted in a tree in the parking lot and, finding the windows to the locker room open, changed back into a human in a stall. I quickly used one of the showers to cleanse and consecrate myself, letting the water wash away any residual darkness on my aura from Amarande's shop lest it disrupt the ritual I was about to enact, plastic bag full of Lionel's ashes hanging from a hook just to the left of my curtain. When I tried the door to the beach, it was locked. After 7 p.m., a sign on the door indicated, people could leave the cove but not enter. Well, I didn't have time for that. I pushed myself against the pale orange wall, coaxed it to soften, and trudged through it like it was made of soft putty. I had to break the wards, too, and the magic was outdated enough that I passed through the silvery sheen like smoke. I knew now that instead of a check from the US Marshals, the only government mail I could expect anytime soon was a hefty fine for tampering with wards on public property. *Shut up,* I scolded. How could I be thinking of that, of all things?

It was totally dark on the rocky beach at this point, and Sarah was there alone heaping sand onto a pile of burning coal, and she looked at me with my THANK YOU THANK YOU THANK YOU bag, and she knew. Of course she knew.

"Oh, god," she said, flinging her arms around me, and I let myself cry into her blonde hair. "Listen, we're packing up the car right now. Do you want me, us, do you need us to be here with you?"

"I don't think so," I said. I didn't ask who she meant by "us." I looked at the Moon, who had just risen above the rocks of the cove. "I think this is something I've got to do myself. I've never tried to bring back the dead before."

"I know, honey," she said. She kissed my forehead and walked toward the locker rooms.

"Sarah!" I cried after her, and she turned. "Am I ready? Can I do this? What's going to happen if I'm not powerful enough? Please."

If anyone could read the stars and tell me whether I could bring Lionel to life, it was her.

"It doesn't matter whether or not you can, does it?" she said, and she was gone. God, no disrespect to divination or its practitioners, but sometimes that cryptic shit really got on my nerves.

I dumped the contents of the plastic bag onto the sand, letting the wind carry Lionel's ashes into the circle of still water that reflected the pearly light of the rising Moon. I knew here, now, full Moon rising, with my fury and anguish as an offering to the feminine divine, I was at the height of my power. I'd told Lionel the full Moon would be feeding me power. I hadn't known I'd need Her for this. I felt crazy, stupid, arrogant—drinking the Moon's power because I'd fucked up so royally, flown too close to the sun (and all his hotheaded aggression), when it was clearly the Moon's healing power I had needed to be focusing on all along. Under Her white stars, I began my work.

Flinging my hand toward the rock-made circle, I caused Lionel's gray shirt and black shorts to hover ten feet above the flat water, rooted by magic to the circle's center, flapping in the breeze like a battle flag.

Theoretically, resurrection is all about remembering someone—the gestures, the face, the quantity of stubble, the preference for yellow roses over red, the asymmetrical arrangements of cookie dough on an oven tray to maximize the economy of space, the readiness of the laugh, oh god, his laugh. I closed my eyes and let his face fill the black expanse of my mind's eye: the dark stubble that prickled my shoulder when he'd lie with his arms wrapped around me, the wire-framed rectangles of his glasses transitioning to dark shadowy lenses in the sunlight, each wrinkle in his smile, the folds of skin under his chin when he frowned down at his dinner. I remembered. I remembered. I remembered him as he was. Eyes closed, I hoped that the shirt hovering above the water was beginning to twist, to fill with his torso, his torso with the small patch of coarse black hair on his chest, those black hairs contrasting with his skin so pasty it seemed greenish in the dark. In my mind's eye I saw the gray sleeves fill with those vascular, skinny, used-to-lift-hand-weights-but-not-anymore arms. Remembering.

Remembering—and rewriting: we didn't go down south to confront Amarande, I whispered to the Moon, to time, to memory. We were going to Callisto the whole time. We flew over the river to the cape as birds and swam down the East

Coast as dolphins—albino dolphins, no less, just for the hell of it—leaping and flipping through the choppy surf. These were the sorts of details that lent authenticity to the rewrite. We lost track of time and got here, to Callisto, just in time to catch Sarah before she left—she was alone, just as before. If my spell worked, Lionel would forget, which was essential. If he remembered what really happened, the spell would fail and he'd die, again, on the spot. Sarah wouldn't forget, but that's because diviners see all the tributaries that branch from the river of possibility; she'd have the good sense to keep it to herself. All the better to cheat time. Whether Amarande would forget was anyone's guess, but I had a feeling he wouldn't be bothering us anymore.

Sarah left Lionel and me alone, I rewrote, and let us watch the Moon, rest, admire each other, kiss. I rewrote and rewrote.

I rewrote his mouth on mine, there, in that moment. His tongue.

He pulled away. I opened my eyes and there he was, in that gray shirt and those black shorts that were three sizes too big, the belt holding them up, the oversized bronze belt buckle shaped like a sun. Lionel.

"Hi, love," he said, looking only a little disoriented.

"I want you to tell me what you remember of today," I said. "Quickly."

"What?" he said. "Of the swim? It was great, babe! Wish we'd gotten here earlier so we could've seen more of Sarah, though. We'll have to have her over next week. Or the week after."

"Think, Lionel." I placed my hands on his head. I needed to be sure. "Do you remember anything besides the swim?"

"I mean, I guess the details are kinda fuzzy, the day went by so fast. I do remember something really random that I probably dreamed this morning. An alley, back in the day. But that doesn't make any sense, it smelled awful and, oh man, my chest hurts, oh my god, I feel like I'm having a—oh god, oh my god . . ."

His eyes squeezed shut, his jaw clenched, his eyebrows

pinched with pain. I pressed hard against his head and sucked air in, drinking the last of the memory.

"Ah, that's better," he said. "That was really weird, babe. What was I saying?"

"About Sarah," I said.

"Oh, yeah. Let's look at the calendar when we get home."

"Yes, let's." I looked around for the plastic bag, the red THANK YOU THANK YOU THANK YOU letters. I'd toss it out without Lionel seeing it. But it was nowhere in sight. Littering aside, I figured that was a good thing.

So I guess sometimes we're not meant to chase down the baddest witches around just because we've got the Gift and grew up with a taste for crime novels. Sometimes, I decided, we don't have to measure our success or our goodness by the evil we erase. Maybe sometimes we can measure it by the things we have the power to do in our own lives to balance out all the bad. If my fiancé ever learns what happened he will literally disintegrate, so I can't talk about what is perhaps the most important event in my life with the most important person in it. But I know Amarande's still out there, and I can offer my story to all who seek to take him down, in the hope that someone, somewhere, will do a better job than I did. So if we ever meet, please, just don't say anything to my husband about what you've learned. I promise, I'll be here in the wings waiting to help you if you fail, and I'm just doing what I can. I'm doing what I can to keep Lionel around as long as he'll stay.

DEADBEAT

I sit up, gasping. His eyes, half open. Body swaddled in Egyptian cotton. Sweat. Sunlight through blinds.

"I just won second place in a speed eating contest in Berlin," I say.

"Just now?" he says. Slow blink.

"It wasn't even just a hot dog eating contest! It was all different kinds of food."

"Mm," he curls toward me. Leg over my leg.

"Aren't you proud of me? I won second."

"Mmhmm." He doesn't mean it.

I lie back on three pillows. Eyes wide. His, closed. He knows I'm not dreaming. Knows that the process of astral projection, of possessing the body of a host, is nothing to laugh at. Used to be impressed. I possess the body of the competitor least favored to win the eating contest, stuff its face. I haven't won yet, but I'm getting better.

"I know," I say. Long exhale. Didn't realize I'd been holding my breath.

"No!" he says, waving away the smoke that seeps from my nostrils. He complains about this sort of thing—the smoke, the smell of burning hair when I lose myself in thought, the summer bonfires that burn too hot when I approach—but I really do my best. He continues, "It's fine, really." He rethinks. "I mean, it's great! Second place is great, it's . . ."

Doesn't say: *First loser.*

"What do I say to your parents?" I say. "It's getting, I don't know. Should I be embarrassed?"

Downstairs, his mom clatters around in the kitchen. *I'm awake!* she screams through the pots. *So everyone should be awake.* Every morning. Every. Damn. Time. We. Visit.

His eyes: still closed. "I just wouldn't mention it."

"Oh," I say. "Great, thanks." *Another deadbeat demon lover leaching off my little warlock,* sings the kettle downstairs. *Can't even win an eating contest in* Berlin. I hear the coffee mugs clink against granite. Their laughter: disappointed but not surprised.

I brace myself for it. Seconds roll past. Minutes? Then, her voice from downstairs: "Boys!"

He forces his eyes open. A naked leg slips from the shelter of the bedsheets. A grumble on the way to the bathroom, something about the word "boy," about whether it applies to him on the year of his twenty-seventh birthday. His bare ass deserves applause.

I spit mouthwash into the sink beside him. Gently (he's not a morning person), I say: "It's just a mom thing. I mean, she said it to both of us, and I'm . . ." ageless. I shut up. We try not to talk about the mortality thing. I try for a topic change, try the real issue at hand. "What do you think I should do about, you know, the contests?" I hate making decisions. He loves making them for me. Makes him less grumpy in the morning.

"Probably take it easier on yourself? You really are getting close, you know," he says, and I'm surprised to admit that he sounds like he means it. "I think you've gotta chill out a little. You've cracked the code, but you're burnt out."

"You really think so?" Something very like relief—I can't say for sure; it's been decades—loosens sinew in my back and shoulders.

"I mean, you literally singed the edge of the pillowcase last night." He gargles toothpaste-water, spits. "Maybe try to sleep for real. Take a nap this afternoon." He looks at me from the corner of his eye. Mouth upturned. Lascivious. "Stay on this side of the planet tonight. I can make you good and hungry for something you can't eat with someone else's mouth."

He turns to me and licks his toothpaste-coated upper lip, raising one eyebrow cartoonishly. In spite of myself, I do laugh. One short burst.

"But seriously. You look like you haven't slept all month."

I consider my mug in the mirror. Dark pillows under darker eyes. All month? If only, child. It's been far, far longer than that.

MASK FOR MASK

As his first swamp tour group of the day approached from across the parking lot, Jean couldn't help but feel like there was something off about them. They *looked* normal enough. A bachelor party, he could tell from far away: the polos and the snap-back hats and, of course, the only skinny one among them at the head of the pack—no doubt the least hungover—struggling with a thirty-pack of beer. The reigning look was your average peaked-in-college "marketing manager" in between the twenty-six and thirty-two range who still used phrases like "gotta make those gains, bro." The picture of normal, red-blooded American masculinity. Except something unsettled Jean. Perhaps it was something in their gait; the typical wide-stance walk of manly man straight guys looked a little stiff on them, the knees not quite bent enough. Perhaps it was a trick of the light, but Jean noticed a certain phosphorescence to their skin tones. At first, he thought the white ones were simply so pale their skin seemed almost sickly green in the bright sun, but even the two with light brown skin had a sort of green undertone that offset their natural beauty. They were certainly good looking, almost overly so. Unnaturally so. That was probably it, he decided. Good-looking young men always distracted Jean, teasing that fine line between envy and lust that was par for the course for a married gay man just north of sixty.

When they were close enough, Jean stretched his face into a

smile and shook hands with the nearest one. "Which one of you poor boys had to drag these assholes out of bed this morning?"

Did it take them just a moment too long to understand Jean was joking? Did they overcompensate, laughing their affected baritone laughs just a little too hard amid their put-on grunts of *broooooo* and *this guy*? Jean shook off the thought. They must've been hungover.

He noticed then that the box of beer one of them held had a logo he'd never seen, depicting a yellow river with two cartoonishly large, red reptilian eyes poking from its surface. It was in a language—no, an entire script—Jean didn't recognize. He didn't fancy himself a worldly man—in fact, his friends and family had always pronounced his name "gene," and upon learning the French pronunciation as an adult he'd chosen to keep introducing himself the old way—but he'd been in the military in his day long enough to tell Cyrillic from Japanese, and this strange script was neither. He made an effort to relax his jaw at the creepy sense that came over him. Shrugged inwardly. Yuppy guys like this were into that Ikea shit, that vaguely faux European style that probably birthed beers with labels in made-up fonts.

Anyway, weird or obnoxious or geeky or rowdy or whatever, bachelor parties had always tipped him the best in his twenty-five years working the swamp tours. They were in New Orleans to waste money already, and Jean was masculine enough and Southern-sounding enough to pass for straight. "Passing" was a point of pride for Jean—his Catholic parents had raised him better than to walk around "all limp-wristed and light in the loafers"—and it meant he didn't run the risk of being stiffed on the tip by more homophobic tourists, of which bachelor parties were an obvious subset. No, he was sure this would be a lucky day for him. Jean would bring home a nice steak for the husband tonight, and they'd have the first good fuck they'd had in a little while.

He was on a real kick these days, trying to be a better husband to Lou. When the two of them had met some years ago—two leather daddies reaching the twilight of their prime out in New Orleans's orgy-fueled kink scene—it had felt less like fate or romance than a mutual understanding that perhaps, finally, it was coming time to settle down. When they'd been married, Jean had been sixty-one to Lou's fifty-nine Now, neither was getting any younger, fitter, or more conventionally desirable, even to those young twinks who fetishized "daddy" types. Jean had already aged out of that category somewhere in his mid-fifties, his years in the sun and at sea weathering him far sooner than he felt was fair. It was even worse now. He was sure he looked every one of his years and more, and those kids didn't want a guy actually old enough to be their father, or grandfather. Mutual respect had come first for Lou and Jean, and something like love had eventually followed. In the two years they'd been married, though, Lou had taken to monogamy easier than Jean had. The two would occasionally talk fondly about the glory days, but Lou never really indicated that he missed them, missed the seemingly endless stream of young men that had been available to him, hulk of a muscle daddy as he'd been before he threw his back out.

When Jean heard about Lou's sexual history, however, he couldn't help but feel like he'd missed out a little bit, not only because he'd spent so much of his own prime in the closet thanks to his navy years, but also because the two had met *after* Lou had thrown out his back. Deep down, Jean thought he hadn't even experienced the best of his husband, at least not sexually. Of course, he felt terribly guilty even for thinking it. Lately, he'd been brainstorming ways he could channel this guilt into being better to Lou. Maybe if he put his mind more on Lou he'd forget about all the wild, rough sex he wished he could still be having and give himself fully to his marriage.

When Jean turned his back on the tour group to lead them across the rocky parking lot to the boat, he beamed. A real smile, an I-can't-wait-to-take-your-money smile. Today, he knew, was going to turn out just fine.

Whatever hungover reluctance the boys had displayed earlier disappeared when the boat started moving. They hollered when the engine kicked up. They kept their beer cans wedged in the ice of the communal cooler Jean kept on his boat, plucking from it liberally.

Each of them kept a stainless-steel bottle between his legs. Every hour or so throughout the tour, they all went quiet and took one small sip, in unison, from these bottles.

"Gotta stay hydrated, huh?" Jean remarked the second time they all sipped simultaneously, directing the comment to the bridegroom himself: a true beefcake crammed into a navy-blue polo whose otherwise greenish, pale face was red with sunburn on the cheeks and nose. The boat was stopped, drifting. Jean resisted the urge to stare at the man's bulging chest.

"What?" said the groom, sealing the lid on his stainless-steel bottle as his companions did the same. "Oh, good idea."

And he tucked the stainless-steel bottle between his legs, grabbing a water bottle from the cooler. Interesting. Jean stared at the bottle squeezed between the man's thighs, wondering what was really in it, until the young man turned to him. Jean looked away, not wanting the groom to get the wrong idea. For what it was worth, Jean didn't care much for what was below a man's legs—size and shape and whatnot—as long as the man was circumcised like a good American.

He caught sight of a gator's nose poking out of the muddy water over by some brush. As the young men watched, Jean speared a piece of hot dog with a long stick, dangled it over the water, and called the creature over with the loud, repetitive, lip-smacking gator call all the tour guides learned. It swam over, tail snaking languidly side to side.

It was a little thing, maybe five feet. He explained to the tour group that you could tell their size from the distance between the eyes and the tip of the snout: one foot for every inch at the nose, so this gator with a five-inch snout had about five feet from head to tail. They went wild about this—they all seemed to cream their pants at any little trivia Jean gave out—but that response was nothing compared to their eruption when the gator leaped out of the water to chomp the piece of hot dog at the end of Jean's stick.

"Ohhhhhhhhhh," they all yelled.

"No way, bro!" someone said.

Another yelled, "Bro, he's so stupid, bro!"

And so on. Jean slipped another hot dog end onto the tip of his stick, dangled it over the water. The young men erupted again when the alligator jumped, this time even louder. By the third time, when the gator jumped for the hot dog and then swam away, satisfied, Jean's strange passengers were going completely nuts.

"Go on, you lazy motherfucker!" screamed one.

"Bro, does he just do this all day, bro?"

"He's sooooo lazy, bro."

"Yo, do you just sit around all day and let people feed you? Fucking fatass."

It started to disconcert Jean, all this overreaction. It struck him more as heckling than anything else, but what kind of man needed to heckle an alligator? It started to nag at him: how they took the gator's behavior almost personally—like they expected better of it—not to mention the greenish hue to their own pale skin, the dryness under their eyes that appeared almost scaly, the combination of camaraderie and superiority with which these preternaturally handsome young men assessed the scaly, ancient predators of the swamp. He pushed the thought down, thinking about the cut of steak he'd buy Lou, perhaps even the six-pack of craft beer the two of them would drink while Jean regaled him with stories of these weirdos.

The passengers took a sip in unison from their stainless-steel bottles. Jean couldn't help but notice all of their large eyes on him.

As mystifying as Jean found their aggression toward the alligators, he began to feel agitated, sexually, at all the testosterone flying around that boat. Try as he might, he couldn't help but think about the all-too-occasional sex he had with his husband because of Lou's bad back and how tired Jean himself would get after shouting about swamps all day in front of pack after pack of wide-eyed tourists. *These* men had something of the vitality he missed, and whether he wanted to be them or jump into bed with them, he couldn't tell. But as strange as these fellows were, they did something to him, something that hadn't been done in a long time.

At one point, Jean brought up apple snails, an invasive species wreaking havoc on the swamps by eating up all the aquatic plants. A darker-skinned guy that Jean took to be Indian piped up. He wore a safari hat and a Hawaiian shirt—unbuttoned enough to reveal a wealth of chest hair and pectoral strength—and became weirdly defensive of the fist-sized snails.

"It's humans that brought them here in the first place," the guy said in a nasally, precise voice. Something about the way he said the word *humans* unnerved Jean. "They're just seizing an opportunity they were given when they were dragged from their own homes against their will. They're not the *invasive species* we should be blaming here."

Everyone else fell silent, nodding along. The boat drifted alongside the patch of duckweed Jean had pointed out, the leaves speckled with the pink eggs of the apple snails, looking like so many chewed-up wads of bubble gum.

"Well, sure," Jean said, trying to sound friendly. "It just spells out trouble for the other critters in the swamp is all. These fuckers lay eggs like crazy, and ain't nobody in the state of Louisiana found a way to get rid of 'em without killing other animals."

"Isn't that just like the human race," said the guy, staring right over Jean's head. "Scrambling to stop a thing they set in motion themselves. Calling it an *invasion*."

Close up, the dark skin on this one's arms and chest was so rough it was almost scaly.

"Well," Jean finally said, shaking away the kind of chill which, according to his mother, meant someone was stepping on his grave. "If you gentlemen'd like, you can take a closer look." He brushed past them to the middle of the port side of the boat, leaned over, and plucked an apple snail off the duckweed with both hands. The brown, wriggling head receded into its shell.

At the dock, each of them shook hands with Jean when exiting the boat—firm handshakes, he was pleased to note—and each of them slipped a bill into his hand, all conspiratorial, like he was a bouncer and they were bribing their way into a club. Like any good gentleman, Jean thanked them profusely without glancing down at how much they'd given him until they were out of sight.

When at last they were out of sight of the boat, Jean looked down into his hand—only to count eight crisp, single dollar bills. He cursed, kicked the side of the boat, considered throwing the meager eight bucks, this mockery of generosity, to the goddamned gators. *Assholes.* He shoved the cash into the pocket of his cargo shorts and sulked to the back of his boat.

That's when he kicked at something that made a scraping sound as it skittered away. Jean looked down. It was one of the stainless-steel bottles these creepy cheapskates had been sipping from. In fact, the boat was littered with them. Jean picked up the one he'd kicked, a pristine bottle that seemed almost to shine despite the shade provided by the boat's awning. He reckoned it to be a liter in size, and still nearly full. It looked like all eight of the guys had forgotten their bottles, and they all held the same amount of liquid as this one. Unlike the box of beer with the mysterious label, these stainless-steel cylinders bore no logo at all—they all had the look of the sleek, refillable water bottles so many geeky tourists swore by, even clipped to the belts of their cargo shorts, but they were devoid even of imprints on the bottom to indicate what company they'd come from. Almost too normal, eerily nondescript, as if daring Jean to look away and think nothing of them.

Now, at this point, a Southern gentleman and upstanding tour guide like Jean would normally go hollering after the group, give them a hard time—*hey, y'all forgetting something?*—all in good fun, and hand over the bottles. But, you see, Jean had eight measly bucks in his pocket from the rich brats who ordered a twenty-two-person boat just so they wouldn't get rained on, and wasn't he getting a little too old to be chasing down healthy, able-bodied young men who had the calves and asses to prove they were perfectly capable of marching over and getting their own damned bottles? Nah, if the bottles were that important, someone from the group could jog over, or call when they got home and realized they'd left them behind. Meanwhile, Jean would play dumb—*In my boat? I never noticed such a thing! Why, I think I'd remember something like that!* Anyway, maybe Jean wanted a taste of whatever psychedelic cocktail made those fools act so goddamned weird. Maybe his coworkers would be willing to share some of their (no doubt more generous) tips to find out.

It was almost as if they had been left there on purpose, daring him to take a sip. He stowed the stainless-steel bottles in his personal cooler, and none of the stingy young men returned.

When it came time to pack up at the end of the day, Jean popped open the lid of his personal cooler. The ice had all melted, and the bottles those young men had left floated at the top like dead fish. Jean pulled one out, thinking he'd give it a try. Whatever it was, it had given the guys who'd left it one hell of a time. And it had been a day. Hadn't he earned the same?

He unscrewed the cap and took a careful sip, which he nearly spat out. The liquid was unbearably bitter, with an unsettling gritty texture and a savory aftertaste, as if someone had sprinkled turmeric in battery acid and called it a cocktail. Whatever they were drinking, it surely wasn't beer. He'd heard people made psychedelic mushroom teas that tasted like shit but took you for the ride of your life if you could choke them down, that youngish rich guys with boring office jobs that hadn't managed to suck the partying souls out of themselves just yet would "microdose" hallucinogens in small quantities to keep a nice psychedelic buzz going without losing their minds. It would explain why those guys had acted so strangely but managed to amble out of the boat and across the dock without incident. Maybe he should pour them out, but then, he thought, why not go on a trip? Didn't hurt those guys. So he swallowed. Only pussies spit, he chuckled to himself.

The sun began to sink low enough that the cypress trees cast crooked shadows over the water, and none of Jean's coworkers seemed to have stuck around. Some nights a hardcore crew of them would sit on a couple of the picnic tables out front, sipping their customers' forgotten beer into all hours of the night. Jean's husband wouldn't be home from the refinery until late.

He plugged his nose and took another, slightly larger sip. Didn't take much with these psychedelic drugs. He didn't feel anything at first, but he knew better than to take more. Instead, he busied himself about the boat, stuffing the bottles into his backpack, dumping the excess ice and freezing-cold water, picking up trash in his boat, and so on. When he was done, he lay on the bow of the boat and stared up at the reddening sky, waiting for the high to come.

Nothing still. He watched the sky change colors—the gases over the swamp made for a spectacular sunset, a spectacle of purples and reds and dusty blues, whether you were high or not—but by the time the sky was a dark, grayish purple, Jean was certain he'd been ripped off again. He felt nothing, saw nothing out of the ordinary, and cursed his customers for getting his hopes up a second time.

As he finished up, a crowd of alligators gathered across the channel from the dock, watching him from the reeds.

On the way home, Jean stopped at Otis's, a little orange butcher's shack that boasted, among other things, the best cuts of gator meat anywhere near the city. The owner, Otis, also sold a decent rib-eye, and though Jean's tips wouldn't afford him anything too fancy, he still had it in his mind that he wanted to bring home steak for dinner.

The butcher's shop was cramped and stuffy, a ceiling fan twirling lazily—too slow to stir the humid air—in the dim yellow light. When Jean had paid for his order, Otis, a skinny bald man about ten years his junior, said, "Bringin' some steaks home for the little lady, eh, young man?"

Jean snatched the bag from him. "Hey, fuck you, Otis," he said and turned away. His voice sounded different to him somehow. Clearer. He shut the rickety screen door behind him a bit harder than he normally would. Otis was one of the few casual acquaintances out here who knew Jean was married to a man, and usually he was cool about it. That he'd chosen today of all days to be an asshole nearly sent Jean over the edge.

His energy sapped and his frustration bubbling over, Jean noticed that his hands were pale, large, and smooth on the steering wheel. He squeezed his eyes shut, shook his head, and threw the car into reverse. He never once looked at his reflection in the rearview mirror.

—~— —~— —~—

Jean and his husband lived in New Orleans East, way up toward the bayou, in a modest house thirty minutes' drive from downtown. On nights like this, when Lou worked late and Jean had some extra steam he needed to blow off, he'd head down to a tolerable—if touristy—gay bar in the French Quarter, nurse a couple Jack & Cokes at the bar, and leer at some of the young, in-town-for-the-weekend ass. After the day he'd had, Jean needed it. Lou didn't know about this little habit, but it wasn't like Jean meant anything by it, and even if he did, nothing would ever come of it. Young, tight-bodied tourists weren't in town looking to hook up with someone Jean's age. Anyway, there was a difference between looking and touching. Lou didn't need to know.

Despite the relative darkness outside, the bar itself hung in that twilight state where the remaining day-drinking tourists trickled out to make it to their ghost tours, and the night birds trickled in from their overpriced dinners. The dimly lit room had a divey feel, all dark wood and beer advertisements, which Jean liked about it. Aside from the single, unobtrusive rainbow flag at the end of the bar, you would never know it was a gay bar from the décor. The clientele made it clear enough, though, and the occasional confused, heterosexual tourists who thought they were in for a drink at an "authentic NoLa bar" soon disappeared. The bar was a breeding ground.

Normally, Jean would get a drink and make himself scarce at some tiny table in the corner, but tonight he felt like taking up space. He parked his ass right at the center of the bar and ordered a shot of well whiskey, followed by another shot, followed by a Jack & Coke. He'd cause a little trouble: hit on some young men, just to freak them out, stare openly at them while they ordered their drinks, maybe smack an ass or two. All in good fun, to the chagrin of the staff who usually interacted with people Jean's age as little as possible. "Olds" were bad for business.

But the weird thing was, the two bartenders—interchangeable little Ken dolls not even half his age—acted all sweet on him, using words like "baby" and "hon" when they took his order, which they often pointedly used only on younger men than Jean, while not even calling him "sir." One of them, when handing Jean his Jack & Coke, even dragged his thumb across Jean's before letting go. Normally, the twinky bartenders at this joint at best barely tolerated old fogeys like him, but at worst they acted downright hostile: shooting dirty looks at him when they thought he wasn't looking, chintzing him with weak drinks, refusing to make eye contact or small talk, never cracking a smile. Nobody could outright kick him out for being old and ugly, but they sure as hell made it known he wasn't welcome. It was one of those things about the more touristy gay bars Jean found most confusing, since out on the bayou it was more often the older tourists who could afford the best tips, but apparently being the type of bar frequented by someone who looked like Jean was a worse risk than being stiffed on a tip for rude behavior. Tonight, though, they treated him like a prince. Maybe they could tell he'd had a bad day and were taking pity on him.

Before Jean could set his sights on a young man to mess with—the bar was still quiet enough—to his surprise, a real specimen of a man ordered a vodka cranberry and scooted his bar stool close to Jean's.

"Hey," the man said. "So." He was olive-skinned, probably half-Latino, Jean guessed—dark hair quaffed up in a heavily gelled pompadour, slender but well-muscled in a white fishnet shirt, probably close to thirty.

"So," Jean said, amused. This man was no twenty-two-year-old baby gay for Jean to freak out, but he'd do just fine. "Business or pleasure? What're you in town for?"

"That obvious I'm a tourist, huh?" the man said. "Well, a

little bit of both, I guess. There's a conference for tech startups downtown, but I'm trying to cross *everything* off my list in the meantime." He raised his eyebrows. So either he was a real, true daddy chaser, or he was messing with Jean. Anyway, he was one of the femme types, speaking with up-endings in his higher-pitched voice and given to large, wild hand gestures. He continued, "How about you?"

"Born and raised here, but I've lived all over the place. Moved back to New Orleans East after I got . . ." Jean paused—he was going to say "married five years ago," but something wicked came over him, and instead he said, "out of the navy. Thirty years ago."

The man was looking at him, puzzled, and then his eyes widened and he started giggling. "Oh, you're so funny, that's funny," he said. "The navy, that's so funny. What'd you do to stay so young, then? Suck Satan's dick?" He was giggling again—a distinctly unattractive quality in a man, in Jean's opinion.

And this was enough. After everything else he'd dealt with today? He blew up.

"Now, you look here," Jean said, getting up. "If you just came over here to make fun of me, that ain't right. I came here for a nice coupla drinks after a long day's work and I ain't gonna sit here while some sissy boy like you makes an ass of me!"

Jean grabbed his drink and marched to the corner of the room, opposite the bar, thinking he'd finish his drink and scowl at this asshole from across the room the whole way through. He could hear the man downright cackling at the bar and feel the heat in his own face. He hated to get worked up like this in public, especially about his age. Hadn't he played into the daddy thing when his skin was still tight enough for the young guys to fetishize him? Hadn't he shunned guys his own age until they were the only ones that would return his gaze at the local leather watering hole? A part of him knew his generation bore as much responsibility for age hang-ups in the gay community as these twinks, but confronting a young, attractive man who only gave him the time of day to make fun of him filled Jean with a rage toward the young that astonished and embarrassed him. He hadn't lived through all of it—the AIDS crisis, "Don't Ask, Don't Tell," his days staying closeted in the military so he didn't get ostracized or worse, the days when "queer" was just a slur for people like him and not some fancy reclaimed word the youths used to describe themselves—so that some young punk could pull one over on him when he'd just come in to relax after a long day of work. He took a clumsy slug of beer while he walked, hoping to cool his anger, but dripped a little foam that splashed on his shoe instead.

When he got to the corner table, though, things got really confusing.

See, on the wall opposite the bar was a long, dirty mirror, and the mirror-man approaching the mirror-table was not the sun-spotted, wrinkled, balding man with a slim frame and a hanging gut that Jean had gotten used to seeing in the bathroom mirror when he brushed his teeth in the morning.

No, the person he saw was smoking hot—mid-to-late twenties, broad shoulders, muscles bulging against the sleeves of Jean's orange swamp tour staff shirt, with a head of thick, dark brown hair. The face was familiar, but utterly not Jean, who had always had thin light hair, even when he was younger. And those cheekbones! Whose were they? They were . . . they were . . . it couldn't be. The man staring at him in the mirror was the groom from the bachelor party on his tour earlier that day, wearing Jean's shirt and cargo shorts. Jean rubbed his eyes and pinched himself, but the unfamiliar reflection remained, mirroring his every action. Damn, Jean thought, whatever psychedelic cocktail those boys mixed up must've been some powerful stuff.

And yet Jean felt completely lucid, or at least as lucid as he could be after three drinks. He felt nothing of the highs or the strange bursts of energy or the general creepy sense that *something just wasn't right* that LSD or shrooms always gave him.

Just when he was wondering whether he should find a place to lay his head *quick*, before the more destabilizing effects of the drugs hit, a man approached him in the mirror and pressed himself against Jean's thigh. It was the man from the bar.

He put his mouth awfully close to Jean's ear and said, "That was a spot-on Southern gentleman impression back there. You were *so* funny. Do you practice in the mirror or something?"

Though Jean's accent was usually mild enough, he knew the South in him really came out when he was angry. He relaxed, considered what he saw in the mirror: two handsome men in their prime, the steam of pheromones practically fogging up the mirror. He smiled. In that moment Jean thought of one thing only. Not his hope that he could be a better husband to Lou, not the fact that this man pressing against his hip was a little too flamboyant to be his type. He could think only of how long it had been since he'd felt so lusted after, and so aroused himself.

Jean turned so that his pelvis rested against the other man's, and their faces were barely inches away. "Why, yes," he said, laying the accent on nice and thick. "Yes, I do."

When Jean woke before dawn, he did not immediately realize he was in somebody else's bed. Initially, he had the thought that his bed was comfier than he'd ever noticed. Then, he opened his eyes to a cream-colored ceiling and an ornate light fixture with the fan's arms looking like fat, gold leaves that he definitely did not recognize. And next to him slept an equally pretty man who was definitely not his husband. And the night came back to him.

He'd never gotten up and dressed as fast as he did just then. Usually, he got up slowly, nestling in the comforts of his warm sheets for as long as possible and wondering which ache from a lifetime on the water would come back to life when he moved.

Today, the horror of his situation propelled him across the room to his carelessly flung-aside pile of clothes and had him zipping up his pants before he even registered the usual twinge in his left wrist—the wrist he always inadvertently favored at the helm on a choppy day and had used to catch himself from falling one too many times over the decades when rough surf sent him wobbling toward the deck.

The apartment was some Airbnb in the French Quarter, renovated to appear even older than it actually was, all crown molding and decadent, gilded furniture. Jean snatched up the silver bottle he'd taken with him, from which he'd taken tiny sips throughout the night just as he'd seen the guys on the boat do. This morning, it was right in the foyer by his shoes and socks—the only clothing he'd removed with any care. On the way out, he caught a glimpse of himself in the oversized mirror. It was him all right, gnarly old Jean, back in his own body.

Out where the street cleaners erased the evidence of Saturday night French Quarter filth, Jean sweated all the way to his car trying to convince himself that the effects of whatever drugs were in that bottle made him do it, or that maybe the psychedelics made that morning's scene appear to be something more than it was. Maybe he'd only imagined, in a drug haze, that he and that stranger had fucked with wild abandon. And yet there he had been that morning, naked in bed beside a man young enough to be his son. What was there to confuse? It had all been real, borrowed body and all. Jean knew that besides a few drinks, nothing had put him out of his right mind except, maybe, that the anonymity of looking like someone else, someone young and hardy and beautiful, meant he could do whatever he pleased. There it was. The truth, staring at him plain in the face.

He got into his old pickup truck. He didn't even dare look at his phone. What must Lou have thought? It hadn't been the first time Jean hadn't returned after work, but he usually let his husband know he was passing out on the yellow couch at work.

No, he distinctly remembered ignoring Lou's texts the night before.

In fact, the man he'd slept with—Ricky, his name was—had demanded they take a picture together before they left the bar. He'd snatched Jean's phone before he could protest (the man's own phone had been dead), and while they were taking the picture, an alert had flashed across the screen, a text from Lou: "Where are you." No question mark. That was Lou's way.

"My roommate," Jean had told Ricky without hesitation, amazed how easy it was to lie when he looked like the kind of man people were dying to believe. "He's always getting locked out, but he can deal with it himself for a change."

Ricky had laughed, typed his number into a new message box, and sent the photograph to himself. "Memories," he'd said. "I won't post it or anything."

Jean started the engine, stepped on the gas. Light was seeping into the cloudless sky. His car was rancid, like a possum had crawled up in it and died: the steaks, Jean realized. He'd completely forgotten about the steaks he'd gotten for dinner last night.

No, there was no getting out of this one. A real man had the integrity, at least, to come clean. He'd speed home, creep into bed before the sun came up, and curl himself up beside his husband. After work he'd confess everything, explaining to Lou how he literally hadn't been himself, show him the effects of the weird elixir of youth left behind by his even weirder passengers. Lou would be mad, probably, but whatever young body Jean inhabited when he showed his husband what the stuff in the bottles did would be irresistibly sexy, and he'd understand. Hell, maybe the two of them would bust the bottles out every once in a while and have the aggressive, acrobatic sex they'd have had if they'd met in their youth, before the beginnings of arthritis and the occasional moment of impotence.

Jean picked up powdered donuts—Lou's favorite—on the

way home, which meant he had just enough time to rinse off in the shower (it wouldn't do to smell like another man's sweat) and no time at all to slither into bed with Lou. But that was all right. Lou was dead asleep. He wouldn't know the difference. He scrawled *sorry* on a light blue sticky note and stuck it to the white donut box at the kitchen table. When he got into his car to go to work, Jean was feeling less frantic already. Anyway, he only had a little bit of a hangover, just a faint ache at the crown of his head. So that was something.

As the morning tour kicked off, this one a mishmash of several groups of three or four, his optimism chipped away to reveal the nugget of dread beneath it. Tours like this, filled with small groups who didn't know each other, were always quieter. The passengers were too scared of embarrassing themselves in front of so many strangers to ask Jean questions or even laugh too loudly at his jokes. This morning, it left him too much space to think about what he'd done. Their blank, squinting stares seemed to ask, *What kind of a man breaks someone's trust the second some shiny new thing looks his way?*

Many of the alligators turned their noses up at his hot dog nubs today, and while Jean knew they had probably just had enough to eat the previous day—they didn't need much, and that made them lazier toward the end of the week—he couldn't help but think the unwashable smell of a cheating-ass husband was really what kept them away.

By the next tour, a high school cheerleading team in town for a conference, the dread soured into irritability, and then resentment. To a man's man like Jean, the only thing more repellant than teenaged girls was a large group of them, screaming and hyper. The grumpier he got with them, the more they thought he was playing the crotchety old Southerner, and the more they ate it up.

After that tour, at lunchtime, he finally looked down at his phone, thinking he'd apologize to Lou again for not saying anything the night before, maybe ask him how his day was going. He wouldn't explain himself just yet, of course. Better in person.

It was then, sitting in his swaying boat at the dock with a ham sandwich in one hand, that he saw Ricky had texted him a few hours prior. He didn't recognize the number, but the text read, "Still sore from last night. In a good way ;) have a good day, stud." Ricky had accompanied the text with a picture of himself on the balcony of his French Quarter Airbnb in nothing but a pair of black briefs. In spite of himself, Jean admired the lithe, lean form and felt a pleasant stirring at the memory of his own hands, smooth and strong, against that tanned skin. There, in the same message thread, was the picture sent from his own phone of the two of them at a table near the bar, Ricky smiling with perfect teeth, Jean (in the body of the groom from yesterday's tour) grinning, close-lipped. There was no mistaking the proof it had all been real.

Except something was off about the photograph from the previous night. There was no flash in the picture, yet in the background, sitting on a barstool past Ricky's right shoulder, a pair of eyes gleamed at them. Jean zoomed in and, in the photograph's shadowy light, could barely make out the grainy face of a man sitting alone at a table, smiling with teeth that seemed unnaturally thin and sharp, glowing eyes a hair too large for his angular face. Jean shivered in spite of the midday August heat, glanced around him with the sudden sensation of being watched, and found that aside from an alligator sunning lazily in the reeds across the way, he was completely alone.

He finally looked at the texts from Lou he'd ignored the night before.

"Where are you," read one, the one he'd seen when he was

with Ricky, followed by another: "were you planning on stopping at the grocery store or what" accompanied by a picture of the empty refrigerator. Finally, around midnight, "guess your having too much Fun 2 respond. Turn off the porch light whenever you come Home."

Jean's first, uncensored thought was, *Damn, what a buzzkill,* and he immediately felt guilty for it. Jean had been out cheating on his husband with a twink after promising to make dinner. Then he thought, would it kill Lou to get off his ass and cook now and then, and why'd he have to be such an asshole about it, and hell, can't a guy blow off some steam after a long day in the sun? For all Lou knew, Jean had been having a couple drinks with his buddies from work. Why'd Lou have to go all Spanish Inquisition on him without even knowing what was what?

The afternoon tours were far livelier, leaving Jean with less time for contemplation. It was hotter today, a true August afternoon in the swamp where the heat sapped the strength and dulled the force of any real worry. But somewhere in Jean, the unbidden resentment at his husband stuck, as if the tricky situation Jean found himself in were Lou's fault for expecting the worst of him in the first place, as if the guilt he felt were unfair and somehow more connected to his husband's judgmental texts than his own choices.

But then, the thing was that Lou never said a word about it that night at dinner. Jean ditched the steaks that had rotted in the car for a fresh pair, and sure, there was a little bit of awkwardness, but one of Lou's best qualities was that he let things go pretty easily. He could be a real bull in the moment, but it never lasted—unlike Jean, who felt the need to come out on top of every argument and held quiet, merciless grudges when proven wrong.

The two ate as usual, telling each other about their workdays. Jean always had more to share here, given the nature of the characters he often encountered at his job compared to Lou's generally humdrum work at the refinery. Jean kept looking for the right opportunity to tell Lou what had happened, to apologize, but his husband was so entertained by Jean's tales of bachelor party boys and screeching cheerleaders, such a damned good audience, such an overall fine companion it was almost infuriating. It wasn't just that there was no chance to bring it up. It was that Lou was such a goddamn treasure that evening that Jean couldn't dream of ruining their night with the news of his infidelity. Not to mention how much trouble it would be just to get him to understand exactly what had happened, just to get him to believe it.

The sex they had that evening was the best they'd had since before they'd agreed to stop sleeping with other people a few years back. What he always loved about fucking Lou was the sheer bulk of his hairy body. Even past his supposed prime, Lou was a paragon of masculinity in every way—deep voice, full beard, bulging arms, hair in all the right crevices of his hulking form. On Jean's worst days he envied and even resented this quality in his husband, but nights like tonight, it made Jean feel like a real man to make someone like that submit, to wrap his hands around a giant's throat and make him beg. Sure, Lou's body had gone more than a little soft, particularly at the midsection. But the body hair was still there, and tonight, Jean imagined him as the bodybuilding bear he must have been before his back gave out. Tonight, Jean fucked his husband like he might have if they'd met a few decades before, still high on the newness of sex and the seemingly endless libido of youth.

When they'd both finished and retreated to their sides of the bed—they both hated physical closeness after sex—Lou, lying flat on his back catching his breath, said, "Goddamn, what the hell happened to you last night?"

Jean's stomach clenched. Here it was: here came the conversation he'd been avoiding. Well, it had been nice while it lasted. He sat up in bed.

"Well, whatever they're putting in the water down at the docks," Lou continued before Jean could let the excuses pour out, "I hope they do it every time you take me to bed."

And then a funny thing happened. A day went by. Then two. No lightning struck Jean. No angry god of monogamous commitment appeared to him in a dream. Lou didn't stand over him in the morning with his finger in Jean's face and declare, "I know what really happened Saturday night, you two-timing motherfucker."

A funny thing happened—nothing.

Except that Jean did get curious. It was Wednesday, and Lou was working even later than usual, and the weekdays were always slower for Jean—mostly maintenance and admin stuff broken up by the rare, sleepy weekday tour. Tonight, Jean was wondering: would those other bottles make him look like the other guys in the bachelor party? He had time to find out. In August, it wasn't unheard of for Jean to drink with his coworkers into the wee hours of a weeknight or two, so he could do as he pleased as long as he let Lou know he'd be gone.

That's how Jean ended up at home, staring at the full-length bathroom mirror at the nerdy but muscular guy who'd had a lot to say about the invasive apple snails. It took some rummaging through old clothes to find something that fit this body well enough—this fellow was a bit shorter and broader than Jean—but this afforded him the opportunity to notice how great this guy looked naked, he thought, in spite of the uncircumcised penis. He settled on a pair of Lou's jeans, but a button-down shirt of his own. Then he *had* to get out of the house, didn't he? Lou couldn't see him like this, not without some kind of warning. It just wouldn't make sense.

On this night, Jean did make it home for dinner, and he also discovered how long the strange juice would last without a second sip before the chariot, as it were, turned back into a pumpkin—it turned out to be about four hours from when Jean left the house. He'd stood, pants around his ankles, against a wall in the back alley of a bar, with a lovely young man on his knees before him, when he felt a wooziness so intense he forgot himself, shoved the young man's bobbing skull away, and stumbled inside to the men's room, pants still half off when he got there. He thought maybe he was having a stroke, but when he got to the mirror with the words *it is a sunny day* ready to tumble from his lips (words you can't say without slurring if you're having a stroke), he felt like his normal self again and, to his dismay, he looked like his normal self again, too.

So the wooziness he must've slept through the first time, and the bottle, well, he'd never leave the house without it again. Not that he planned on leaving the house in someone else's skin again. Dammit! No, this would be his last time. This ought to be his last time. This couldn't happen again.

But then again, he realized a few days later, *then again,* if that was to be his absolute last hurrah, it wasn't much of a hurrah, now, was it? Caught with his pants down, as it were, unable to finish the job. If he planned to cut himself off, dump the contents of the stainless-steel bottles into the muddy waters of the swamp where they belonged, shouldn't he have one last real, hardy, steamy little adventure? Where was the real harm in doing it one more time?

This was how it began. He waited a few more days. He was *so* well behaved, really! And then he had his hurrah, in the body of one of the bachelors from the tour who was taller and a bit slimmer. But this guy was still more muscle and sinew than slenderness. It was easy for Jean to find a willing vessel of a man.

And the morning after that adventure, he wondered if it wasn't a bit rash to get rid of the bottles entirely. Their contents could be worth an awful lot of money, lead to some serious scientific discovery or other. And eventually, one little slip up here and there became two or three, and Jean was moonlighting in these bodies a couple times a week without much remorse. It amazed him how quickly the guilt disappeared and the earth-shattering thrill of Doing a Bad Thing gave way to mere habit. It was like smoking into his early twenties. He knew he could quit at any moment.

One thing never ceased to disturb him, though, and that was that no matter how used to the outings he might be, he could never shake the feeling of being watched. Never keen on being seen in the same body twice, he hopped bars all over the French Quarter's Fruit Loop and beyond. Still, from the upstairs leather lounge at The Phoenix to the crowded Golden Lantern, he'd often spy, out of the corner of his eye, some disconcertingly pale hunk watching him. Always a different face, always stunningly attractive but for the large eyes and pale, was-it-greenish-or-a-trick-of-the-light skin. If Jean snapped a subtle photo, disguised as a selfie with his would-be watcher in the background, the eyes almost always glowed like a cat's in the picture—no, he realized, like a gator at night. Most often, when he'd look again, the guy would be gone or on the way out the door, but the curiosity lingered. Who else had discovered the secrets of youth he had? What did they look like under all that muscle? What would happen if Jean spoke to one of them? He never got the chance. The moment he spotted that fixed stare, it was always too late to catch whoever it was, and the strange moment would pass, and whatever young buck he'd been chatting up would command his attention once again.

He was really getting the hang of it. He'd labeled the bottles by the body to which they corresponded, figured out just how much he needed to drink to get the most mileage out of the transformation (truly, they went a long way, one tiny sip every hour). And now, it was Real Men only for Jean. Nothing like that pansy Ricky (handsome as he was) from the first time. Muscular men, with deep voices, rarely a day over thirty-five years old.

In his borrowed bodies, Jean could afford to be choosy. Masculinity, fitness, and youth were a particular kind of currency on the gay cruising market, and Jean had credit to spare.

It turned out that, of all the bodies in the bachelor party, the chubbier, least attractive one with the bad skin had the greatest advantage in the enormity of his cock, and when Jean walked around in the right fit of pants, with the confidence of the well-endowed, finding a suitable mate never became a problem. The mere thrill of wielding these bodies, as well as the effortlessly erect members attached to them, added an extra element of excitement beyond the fact that Jean was having sex with the most attractive men he'd ever come into contact with. *Being* these younger men was its own thrill. A few times, Jean just stood in front of the full-length mirror and jerked himself off, marveling at the hairy musculature of the body he was in or, in the case of the one skinny guy, the waistline he hadn't dreamed of in years (Jean himself had been on the lean side in his younger years, and while being in this skinny body wasn't as exciting a fantasy to him as the hardier bodies, it did have a certain nostalgia to it). *Mine,* he'd think while he stared at himself in the mirror, touching himself. *This body is mine.* But masturbating proved the least gratifying use of these bodies, and though Jean conserved the contents of the metamorphic bottles as best he could, he knew supplies were limited.

So it went. In the city whose visitors blew through for a weekend and did unspeakable things with the guiltless abandon of the anonymous—the belief that without the possibility of proof there was no real possibility of consequence—it was easy enough for Jean to join the masquerade. Donning the mask of the borrowed bodies, Jean let that other mask, that of the faithful, honorable husband, fall away for a while.

But back in the faithful husband mask, he tried to make up for his cheating, at least for a while. He and Lou consistently had the best sex they'd had in ages, and Jean attacked his marital duties with fuller force, making his husband eggs in the morning, bringing home the good cuts of bacon that added an extra twenty minutes to his evening commute. But the more he snuck away in his borrowed bodies, the more exhausted and jealous for time he became, and he realized such gestures of affection were lost on his husband who, after five years of marriage, ate whatever Jean put in front of him with neither praise nor complaint. As for the sex, well, after enough time driving a fancy red Cadillac, it's a little hard to go back to riding around in your beat-up old pickup, now, isn't it?

On a Tuesday night at a little before six, Jean stood in front of the mirror in the bachelor's body, wearing nothing but boxer shorts. As it was the first body he'd worn, he was particularly fond of it, and while the other bottles had half left in their tanks, this one was nearly empty. This would probably be his last night with it, and he'd taken his first sip at home, so he could look at himself in the mirror one last time. Before pulling on a pair of blue jeans, he stared wistfully at the meaty thighs on this body. He had tomorrow off. He'd make this night count.

As he rooted around in the closet for a button-down, he heard the front door open and shut. But that wasn't right. Lou wasn't supposed to be home until eleven, and it was only . . . he looked at his phone to check the time and saw a text from Lou, "Stomach felt pretty Loose if you know what I mean. No more tacos for a While. Coming home."

And then there was Lou, in the bedroom doorway, squinting at Jean like he was a mirage.

"Who the hell are you?" Lou said. Jean knew all Lou could see was the body of the bachelor that Jean inhabited: half-naked, wearing Lou's own blue jeans. It was clear exactly how this looked

"It's me," was all he could think to say, lamely, even though he knew how little sense it would make. But if Lou could just see, if Lou could just understand. "It's Jean."

"What's this about my husband?" Then, something seemed to click in Lou's mind. His expression went dark, brows furrowed.

"If you'll just let me explain," Jean pleaded, "I promise it'll all make sense."

But Lou wasn't listening anymore; he was advancing. "He tell you he had a husband? He tell you, you was fucking with a married man? Well, you best get outta my house before I blow your brains out and make my pussy of a husband eat 'em."

"Lou . . ."

The two stood inches away. In one last fit of desperation, Jean reached out, grabbed the back of Lou's head, and pushed Lou's face toward his own. As if it was a fairy tale, as if true love's kiss would turn back time, as if it would turn Jean back into himself, as if no matter what he looked like his husband would recognize him in this most vulnerable act. And for a moment,

Lou didn't react, and Jean thought it might work.

Then Lou shoved him away and punched him square in the face. For all Lou had softened over the years, the punch hurt like a motherfucker, like Jean's nose had sucked up every nerve in his body and set each one on fire. And that was it. What could Jean do? He wasn't going to convince Lou of anything when he was like this, and Jean wasn't about to get in a fist fight with his husband. Hadn't he done enough? Anyway, he felt like the hit was the least he deserved.

So Jean crept out of the room as his husband watched, feet planted, his head the only thing that moved, like a gator trying to decide whether the tiny bit of hot dog was worth the effort. Jean thought it best to just leave, as he was, shirtless. He had work T-shirts in his truck, and the quicker he got away from Lou, the better it would be for both of them.

"Shameless pussy of a home-wrecking manwhore," Lou was saying as Jean opened the front door and scampered out. And the worst thing was, Lou hadn't even guessed the half of it.

Jean slept in his car on the side of the road by the swamp that night, squirming in the stuffy August night but smart enough not to open the windows and let the bugs in. He'd sleep on the couch in the office behind the gift shop for a few nights, then come home and explain everything, beg Lou to take him back, show him the bottles and say, honestly, my duck, would you have done any differently?

If he was honest with himself, Jean knew Lou would have, though, and in the morning, he awoke to see Lou had sent him two messages.

The first read, "I'll be at the Refinery till 10 tonight, you can get your stuff before then. Don't bother sticking around trying to Apologize or explain yourself. I don't want to know."

The second message read, "Funny thing is I can't say I'm surprised."

Jean started the engine and blasted the air conditioning. It was the second message that got him. It wasn't the brisk, efficient coldness of the first text. It was that Lou had already suspected that deep down in Jean, somewhere, lay a cowardly half-man who would cheat on his husband and hide it.

At the house, the first thing Jean did was write a note at the vanity next to their bathroom, plopping one of the silver bottles next to the note.

"Lou, I'm the sorriest sack of shit there ever was. I know this. I won't try to sugarcoat it. I messed up real bad. The worst. But there's something I need you to understand about what happened. Remember that bachelor party from a few weeks ago? These guys, they left behind these big bottles. I figured it was something psychedelic in them, gave it a try myself, and . . . I can't explain how it works. Hear me out. It's something in these bottles that turns you into a young stud. That young man you saw in the house, that was *me,* Lou, honest to god. I was planning on showing you sooner, but I had to figure out how to use them before . . ."

No. The time for hiding the truth was past. A real man would come clean when he was caught red-handed. He crossed that last sentence out and kept writing. He told Lou all about what he'd done, his moonlighting in the bodies of these men. It hurt him to write it, to commit it to paper and look directly at how awful he'd been—something he'd managed not to do for weeks. He imagined how disgusted Lou would be. But he had to tell the truth. Finally, he finished:

I couldn't help myself, Lou. I really was planning on telling you. But then, I don't know what came over me. It's been years since anyone looked at me the way they did when I looked like that. I'm not trying to make excuses, just make you understand. It's awful, what I did. I'm sorry. I'm so, so sorry. But think about what these bottles could do for us, that's all I ask. Just think. I swear I'll make it up to you if you give me the chance.

I left you one of these bottles so you can see for yourself. Just a sip is all it takes.

Love,
J.

As he was writing, he considered leaving all of the bottles as a token of good faith, but then, there was no telling what Lou would do when he was mad. He might dump them all down the drain, and then where would they be? The juice could really be worth something.

At least, that's what he told himself when he threw the rest into his backpack.

When Jean zipped his bag and looked up, his first thought about seeing the massive alligator standing on its hind legs in the mirror behind him, besides *what the fuck,* was to wonder how long the impossible creature had been standing there. He spun around to face it, falling back against the vanity, cracking the mirror's glass and knocking over bottles of shaving cream and cologne and aftershave as he did so. It wasn't exactly a gator. Its color was a paler green, like the dull side of a leaf. Its snout was disproportionately long, and it was much, much thicker than a regular gator would be. It was so tall its head nearly touched the ceiling. Its mouth was open in what looked like a grin, but Jean knew better than to equate face shape with real emotion when it came to reptiles. It was absurd—nothing with such mass should've been able to stand on such tiny hind legs. No beast of such size and strength would wait until Jean was aware of it to strike. And yet.

The craziest thing, though, was that in one of its forepaws it held a stick, with which it dangled the end of a hot dog right in front of Jean's face.

At that, Jean blacked out. The last thing he saw was that stubby hot dog, dangling in his face like the lure of an angler fish, and the reptilian teeth behind it borne in the alligator's silent laughter.

Jean awoke, lying on his back on a pile of sand. Directly above him, a harsh spotlight hung from a black ceiling. He was in a circular indoor pit, like an animal on display at the zoo. The paneled walls of his enclosure were blue, painted with a crude child's drawing of clouds, and about fifteen feet up, the walls flattened out to a balcony from which monstrously large alligators watched him—some on all fours, some on their hind legs. Jean counted eight in total.

"Brooooo, I can't believe how ugly it is, bro," came an all-too familiar voice, although there was not a bachelor partyer in sight. It was as if the voice came from inside of Jean's head.

On hearing—sensing?—the gibe at his appearance, he became acutely aware of his nakedness, of sand in crevices he'd rather not have on display under such harsh light. He knelt with his hands over his crotch, wishing more than ever to mask himself in one of those borrowed bodies.

Another voice. "That's just because it's old, bro. The DNA will be whatever, bro, like, we can still use it."

A third voice, distinctly (impossibly) more nasally and precise than the other two, the voice of the man who'd been so defensive of invasive species, said, "We wanted one that would fall for the bottles, didn't we?"

The alligators from above nodded in agreement.

"Well," continued the defender of apple snails, "I ran all the metrics on its old photographs, and according to standards of human attractiveness, this one's facial structure is aesthetically pleasing enough that, with some work on the musculature, it'll make a decent enough specimen if we isolate it at around twenty-two to thirty-five years—that's their term for how many times their planet has made a rotation around its sun."

While the apple snail-lover eviscerated Jean's physique, he watched the other captors busy themselves with machines and clipboards, nodding their reptilian heads at appropriate intervals in an astonishingly human display of feigned interest.

"Besides," said the same nasally voice. "Turns out, this one's as cold-blooded as we are."

Roars of laughter. Jean had little time to connect the dots—the bachelor party's obsession with the gators' laziness, their protectiveness of "invasive species," the seemingly coordinated serendipity with which they'd discarded the bottles.

The understanding barely had time to congeal before the testing began: unspeakable horrors of probing, absurd tests of strength. The creatures sometimes worked in silence, looking at each other and nodding through some silent communication, but sometimes they made their speech known to Jean as they had upon his waking, jeering at his stupidity, his ugliness, his physical inferiority. Occasionally, they'd toss a lukewarm hot dog into the sandpit, which Jean would brush off and, famished, eat with humiliated desperation. Occasionally he awoke in a sandy maze, at the end of which lay a pile of the lukewarm tubes of meat. He never seemed quite able to clean his meals of every grain of sand.

Jean gave himself over to the humiliation. It wasn't so bad, once he got used to it. It felt like penance. Even if the punishment outsized the offense, even if he was caught up in something that wasn't intended as a punishment at all, even if he knew wealthier men got away with much worse and he'd never harmed his husband physically as his captors harmed him, even if being punched and kicked out of his own home and left utterly alone felt like penance enough, he tried to tell himself he'd earned his plight. And that maybe, at the end of this, he'd have suffered enough to earn his husband back.

By night—or what he assumed to be night—when the

lights were out and the alligators left him alone to nurse the aches all over his body from pinching, probing, pricking, and prodding, he thought only of Lou. He thought of Lou moving on with his life, of whether Lou tried to reach out to him once he disappeared, of whether Lou had taken a lover (it would be well within his right, Jean thought sadly). But he thought if he subjected himself to enough of this torment, willingly and uncomplainingly, maybe they'd let him go. Maybe Lou would see he had suffered, sense he had changed, and take him back.

But for now, each night before going to bed, he wrote the same phrase over and over again in the sand, starting from the outer edges of the pit and spiraling inward until he passed out from exhaustion, like a child in detention hoping to shorten his sentence: "I am no better than an alligator."

It was the first lie he told himself that he never managed to believe, and he thought maybe that, in itself, was a start.

The true test happened weeks, maybe months, later. It began subtly at first, the aches in his bones easily chalked up to the constant "research" done on his body, the nonstop itching likely caused by the sand he could never quite wash away (what passed for a shower here was his daily wakeup call: water sprayed unceremoniously from the walls all around him with what felt like fire-hose force). He tried not to scratch too much, but when he awoke in the pre-testing dark before his hose-down so itchy he could gnaw off a limb, he thought he saw a ridge of scratched skin along his forearm so high it seemed the flesh had split open. He squeezed his eyes shut and opened them again, hoping to adjust his eyes to the darkness. Before he could check again, though, the harsh overhead light that marked the start of his days scorched his eyes, and the water blasted all around him in a chaos of haze and kicked-up sand. He had no choice but to rise, although his aching joints popped and creaked and protested in places he never realized they could. He felt off-center, as though his spine curved forward and forced him to stoop, but when he tried to stand up straighter in the pounding jet streams, he lost his balance and nearly fell backward. In spite of all this, he sighed with shameful relief as the pressure washers scratched every itch from every corner of his body.

When the water finally stopped, he looked around him. Each wakeup wash left only a circle of wet sand around him no wider than his wingspan, while the rest of the sand pit went through a mysterious changing of the guard, and a pit of pristine, dry sand always sparkled like virgin snow in a way that satisfied Jean's eye in spite of his circumstances. Today, though, when he went to make his mark on the unspoiled sand, something wet and slippery squelched beneath his feet, and he lurched forward with a yelp from the shock of it.

There, in the circle of wet sand where he'd just been standing, lay a pile of what Jean recognized immediately, somehow, as his own skin. Before he could vomit or pass out or even process what he was looking at, a voice above him boomed:

"Broooooooo, get in here, my dudes!" said one of the alligator people keeping him captive. "The ugly motherfucker finally shed."

Moments later, a congress of prehistoric faces crowded the balcony all around Jean, eyes staring hungrily, mouths identical masks of open-mouthed grins. At the wall near him, a panel slid down to reveal a head-to-toe mirror. Jean stood slightly off-center in the pit, so he could not yet see his reflection. But the faces above, the unfathomable pile of skin in the center of the circle, the mirror inviting him to take a look at himself all told Jean what he would see. For a moment, he thought of resisting, of ignoring the obvious trick dangled before him like a hot dog on a stick or a stingy cash tip from a bachelor party on a muggy August afternoon. But he'd spent enough time at their mercy to know how resistance went, and they'd get their rise out of him whether they had to prod him with electric shocks to get it.

Swallowing—his throat felt dry and somehow . . . narrower—

he stepped into the mirror's line of sight.

Jean wasn't sure what reaction his observers wanted, but the uproar of sound in his head suggested he gave it to them. Cries of *Yeeeeeesssssss, bro!* and *Take a look at that mug now, you ugly motherfucker!* erupted, but one taunt, which eventually grew into a chant, caused his stomach to drop the moment he reached the mirror: *One of us! One of us!*

The transformation wasn't totally complete—his current scales had a slight beige tint, and his oddly flat snout jutted from beneath hazel green eyes that were distinctly human—but it was clear enough. The long game of his captivity, his near-addictive dependence on the bottles, which allowed him a sexual power he hadn't possessed even in his various primes (first in his youth, then in his golden years as a "daddy"), had led to this. So desperate to wear the mask of his bachelor party alligators, or alien invaders, or whatever they really were, he had become one of them. Or at least what they really were underneath.

And the implications of what else he'd become, what he'd really done long before his body transformed, slammed into him when the whooping crowd broke their chant and devolved into excited chatter, because one of them spoke—Jean supposed he would have to learn how they spoke into his mind—a little louder than he should've.

"Bro, we've gotta get more of the gay ones to spread it, bro," Jean overheard. "They don't even use condoms anymore because they, like, cured that sodomy plague or whatever, gave them like a pill for it and now they, like . . ."

Jean's head snapped toward the source of the voice, fury and humiliation rising in him. After all the friends he'd lost in the '80s while the president did nothing, after the years he'd forced himself back in the closet so his military colleagues who worshipped that same president wouldn't suspect him of carrying it, Jean couldn't abide talk like this, not from some fucking breeder whether he was the next alligator overlord or—

But when Jean went to tell this man what was what, only a low growl rumbled from his throat, and one of his captors shushed the room (*Bro, shut the fuck up, bro!*). Then, Jean understood the implications of what that man had said. Whatever transformation he'd just undergone, whatever he'd drunk in those bottles, he'd been spreading something. And to how many? To Lou, to anyone else he'd topped. Deep shame crept over him, shame he hadn't felt since an HIV scare in his thirties when he'd learned belatedly of a possible exposure after a particularly wild weekend, and for once in his life he had feared almost as much for the people he might have spread it to as he had for himself. This shame had him raising his shrunken arms to his face before he realized in horror that his fingernails had become talons.

When his hands flinched away from his face, the room erupted once more in taunts and gibes until one of his captors waved a claw, and the majority of his watchers ambled reluctantly away.

"Don't worry," said the one remaining alligator in a familiar, nasally voice. "You'll be back to your old self soon enough. If you play your cards right."

The panel slid over the mirror and then slid away again to reveal a screen, on which Jean saw . . . himself, in high definition. Except it wasn't Jean as he was these days. It was Jean just over thirty years ago, still in the navy, as fit as he'd ever been, with chiseled cheekbones and the muscles rippling over his naked body. The young Jean on the screen stared out with glassy eyes and rotated slowly like a mannequin on display, giving Jean an eyeful of every inch of himself as he'd once been. Not perfect by any means—he thought his nose was a bit hawkish for his narrow face, his eyebrows were a little bushier than he'd like—and he'd never been one for sissy habits like plucking; his legs were a little too skinny compared to his arms and shoulders, and all the other minute imperfections he'd even had the vanity to pick apart in the barracks—although he always felt he'd wasted his hottest years surrounded by a bunch of straight guys playing war in a time of relative peace.

He noticed that the pale skin on the screen before him had a greenish sheen to it, and that's when he realized what his captors offered him now that he'd apparently cracked out of the cocoon. *We've gotta get more of the gay ones to spread it, bro.* Whatever they wanted him to do had barely begun.

"Of course," continued the nasally voice simultaneously above him and within him, "the transformation is much more painful from your current form, and the upkeep on it can be a real pain."

He could go back to Lou. He could explain what had happened, for real this time, dig up an old military photo as proof, assuming his husband hadn't gotten rid of all his things by now. They could run away together, start fresh, find somewhere to live out their last days before the alligator-alien-shapeshifter-virus apocalypse found them.

But Lou wouldn't see reason, would he? He was steady, loyal, reliable, protective, affable unless provoked, but Jean hadn't married Lou for his complex reasoning skills, had he? And then again, he and Lou were too poor to "run away together" like they were kids with their whole lives ahead of them. Well, Jean might have his whole life ahead of him yet again. Who knew? Plus, Jean would have to steal an awful lot of this go-go juice to evade his captors, living in a young and perfect body while he watched his husband wither and die. Hell, maybe he'd infected Lou already and they'd find themselves somewhere in the alligator-alien power pyramid scheme before they had a chance to make their escape. Wasn't it too late for Lou if they'd already slept together after Jean had begun his unwitting transformation?

Jean could ask. As soon as he learned how to speak in this form—or in the mask of his younger, human self—he could ask whether Lou was safe, what he could do to make sure Lou was safe. He could yell, *I won't be your pawn after what you bastards did to me!* and live a noble life here, in captivity. Alone, as hot as he'd ever felt, where sand would no doubt harsh his mellow if he tried to masturbate *if* he was lucky enough to drink the potion that got him to that form after refusing his captors.

Instead, with the charm he'd used on his navy recruiter all those years ago, he found his voice somewhere well above his throat and said, without moving his leathery lips, "Where do I sign up?"

HOUSEGUEST

He's not one of those harmless-looking old guys—he's not *that* old. But pretty old. Gray hair, just a little chubby, but still that light in his eyes, like he's not too old to have a purpose. So he just shows up at our door, tells Dad, I'm a family friend, old pal, don't you remember me? We're all standing at the door and he shakes hands with everyone at the door except me and touches their shoulders one by one. And that's all. Dad greets him with a bear hug and expects us to do more or less the same.

It's kind of awkward, dinner that night, with him. Everyone's all chummy and familiar with the houseguest—Mom, Dad, my sister Libby. And I'm kind of quiet because I'm thinking, did I miss something? Am I the only one who's never seen this tool in my life? Oh, and there's the way he looks at me, too, like he knows he's bugging me. I don't like it. Dad asks me why I haven't eaten much and I say, I'm not really hungry, and the houseguest looks at me and says, growing boy like you ought to eat his greens, or something way out of line like that. Just before I can say, who are you even, I mean you don't even *know* me, he winks and picks up his glass. Except the glass is empty and he looks at me and opens his mouth like he's gonna say something else and bites right into the glass, takes a big old chomp out of it. Then he crunches it and crunches it, real loud, and blood sort of leaks out of his mouth like he's drooling or something and it dribbles down his chin and slides down his neck and stains his white collar.

Mom just looks at me and says, sonny, now you shut that queer mouth of yours and stop gawking at our houseguest, he's right you know, now wipe that shitty look off your face and spoon yourself some goddamned peas. And the houseguest smiles at me with his bloody lips and swallows the chunks of glass and I just can't help but watch the big sharp ends poking out of his neck as they slide down his throat. Nobody says a word about it.

Anyway, that's dinner, and afterward Mom and Dad say to the houseguest, hey, make yourself at home, you can sleep in our son's room, he can sleep on the living room sofa or something, don't even worry about it. So the house is quieting down and I have started brushing my teeth when he waltzes right into the bathroom, shutting the door. Then he drops his trousers just like that, like it's the most natural thing in the world, and starts taking a piss in the toilet right there in front of me and he says, now I'd hate for you to be put out sonny so I'll share your room with you if you like. I spit in the sink and leave without even rinsing.

I go to sleep on the lumpy couch in the living room, only I don't really sleep much because I hear the houseguest bumping around, bumping around, bumping around. I know it's him because once during the night he walks down the stairs and stands in the doorway and just watches me. And all I can do is almost close my eyes and lie still and pretend I'm sleeping and hope he goes away. He stares and stares for god knows how long and his eyes are kinda like almost glowing or at least that's what it looks like and he knows, he knows I'm awake and he knows I'm scared of him and he knows I know I'm the only one who knows something weird is going on.

Early in the morning I hear some bumping around again and I hear the front door open and shut and at breakfast, Libby is missing so I say Mom, Libby's gone, I'm going to find her so she can eat too; I mean why the hell didn't anyone tell her we were having breakfast? My parents and the houseguest stare at me as I get up and leave the dining room. I don't find her anywhere in the house and I just know it's the houseguest, but I don't say anything about it. Instead, I say, I'm going out to find Libby, thanks a lot for the help. I'm out the front before I have a chance to add, assholes.

I'm walking fast at first but running pretty soon, calling her name frantically, not caring who I wake up in this stupid suburban hell because Libby's gone and I'm pretty sure the houseguest killed her. Soon Dad's driving behind me beeping the horn, and I glance back only once and, ugh, sure enough, there's the houseguest sitting shotgun, looking at me with that vague smile. What a freak. So I keep on running and trip over a crack in the sidewalk and stumble and there's Libby, curled in a fetal position by a big oak tree in that strip of grass next to the street. Her black hair is all mussed up, and blood-caked patches of it are torn out and lying there in the grass all around her. Her skin is muddy and there's lots of dried-up blood all over her and there are finger marks imprinted on her arm.

The car door slams, and Dad and the stupid houseguest are next to us, and I'm pretty bugged out of course, but Libby sees us and pops right up. All of a sudden we're in the car and Libby is chattering away all cheerful, good morning guys, acting like nothing happened and I say, Libby, hold the phone, *what* was that all about, are you all right, Christ, what happened to you? And she says, what, I was just going for a walk, calm your tits, will you? And I say, bullshit you were, you're all covered in blood, I mean really, what the fuck happened? She merely glares and says, watch your filthy mouth before I smack it, little brother.

We walk inside the house and Mom is in the middle of stacking up breakfast plates in the dining room. Didn't even wait for me to eat but I'm not hungry anymore, anyway. Well, the houseguest pushes past me, smacking my sister upside the head on the way with a toothy grin, which makes her flinch without really noticing, and he walks into the kitchen. Two seconds later, he walks up to Mom with a big shiny knife in his hand and very casually thrusts it into her gut and pulls it out and stabs again and pulls it out and stabs again and I'm just standing there, frozen. Then a big glob of blood spills from her mouth and pop-splashes on the stack of plates, and he stabs her again, and she looks at me and says, well son, don't just stand there, help me clear the table you good for nothing little fairy. Then she falls to the floor.

I shout, Mom! and then kneel over her to help or something and I don't know why I'm not crying yet but I think I'm saying *no* over and over and the houseguest just steps over her and moves past me. He's walking over to Libby when Dad says, now son, what on god's green earth are you doing down there?, what are you going on about?, get up off the floor and clean up like your mother told you. And I say, Dad, can't you see, the houseguest stabbed Mom, quick, grab him, call an ambulance, call the police, oh my god oh my god oh my god Mom are you still breathing? Now everything's blurry, which I guess means I'm crying, and Dad is going on about kids and their goddamned overactive imaginations, which is so unfair because first of all I'm not a kid, I'm eleven years old, dammit, and second of all even if that as a general statement is true I'm not making any of this shit up, it's happening right in front of us, as sure as I'm standing here, but it doesn't matter because the houseguest has got Libby by the throat against the living room bookcase.

No! I grab the plate Mom blood-puked on and chuck it at the houseguest and it bounces off his back, shattering on the floor. Libby isn't even struggling, she's just getting pale and sort of dry-heaving like a cat with a hairball. And so I throw a plate, and another, and I nail the houseguest in the back of the head so I keep on throwing dishes and then bowls and then platters at him. Dad steps toward me real pissed but kinda confused and says, son, you stop it right this goddamned second before I beat you, I won't have you humiliate me in front of my houseguest, if you throw one more plate I'll beat your ass so hard you won't sit down for the rest of your goddamned life, etc., etc. I step a little to my right so as not to hit Dad with the plates. Suddenly Mom chimes in all gurgly from down on the floor and says, really, son, you're grounded, what the hell are you doing that for? That kind of shit. And blood is seeping through the gory shredded holes in her floral print dress and dripping all over the hardwood floor. Libby collapses with her face bloated and kinda purple. The houseguest whips up the knife again and turns to Dad. Libby starts scolding me too, her voice thin and dry and cracked.

That's it; I've had it. I go for the gilded lamp next to Dad's comfy leather chair as he asks me what the hell I'm doing, again. Gripping it tightly like a baseball bat I swing full force at the houseguest's head. It goes straight through him and smashes into the bookcase, shattering the bulb. Goddammit all! Dad says, you're paying to get that fixed, now put it the fuck down, why, if our houseguest wasn't here I'd knock your teeth out right this second, one by one, you should be fucking thanking him, you psychotic little shit. I swing again. Nothing. Even as my dad snarls at me and starts to undo his belt to beat me with it, the houseguest cuts his throat open unceremoniously and flicks his tongue out to lick the knife, real quick, like a frog snatching a fly. Dad goes down in a gush of blood and a barrage of threats.

I know what's coming so I stoop down and grab a shard of broken plate and square off to face the houseguest. Everyone is shouting except for us: tell the houseguest you're sorry for all the trouble you caused him, I am so ashamed of you son, go to your room, we're never letting you out, you fucking little brat. But me and the houseguest, we're staring each other down. I'm waiting for him to come at me as he smiles and his eyes gleam like Santa's when suddenly the plate shard is at my throat and it's my *own* hand that pushes the sharp ceramic against my will, as if someone—the houseguest!—is taking a joy ride in my cerebellum. And then it feels like I have this whole big rush of mucus in my throat except when I breathe a little and try to clear the phlegm it flows out of the hole I made with the plate. My throat itches a lot so I cough which makes my vision go darkish which makes me thump on the hardwood floor, all the while listening to my family's impassioned cries, you're an embarrassment, now he'll never stay with us again, that's disgusting son, what do you think you're doing, what's gotten into you boy, maybe you should just leave and never come back.

THE GIRL THE CROWS FOLLOWED

But first, Cecilia was the flower girl at her resurrector's wedding. Even back then, the crows lined the roof of the wicker-woven pagoda beneath which the couple said their vows, brows trembling. Lined the white fence behind the pagoda. Crowded three-to-a-seat in the back where the infamous Thompson family failed to show up after yet another RSVP of yes. The crows shat in the spongy green grass, shat on the train of the bride's dress (*Must be good luck!* the maid of honor laughed).

The bride: Katrinka, twenty-five, still only a sorcerer's apprentice, crow-colored hair. The groom: Christian, twenty-two, son of a banker, dark-featured himself. Sprinkling petals on the ground: Cecilia, four, daughter of a family friend, pink pinafore dress. Frown of concentration on her wide-eyed face. Followed everywhere by crows.

At the kiss, the crows exploded into the air. Circled above, counterclockwise, like a cyclone. Everyone thought it quite romantic, spooky, befitting of a soon-to-be sorceress's wedding. That is, until the birds began to rain shit down on the wedding guests. Even then, Cecilia felt responsible. The crows had followed her there, after all. But there was a charming cabana on the property, and the reception moved indoors without much fuss.

After the obligatory first dances—bride and groom dance,

father and daughter dance, groom and grandma dance—jaunty, crow-haired Katrinka asked Cecilia to dance, squatting down on the shining wood and waddling in circles with the small girl. The crowd cooed. The crows tapped the glass, as if in warning.

Quietly, Katrinka told Cecilia, "In return for being my flower girl, I vow that from this day forward, I, Katrinka Orin, owe you one favor." Katrinka leaned closer, whispered: "I'd choose wisely if I were you. I'm going to be a powerful sorceress someday."

Cecilia frowned. "Christian's so tall. Is he your brother?"

But the girl the crows followed would remember.

Twenty-one years later, Cecilia stood pressed against the dirty brick wall in the alleyway behind the bar where she worked. A man with feathery black hair and many patches on his denim jacket cupped her breast beneath her wine-colored jumpsuit as she pressed her mouth to his sharp jaw. Neon light reflected from a greasy puddle a few feet away, and yes, crows lined the ripe-smelling dumpster. Fast and loose Cecilia, living wildly under the ever-looming threat of her mysterious, unfulfilled curse. *I'd rather fuck up my own life than have the crows do it for me,* she liked to joke. The crows, which had done nothing else but shit, screech, and stare at her all those years. At least, nothing else yet. When the man pulled a knife, Cecilia was barely surprised. She half expected a hilt sculpted after a crow's feather. In her last moments, she thought of Katrinka's promise.

Katrinka was scrying into a bowl of water in her study at the time. The water displayed an image of her second husband, who was naked with a married woman uptown (there are some things even the magic of a powerful sorceress can't change). Mirror, mirror. Cecilia's freshly dead ghost appeared at the window, bloodied chest, jumpsuit the color of merlot. Even after two decades, Katrinka recognized the ghost's sweet, determined face, the wide eyes, the brows furrowed in concentration. It was something of a relief to see her murdered flower girl, translucent and silent in supplication. Here was something Katrinka could bring back. The image of writhing flesh in the scrying bowl faded. The sorceress stood, legs stiff. Wiggled her fingers.

When Cecilia's resurrected body appeared, naked, on the floor of the study, the crows were gone for good. A debt repaid.

Katrinka brought Cecila a billowing black dress, and nothing more. She owed Cecilia a single favor. She'd promised.

AH, WELL

"The moon grows pale, and paler.
Somewhere in the night someone's drumming.
Out where the grass grows pretty wet,
A well stands lost in thought."
—Itsik Fefer, "The Well"

Down in the dewy valley, he drops coins into the wishing well until the grass goes brown and the leaves turn from green to orange. He is twenty-four, too old to wish but wishing his life away anyway. He comes here every day as the sun falls and drops a coin, two coins, ten coins into the well and wishes not for fortune but for escape. His name is Linden. He has been at this for six years and he is still a waiter at the Almond Tree Inn. This is the only inn in town, and he is the only waiter for breakfast and lunch.

Winter approaches and the seventh year of wishing begins.

The dining hall of the Almond Tree Inn is old, all dark wood and dusty air and windows with giant panes. Today, two middle-aged women order poached eggs and talk about werewolves in the next town over.

"Yesterday, two bitten!" says one woman as Linden approaches to refill her water. Her hair is bright orange and curly with a gray streak over her left ear. Crumbs spill from her mouth as she speaks. She wears a white blouse with tiny pink roses printed on it.

"I telephoned Maurine last night, and do you know what she said?" replies the other, who has straight blonde hair and wears a pretty black dress with short sleeves despite the cold. "She said she gives Havensville to the end of the week until the whole *town* catches lycanthropy!"

The two women shriek with scandalized laughter.

Linden says, "When did they know it was werewolves?"

There is a sharp pause. Then, the blonde says, "Well, immediately, dear."

"The whole city is walled in against wild beasts, but a *werewolf* could walk right through the gate on a full-moon day and wreak havoc on the town the very same night!" squeals the orange-haired lady, too delighted to realize she's talking to the hired help.

"It could never have been anything but werewolves. Wild wolves simply couldn't get past those walls," says the blonde, warming up to Linden as well.

"Or eat all those sheep!"

"Head to toe!"

"Tragic!" howls the orange-haired woman, and for a quiet moment in the six-table dining hall, it seems all eyes are on them.

"And witches are so expensive nowadays," says the blonde quietly, kicking her friend under the table as the other patrons ignore, or at least pretend to ignore, the conversation.

"They'll all eat each other alive!" says her counterpart, only a little softer than before.

The blonde looks conspiratorially at Linden. "You should really take a day trip there."

The orange-haired woman claps. "I hear the whole town is in total disorder!"

"Really something to see."

"*We're* going."

Linden politely replies that he is the only daytime waiter and that the Inn runs most smoothly with his consistent presence. He adds that he has never taken a sick day in his six-going-on-seven years working at the Almond Tree Inn. This delights the two ladies even further.

"Oh, then you *must* go at night!" cries the blonde.

"Even better!" says her companion. "The moon is almost full!"

"It'll be *such* an adventure!"

Linden smiles and returns the pitcher of water to the kitchen. When the women leave, they tip him forty percent. One of them leaves a note on the receipt in green ink and neat letters:

"You'll need the money for the gas, dear."

She has drawn a happy face with its left eye winking.

Linden sighs. He had wanted to be a magician himself, but when the recession hit, his parents simply could not afford to send him to college, and Linden has always been terrified of taking on loans and living in debt forever. His father, a marginally successful accountant, was a slave to his own debt, and only the death of Linden's paternal grandfather allowed Linden's father to pay off his loans and retire on his pension. The second-best program in the country for a Bachelor of the Arcane in Medical Witchcraft offered him a scholarship that would have covered half of his tuition, but even that had felt too expensive. Plus, he wasn't sure if he was ready to commit so wholeheartedly to medical witchcraft as a profession, and the scholarship was specifically in that discipline.

Linden does not go to Havensville. He hopes that the women do, that they become werewolves, that they bite him. They tipped him well, though, so he knows that they will not bite him if they do become werewolves.

That evening, at the well, he wishes for werewolves. The next morning, the ladies have gone.

Linden's favorite thing about the Almond Tree Inn is that it's always full of strangers. This young man has the look of a wanderer. His colorful clothing is dusty and doesn't match: red pants, a yellow button-down shirt, a vest with blue and silver stripes, many gold rings. He drapes a black fur coat over the back of his chair. His hair is the light brown of someone who used to be blond; he has a thin, patchy beard; his voice is high-pitched, so that if Linden closed his eyes he would not know if he were speaking to a man or a woman. The young man tells Linden he is a professional magician.

"Ah," Linden says, placing a menu in front of the young man. "I always wanted to be a magician."

The magician looks at him, puzzled. "Then why don't you?"

"Well, you know," says Linden, suddenly shy. "I couldn't afford the education."

"Education!" giggles the magician. "Who said you need an education to get into magic? I mean, magic is magic, baby, whether you learn cheap parlor tricks in a classroom or figure it out in the real world! You know, I tried the whole higher education thing and it just didn't work out for me. Went to community college for a little while to save up money for the big pond, you know? For a big 'university.' Ha! After half a semester I thought, goddammit, you can't teach this shit in a classroom! Finished the semester up and then dropped out. I'm always reading, of course, but yeah, I'm a self-taught magician. Hey, you're a Virgo, huh?"

"How would you know that?" Linden wants to get out of there, run, run to the well, get away from this man who is younger than he is by at least three years.

"Wanna know what I'd do if I were you?" says the magician. "Get the hell out of here and *do* it, you know? Or start small. Get some books on basic magic theory, the power of intention, see if it's for you. Hey, I can lend you a couple books if you want. But you just gotta *go* for it."

Linden wants to snap, *Of course I've read all the basics! Everything I could get my hands on when I was half your age, you twerp!*

Instead, he looks down and says, "I'll be right back to take your order."

There are no other customers in there at the moment. Linden goes into the kitchen, washes his hands, washes his face, dries his hands and face with a dish towel for three minutes.

When he returns, the magician says, "You could travel with me, you know, learn a thing or two. I know it sounds kind of bougie, but I could actually use an assistant. I'll pay you, all that, at least as much as you're making here."

"You do pretty well for yourself, huh?" says Linden doubtfully.

The magician smiles, closing his eyes, and his chair begins to rise from the floor. It hovers there, perfectly still, as Linden tries to conceal his wonder and his vague but growing hostility. The chair sinks again to the floor.

"By the way," says the young prodigy. "I'll take a turkey burger with bacon and avocado, please."

"It comes with sweet potato fries. Is that all right?"

"Just regular fries, please. You know, I feel like sweet potato fries are such a stupid diet scam. Like, they're actually more calories than regular fries, and they're not really even that much better for you. I mean, I've got a bad heart. It's congenital. My dad died real young of a heart attack, like when I was still a baby and stuff, so I'm supposed to watch out for my ticker or whatever. But I do a lot of cardio, so every now and again I feel like it's fine to just, like, have some friggin' fries, you know?"

"I didn't know that about sweet potato fries," says Linden and walks off.

For the rest of the magician's meal Linden avoids his gaze. The magician reads from a thick purple tome, smiling to himself but openly staring at Linden each time he comes to the table.

When Linden brings him the check, which is only after

he has eaten a bowl of ice cream—Neapolitan style: chocolate, vanilla, strawberry, all house-made—the magician grabs Linden's wrist and says, "Well?"

Linden's mouth hangs open for a moment. "Well, what?"

"Well," he says once more with a knowing twinkle in his smile-creased eyes, as if aware what the word means to Linden beyond these walls. The magician seems to notice that he has grabbed Linden's wrist. He lets go and smiles unapologetically. "Are you going to come with me?"

"I, uh," Linden says. "My, um, place is here, I think. At least for now."

The magician pinches his eyebrows with what looks like sympathy, which makes Linden feel insulted to the point of infuriation but simultaneously tempted to go with him, to swallow his pride and learn from this young man, to follow him to the ends of the Earth if it means being anywhere but here.

"I'll . . ." Linden says. "I'll think about it."

The magician stays at the Almond Tree Inn for two more days, but Linden no longer talks to him about being a magician, although he does think about it often. He has always had negative opinions about self-taught magicians. Out of all the most famous, most successful magicians, the ones everyone talks about are the ones who drop out of college, or who never tried to get a degree in the first place, or who flunked out of their first practical magic class and went on to cure cancer with a teaspoon of goat's milk and half a handful of mandrake roots. But Linden always says that for every college dropout mage there are fifty better sorcerers who paid their dues at a four-year program. And how much better could those self-taught magicians have been if they had honed their craft at a university? How much more could they have achieved? Not to mention that these "Magickal Geniuses" often have more innate leadership qualities than actual magical talent, with teams of well-educated magicians working under them for none of the credit!

For each night of the magician's stay Linden goes to the well, stands in the muddy grass, and wishes for the money to go to college.

At the end of the magician's last lunch at the Almond Tree Inn, he says to Linden, "Look, so, I'm leaving today, and honestly I can find any assistant anywhere, but I feel like I'd want it to be somebody who could really benefit from traveling with me, really have an adventure, you know? I'm not trying to be weird, like I'm not going to, like, I don't know, jump your bones or whatever while you're sleeping. It's not like that. It's just I need an assistant, and you're into magic. You can always quit and come back. The Almond Tree Inn isn't going anywhere."

Linden frowns. "I appreciate the offer, but I think if I do decide to pursue a career in magic I want to go to school for it."

"Understandable. I'll leave you my card, anyway. No pressure. Hey, what's your name?"

"Linden."

"Well, Linden," the magician says, placing a wad of cash on the table and slapping a playing card on top of it. "I wish you luck."

The magician vanishes before Linden can say, *I've been wishing since the day I started working here, and it hasn't done me any good.*

The playing card is an Ace of Hearts, and it says "Sydney Alders—Freelance Magician." There is no telephone number. Linden counts the cash on the table. Glances at the check. Counts the money again. The magician has grossly overpaid, which is to say that he left a three hundred percent tip—and with a four-course lunch plus a bottle of the restaurant's second-finest cabernet sauvignon (Linden had had to ask awkwardly for Sydney's ID, finding that the "boy wizard genius" had in fact very recently turned twenty-one), the meal wasn't cheap by any means.

That evening Linden wonders if he has made a mistake. He

thinks not only of the seductive possibility of learning magic, albeit sloppy, unacademic magic, but also of the generosity of the magician versus the transient nature of all the connections in his life to date. He thinks about being the youngest employee at the Almond Tree Inn by seventeen years, how all the young people in Glynwood leave, how soon enough, perhaps, he will not be able to call himself young. It is the beginning of the seventh year of wishing, after all.

The evening is cold and damp, and at the well he wishes that the magician would come back.

The water of Linden's shower is temperate as always. He never likes it hot, even after chilly visits to the well when he could use a little scald. Tonight, he stands under the warmish water and looks at his feet for some time. He sees the water swirling clockwise into the drain as it passes his toes. He watches it drain and drain and disappear like his coins in the well. He turns the shower off without washing his hair.

Instead of going straight to bed, he sits in his faded orange armchair and opens an old book of magic titled *The Basic Creation and Manipulation of Coloured Light.* His parents bought it for his nineteenth birthday before they sold their modest-sized Glynnwood home, Linden's childhood home, for a houseboat. He hasn't seen them since, though he does occasionally receive a postcard with a photograph of an obelisk or a particularly compelling arrangement of cliffs from their retirement travels. He has read this book a hundred times over but has never tried any of the spells.

Now, he turns to one—the simplest spell: "White Light from the Left Hand." He has read the spell aloud countless times without ever having the courage to cast it, and magic, of course, is all about intention. He has read it aloud because he likes the way it sounds; it is nonsense, filled with words like *slip, triple, flip, fuel*—words strung together that articulate no coherent thought but the secret logic of the sounds of words. So tonight, he reads it not to relish the words and imagine he is a magician. Tonight, he reads it to be a magician himself.

He hasn't cast a spell since high school because he hasn't felt comfortable doing so without instruction, so the first time he reads "White Light from the Left Hand" and focuses his intention, he stutters and botches a few words although the text itself is quite simple to pronounce. He takes a deep breath.

The second time he reads it, he clears his throat and speaks with authority, and his left hand radiates light as bright as any bulb, so bright Lindon has to look away as his breath escapes him. As he glances sidelong at his glowing hand, Linden feels glee in his chest as though his diaphragm is a hot air balloon. It is the almost painful glee one feels when kissed, really kissed, for the first time. Or so he thinks. Linden himself has never been kissed. The spell lasts only fifteen seconds, but the giddiness lingers.

Linden casts it once more. Twice. He lays down in his bed. He squirms. Eventually, he sleeps.

In his dream he sees a wizard, the archetypal cartoon wizard with a long white beard and a long blue robe and a voice like tired wind. The wizard says, "You wouldn't know an incantation if I used one to turn you into a toad. Why don't you just get a goddamned education?"

The wizard laughs a breathy, pathetic laugh. Linden looks down at his tiny, slimy green frog feet, and when he looks up again the wizard is gone. In his place is the young magician in faded red pants and an oversized yellow button-down.

Sydney towers over him. "Hey, don't worry about it. I'll change you back, no pressure. You won't owe me one, like, I'm not going to expect you to be my assistant because I turned you back into a man. By the way, are you seeing anyone? Not that you have to kiss me to break the spell or anything. I'm just curious, you know?"

Linden grows and grows until he is face to face with the

magician, who stands a couple of inches taller than him with his lips slightly parted. Warm breath that smells like coffee and cinnamon covers Linden's face. He touches Sydney's hands with his hands, touches Sydney's mouth with his mouth. He closes his own eyes for the kiss, but in his dream he knows that the magician's eyes are open wide with surprise.

Linden wakes up. He calls in sick to the Almond Tree Inn for the first time in his six-going-on-seven years and spends his day in his small studio apartment playing with light. Blue light drips down the pale yellow walls; green and yellow and purple dot the white carpet like flecks of sun caught in stained glass; orbs of white light hang about the apartment in midair, ranging from the size of a gumball to the size of a fist; all the curtains are closed. For the first time since he began at the Almond Tree Inn, Linden remembers he is *good* at magic, remembers why he got into some of the top schools in the first place, remembers how magic is a muscle you have only to flex a few times to realize you still have it.

Linden does not want to go to work the day after that, but he does. He has a new verve to him. He drums his forefingers at the bottom of plates as he brings them out and sets them down. He smiles more widely, flashing bright teeth. He taps his feet as he stands waiting for an order but does not appear impatient. Through the mirror behind the bar, he appears to glow though he tries not to show anyone he has been working magic without the supervision of a professor. He fears it will be obvious to everyone that he has gone against his own principles. His hands feel dirty. His heart feels joy.

And the ladies who went to the werewolf town have returned.

"Well, I think it was a great idea," says the blonde. She is wearing a long silver gown and has a wild look about her.

The redhead wears black pants and a billowy black shirt. "Yes, dear, it's just—"

"Oh, *god,* so what? Don't you dare say it out loud in here."

"It's only, well," stage-whispers the redhead with a slight grin. "It's only that it doesn't make you the easiest traveling companion."

"Shush, dear. Here comes our waiter," says the blonde, but Linden has heard the whole thing.

He smiles. "How was your trip to Havensville?"

"Oh," says the blonde. "It was a scream."

"What she means is, it was a *howl!*" says the redhead, and both women burst into laughter. Throughout their lunch, Linden continues to smile but say little, and the ladies tip him handsomely again.

After the sun goes down, Linden realizes he has forgotten to pick up his paycheck from behind the bar at the Almond Tree Inn. Since tomorrow is Monday, the restaurant will be closed, so Linden waits until after midnight to return. He wants to practice light magic with no one around. He creeps into the dark, silent restaurant and lets white light leak from his left hand (he has grown fond of that spell, his first spell as an adult, simple as it is). When he gets behind the bar he releases a tiny ball of white light the size of an olive from his palm, which hangs next to him as he unlocks the strongbox where the checks are kept. There isn't enough light for him to read the names on the pile of checks, so he allows the ball to grow to the size of a plum. It hangs in the air below the lip of the bar. To the unwitting, it could be the light of a lamp, a flashlight—anything. Not magic.

"I'll take a whiskey, neat," says a familiarly androgynous voice.

Focused so entirely on maintaining the ball of light in the air while finding his paycheck, Linden does not even glance up as he says, "I'm sorry. The bar is closed."

Just as Linden finds the envelope with his name on it, the visitor says, "But Linden, didn't you miss me?"

Linden looks up to see the young man's grin right across

the bar, bathed in the dim white light, leaning so close Linden can hear the magician's calm breath. The orb of light winks out and Linden drops the pile of checks to the floor. Fumbling, he crouches down to collect them, and when he realizes he can't see where his own check fell he decides he will pick it up in the morning. He begins to shuffle the checks together so he can put them all away and get the hell out of there.

"How about some light on the subject?" says the magician, and a melon-sized ball of light illuminates the entire room.

"Put that out!" hisses Linden. "You're not even supposed to be in here."

"Do you want me to go, then?" says Sydney. The light winks out. Behind him, the full moon glows through a window.

"What are you doing here?"

"Checked into the inn this afternoon."

"Why? I thought you left two days ago."

"Passing through? Was gonna go to Havensville, but when I found out about all the werewolves, I thought, well, you know, with my heart, all that excitement wouldn't be too good for me. Goodness, Linden, is that how it is? You're not working for tips, and suddenly you're all . . ."

"Listen, I'm sorry. It's just—"

"Surprise? You're surprised to see me? Magicians, Linden. We, you know, we do that thing where we surprise people. Expect the unexpected, all that shit. But it looks like you'd know a thing or two about that, huh? I don't imagine you learned your little light tricks at school, unless you're taking night classes." The magician giggles.

As the red warmth of shame blossoms on his face, Linden is glad for the darkness. "Oh, I—it was—I wasn't planning on—I don't have the money now, but when I *do* . . ."

Sydney leans over the bar and touches Linden's arm. "Hey, buddy, you don't have to tell me. You don't owe me anything. By the way, I'm just curious. Are you seeing—"

A howl from outside interrupts the magician, who flinches in surprise. He gives one slow blink, and then says, "Are you seeing anyone? Just, you know, out of curiosity."

Linden considers the wolf outside. Swallows, hands shaking. Isn't sure what he's afraid of: the wolf or the young man. Thinks, *How absurd.* Says, "No. Glynwood isn't exactly, well, there's not really a lot of people my age around, you know, and I . . ."

"Let me take you out sometime?" says the magician.

Another howl from outside. "I—well, okay, sure," says Linden, amazed with himself, perhaps riding on the tide of his newfound magical freedom. "How long are you in Gl—"

The sound of breaking. A mass of fur leaps through the window, showering the opposite end of the restaurant in broken glass. As Linden calls light to his left hand—*slip, triple, flip, fuel*—Sydney turns and inhales a ragged gasp. A large, hairy wolf weaves slowly through the tables, growling and grinning all at once. Its coat is a light brown, almost blond color. It wags its tail. It prowls toward them.

With the magician frozen in fear, Linden recalls more light spells and flings them around the room. He hopes to disorient the creature, but it seems he only succeeds in further frightening Sydney, who stares at him with a look of pain and clutches at his chest. The wolf continues unperturbed, perhaps blinking a bit more. Flashes of blue and yellow splash from Linden's hand; globes of white orbit the wolf's head; the magician is blinded; the wolf continues to approach. It comes within a few feet of the magician, lets out a low growl, and licks its chops. The magician collapses with a cry that sounds half pained, half terrified. This magician—this grand, self-proclaimed prodigy who levitated in his chair and overtipped his waiter, who would have known *some* defensive magic if he were half the magician he claimed to be—faints out of fear and condemns himself to the mercy of a wolf! And here is Linden, poor Linden, flinging disks of yellow light impotently at the shining eyes of the animal.

The beast begins to sniff at the magician's feet. Wags its tail. Licks its lips like a harmless puppy.

Linden stops his light tricks and grabs a pint glass. He hurls it to the opposite side of the room in hopes that the shattering of more glass will alert the wolf and fool it into thinking that there is a more titillating foe on the opposite side of the room. But its focus remains on the magician.

Linden raises another glass. Should he throw it at the wolf? If he hits its head, knocks it unconscious—then what? He will likely miss, and the wolf will attack him, and he will die. Should he smash it and attempt to impale the wolf with the jagged shards? Even if he succeeds in stabbing the wolf with a broken pint glass—also unlikely—look at the beautiful creature he would be hurting! It sniffs at the magician with more curiosity than malice. It licks the leg of the magician's lavender-colored dress pants. It nudges his ribs. Just as it bares its teeth and growls, just as Linden pulls his arm back to throw the glass god knows where, a piercing whistle fills the bar. The wolf looks up, turns around, bows its head. Sticks its tail between its legs.

The redheaded woman from lunch, wearing a gray nightgown, leans into the broken window with a silver whistle in her mouth. She is shivering. She snaps her fingers. The wolf shuffles guiltily toward the window.

"Virginia, will you hurry up?" she hisses. "The grass is wet and my toes are going numb. Honestly, dear."

Then she looks over at a shocked Linden, who lowers his glass and places it with shaking hands on the bar. "I'm so sorry, young man. Virginia *told* me to lock her in the trunk of our car! She said, 'Really, Lois, there's no telling what I'll do when the moon is full! Just lock me up and be done with it.' And sure enough, she's gone and ruined your window, and it looks like she's given you such a fright! And your poor friend. She didn't *bite* him, did she?"

"No, she didn't. And he's not my—"

"You tell me how much it costs to replace that window and I'll write you a check. Oh, my. This is all my fault! All right, Virginia. Hop on over. We're so, *so* sorry!"

And just like that, Virginia the lady werewolf leaps effortlessly through the window and the two are gone in the moonlit night. Linden makes his way to the magician—Sydney?—and feels a sense of dread.

Perhaps it is a prophetic instinct, or perhaps it is something he heard the magician say about his heart. But Linden knows that he will not be able to wake Sydney.

The magician wears a look of concern and does not appear to breathe. Linden shakes him gently by the shoulders, and the look of concern slackens, but the magician's mouth hangs limply open. After a moment's hesitation, Linden makes his way to the bar and fills a glass with cold water. He spills a few drops on the magician's forehead. When that doesn't work, he dumps the whole cup on his face, hoping that the magician will gargle into consciousness. No such luck. He lights a match that he finds behind the bar, holds it close to the magician's nose. No draft from the young man's nostrils stirs the steady flame. Linden feels Sydney's neck for a pulse. There is none.

The magician is dead.

Linden leans over his face and wonders who in the world will mourn this poor young man. He feels sad, but mostly he feels fear of his own death and what comes after death and what, most importantly, comes before. He looks at the magician's mouth, and in his head he hears the curse from the old fable: *"With a kiss you shall awaken."*

Linden shakes his head, collects his paycheck from behind the bar while carefully returning the others to the strongbox, stuffs his paycheck into his pocket with shaking hands, cradles the magician (who is rather light for his height), and makes his way toward the window. Clumsily he props Sydney on the windowsill and, placing his hands under the magician's armpits, attempts to lower him to the ground outside. When the magician's feet touch the ground, Linden cannot reach any further down, so he drops the body in a heap. He winces in sympathy for the ragdoll of a man although Sydney is dead and can feel nothing. He looks at the magician's contorted form on the ground and thinks, *heaps, we are all only heaps in death, and there is nothing left. He feels despair.*

Carrying Sydney to the well is not too difficult—it is a mile downhill—so Linden manages although the barely living grass squishes, soggy, beneath his feet. Nor is it difficult to pluck out a pair of hairs from the magician's head and place them carefully in the envelope containing this week's paycheck.

In years, he will use the hairs to divine the cause of the magician's death and will find that it was indeed a heart attack, that the magician's heart suffered constantly, that had Linden studied medical magic he perhaps could have helped this young man, resuscitated him, cured him. Heart magic is difficult and complicated, life-and-death magic even more so; medical magic is seldom self-taught, seldom developed outside of an academic community. Later, Linden will gather the resolve to reapply to programs in medical magic, debts be damned. Later, in the middle of a successful career as a witch doctor, he will wonder whether medical magic was the right choice. Later, later. All later.

Now, there is a dead man in his hands who could ruin the lives of two ladies. There is a mess of glass at the restaurant. There is a broken window. And then there is Linden, who drops the magician into the wishing well and never returns.

THE COLOR OF CREAM

Every Saturday at 10:45 p.m., long after his wife has fallen asleep, Bartholomew creeps out of bed and heads downstairs to the kitchen. There, he fills the same royal blue ceramic bowl with croutons from the Secret Bag he keeps behind the cleaning supplies under the sink. His wife will never find them there. These croutons he smothers in Creamy Caesar dressing. Then, like a child watching Saturday morning cartoons with a bowl of sugary cereal, he takes his bowl into the den to watch the milky-eyed medium from Florida.

She sits in front of a live studio audience atop a crystal couch, blue calcite in giant geode chunks, smoothed over and carved into the shape of a loveseat and adorned with a sky-blue cushion for her to sit on—to aid, she says, with communication and clarity. Behind her: video feed of mist thickening over cliffs by the sea. Waves crash against the cliffs without a sound.

"In the morning," she says, tonight, on This Saturday of All Nights. "I sit on my porch and stare closely at the dew in the grass. And I wish, I think if that dew could just . . ." here, as she hesitates, she pinches the air with her thumb as though to pluck the right word from the ether. "Melt! If that dew could just melt into the grass, well, that would be just fine."

She smiles a warm, firm smile without showing teeth. Bartholomew loves her smile. Secretly, he does not trust women who smile with teeth. They remind him of sharks.

The mind reader with milky eyes reminds him, a touch, of Mia Farrow in *Rosemary's Baby* after she gets her hair cut short: spritely, with a hollowed-out face and wide, bewildered eyes. But this woman wears cream-colored pantsuits and has lighter hair and carries herself in an altogether more still, self-possessed manner, and most importantly her eyes are foggier and grayer than Mia Farrow's, with only a touch of blue. She sits upright, never slouching forward or slumping backward; her back never touches the back of the crystal couch. She calls herself The Semi-Psychic in half jest; she abhors the word "psychic," finds the art of seeing into the mind or into the future to be much less precise than that label implies. Really, she says, her eyesight is especially powerful—she can sort of "zoom in," as she puts it, close enough to see the molecules in dewdrops or the lighthouse miles away or, when she looks hard enough, the fuzzy shapes inside your head. Like peering at shapes through a fog. This is Her Gift to us. Her eyes glisten constantly, as though she might cry at any moment.

"And someone in here," she says, pointing at someone in the audience, "is hoping two different kinds of matter might melt into one another as well."

The camera pans to a pretty woman with long brown hair and a silky red dress in the audience. This woman covers her mouth with her left hand, laughing with what appears to be shock.

"Is that correct?" says the medium, her voice soft and smooth, like butter left at room temperature overnight.

"Yes!" says the brunette and bobs her head up and down. A man in white linen pants and a loose white shirt holds a microphone to her red lips. "Yes, yes! Yes it is!"

She flicks her left hand out, palm down, and wiggles her fingers. The TV screen fills with her hand, with the thin ring and its chunky diamond. She has bitten her nails to the nubs and chipped the red polish.

The camera pans to the clairvoyant in her cream-colored pantsuit, who says, "You're worried that you won't be able to melt, like how dew gives the appearance of melting into the grass when, in fact, it evaporates, losing itself in the morning haze."

The camera pans to the woman in the audience again, whose head bobs up and down. The milky-eyed medium continues to speak.

"But I'm asking you not to melt, not to—" here, she plucks the air again, "—worry, not to worry about melting. Material wealth," she says, apropos of nothing, "is only as powerful as we allow it to be. You don't need to become him or be a part of him to be with him. And you mustn't allow yourself to disappear."

The moist-eyed medium looks down, then looks up at the camera again with a steady gaze. "Tonight, we will talk about union."

If he could do it all over, Bartholomew has always thought, he would find someone like this woman, with her foggy eyes and the kind of soft, comforting skin that reminds him of drinking warm milk before bed. He's never felt like much of a looker himself—his Armenian genes showing up strongly in his squat build and prominent nose. A blue-collar man from a blue-collar family, he's never entertained serious aspirations of being wealthy enough to hook a trophy wife. He likes to think he's a bit rough around the edges, the kind of man you'd have to get to know in order to understand his charm. But the foggy prophetess, of course, Sees Beyond all that. She wouldn't care about money or looks. She'd See the good in him right away. She Sees the good in everything.

"You know," she says, "NASA once asked me if they could inhabit my dreams. I told them, well, if you can find the dream where I left my ex-husband, you've got a deal!"

Pan to the audience, hollering with laughter, practically

falling over themselves. She's so smart, Bartholomew thinks. Half the things she says go right over his head. Or right through, like arrows through the mist. He could listen to her talk all night.

She points to someone new in the crowd, a young man in a pair of pink seersucker pants and a white shirt, who, she tells the audience, "wonders whether the one he's seeing is the one who inhabits his dreams."

This man stands, hands folded in front of his crotch, head down, face as pink as his seersucker pants. When she asks if this is true, he nods but keeps his head pointed toward the floor.

It's not that Bartholomew's wife, Patricia, doesn't see the good in him. She doesn't seem to mind how much money he makes—she's a working woman herself—and she never nags him about his preference for meat and potatoes over greens. She's mild; there's not much about her, really, to find fault with. At times she's even pleasant. It's just that sometimes, in her unassuming way, she can get jealous. It's nothing major. Just the edge in her voice when she says she thought he got off work at six, not at nine-thirty, tonight. The way she looks a little hurt when he says it's only going to be him and the guys watching the game at Jim's this time, that Jim's a single guy so it makes him moody when they bring their wives. Bartholomew doesn't understand what he's ever done that cost him Patricia's trust—0she's never outright said she does not trust him. Years ago, when they realized they could not have children, they simply stopped seeing the need for sex. He simply isn't interested, and as far as he knows, neither is she. But if he broaches the subject, there's always the risk she'll withdraw and act wounded, thinking he's stirring the pot because he's unhappy with their marriage. This always seems to be her conclusion. It's not that anything's wrong with Patricia, it's just that he doesn't always think she sees inside of him the way your spouse is supposed to.

This clairvoyant, with her ash-blond hair, would See right into the corners of his mind. She would Know everything about him, even the worst things, and love him anyway. There's no room for mistrust when you know exactly what your husband is thinking. Things simply Are or Are Not, as the milky medium always says. He wishes Patricia could understand this. But she won't watch the medium with him, so perhaps she never will.

"I want you," says the semi-psychic from her Florida studio inside the TV. "I want you to . . . to put those dreams in the shoebox under the bed, where you keep your emergency underwear, and forget about them for a while. This woman you've met—" and here she winces, squints at the young man in the audience, closes her eyes tightly, and opens them again. "Oh! I'm sorry," she says. "I'm so, so sorry. I mean, this man. He is a man, isn't he?"

The young man in pink seersucker nods, still staring at his shoes, still protecting his crotch with folded hands.

"I'm so sorry," the foggy reader of dreams repeats. "I'm so very sorry I assumed. Well, either way. Dreams. I want you to put those dreams into the shoebox, because this man, he's something else, something entirely different. Let him inhabit a new sort of dream."

In the video feed behind her, the mist has thickened so much that the waves breaking against the cliff are hardly visible. The blue of the sea has faded from a deep dark to a pale, grayish blue.

Bartholomew has begun to touch himself. He does not typically do this when he watches her show. Normally, she stirs a different kind of longing in him, a lust to be Seen and understood. But something about her conversation with this particular young man really gets him going, and before he realizes what he's doing, he's unbuttoned his pajama bottoms and reached inside. On the dark wooden coffee table in front of him, a few abandoned croutons remain to sop up the puddle of Creamy Caesar that sits at the bottom of his bowl.

She continues speaking to the young man, whose shy demeanor and refusal to look at her or the camera excite

Bartholomew—just as much as her short hair and the billowy fit of her eggshell-white blazer. "En route to the highway of our dreams," she says to the young man, astounding Bartholomew, "we learn, sometimes, that what we really need to do is stop at the bakery for a warm baguette before we can continue on our journey."

The young man weeps openly as he sits back down in his seat. The camera pans to the hazy medium, who wipes a tear from her pale, pale eyes. This pushes Bartholomew so close to ejaculation that he stops, returning to his croutons so as not to make a mess on himself before the end of the twenty-five minute program, which inexplicably runs uninterrupted by commercials.

Bartholomew loves his croutons, especially after they've been sitting in dressing for some time. Caked in cream from neglect, they become mushy on the outside. On the inside, though, they maintain their crunch. He wishes, desperately, that Patricia would understand this. Instead, he must hide this part of himself from her. Once, she came home early from work and caught him munching on his croutons. For days, they said little, and Patricia slept on the couch. After this, he proceeded with caution. He tried, for a time, to break the habit. They stopped buying croutons for salad and even switched to balsamic vinaigrette. Eventually, though, he could not walk past croutons or Creamy Caesar at the grocery store without quivering. Finally, when buying groceries alone one day, he put them in his cart and asked the cashier to place them in a separate bag, his voice thin and hoarse with guilt. Since then, he has always hidden them with the cleaning supplies. It is Bartholomew who does the cleaning in this house. The presence of the Creamy Caeser, Patricia tolerates. Or, at least, she pretends to.

He crushes the final crouton between his teeth. He swallows.

With just a few minutes of the TV show left and an absence of croutons, Bartholomew sees no reason not to continue masturbating. The medium finishes up with another man in the crowd, this one even more diminutive than the last. When the slender, hunched-over man appears on the screen, Bartholomew grows as hard as he was before in mere seconds and hardly hears the bulk of the conversation.

But she finishes with this: "Wedding dresses, like doves, need not always be white," she says. "A dove in the dark is no different than, let's say, really, a pigeon!"

The audience bursts into laughter once more. She sighs from her crystal couch. "Folks," she says, "the time has come."

At the end of each episode, the milky-eyed medium directly addresses a home viewer, calling their name specifically and speaking extemporaneously on an issue inside their head as though they're in the studio with her. The lottery thrill of watching, knowing that during any episode she might call you by name, has earned her a viewership beyond that of any other television psychic. She has never failed, not only to name a viewer accurately, but also to speak to a specific issue that the viewer cannot possibly have shared with her. Her perfect accuracy separates her from any medium or mentalist or psychic out there. She is The Real Thing.

"As many of you know," she says, eyes even wetter with unspilled tears than normal, "I went through a divorce myself. It's why I moved down to Florida in the first place. The thing is, we were still living in the same house when we signed the papers, and from then until I moved out, it's like everything was . . . nice between us again. We'd have dinner together. Only in divorcing did we find we were able to love each other again. Not as spouses, mind you, not as lovers. Not a love that made us wonder whether we were making a mistake. And it just, the divorce, it made me—us—it just made us both so horribly sad."

In the video feed behind the medium, the mist has crept in so thickly that Bartholomew can barely make out the dark shape of the cliffs. He is masturbating again. She allows a tear to slip down her cheek, which she wipes away without sniffing.

She looks down again, then up, through the camera, through the screen, right at Bartholomew (he swears she's looking right at him), at Bartholomew who is so unbearably close to climax, his member exposed, his hand moving back and forth. She looks at him with her wet, wet eyes, takes it all in without judgment.

"I'm speaking to you," she says, pointing at him. "You know who you are. I tell my friends sometimes not to get married just so they don't have to risk the pain of going through a divorce. But I want you to think about what you're prolonging, by hiding who you really are from the world. By not filing for that divorce. I want you to be brave. You know who you are, Robert Salvatore Fleming."

Right at the name, which Bartholomew is sure will be his name, he ejaculates all over his light blue pajama shirt, even shoots so far that a glob of his own seed hits his chin. At once, he realizes two things. One, that she's called someone else's name even though he was expecting to hear his own. Two, that Patricia stands watching him in the doorway—long dark curls a mess, hand on hip, breasts peeking out from the opening in her puffy gray bathrobe. He has no way of knowing how long she's leaned against the door frame, but he can guess it's been long enough.

Years from now, after one drink too many, he'll tell his friends that this moment, in particular, caused the eventual collapse in his marriage—not the moments to follow. This, he'll say, was the moment when he let his wife come to her own conclusions, when he didn't bother to try to explain to her about the croutons or about how it *wasn't* that he was sexually attracted to the medium, or about how masturbating while watching the medium did not reflect any negative feelings he had toward his wife.

Instead, he opens his mouth to speak, but his voice catches when he hears the foggy woman on the television: "Bartholomew Simonyan, that goes for you as well. I want you to pick up that blue bowl of croutons, pour yourself another round, and cover them in the cream you really desire."

Behind the medium, even the outlines of the cliffs have disappeared beneath blankets of mist. The show ends as she rises to her feet, nothing behind her but empty white.

TEA LEAVES

The dead body stares at me with brown eyes. It frowns. It lies on the white table on its back. It exposes itself to me—its purple neck swells; its clavicle jabs my hand; its ribs poke out; its feet stink; its cock looks like mine. I carve a neat "I" into its abdomen with a scalpel and pull apart the flaps. The belly opens for me. I reach in. I am not wearing gloves. Even the insides speak to me. The bits of viscera steam against the table one by one as I remove them, wet and flimsy and grayish-brown. They warm my cold hands. I can read them. I do.

A new romance will enter your life very soon, reads the large intestine.

Wonderful, I say.

You have lost something important to you, begins the small intestine, which is of course much longer than the large intestine. Funny.

That is true, I say.

If you wait patiently, it finishes, *it will come back or something new will take its place.*

I don't want something new, I say.

Your temper will get you into trouble if you don't control it, reads the kidney.

Fuck you, I say.

Hush, reads the gallbladder, *and listen.*

I say nothing.

What are you doing? says the dead man. It is the voice of my younger brother. He is looking at me. His eyebrows pinch. His glassy eyes glance down at his torn-up midsection. His blue lips part.

Nothing, I say. I'm doing nothing.

He believes me. He relaxes. I lay his entrails carefully back into place, sew his belly back together, carry him to his bed, tuck him in, kiss his forehead, leave his house. Tomorrow morning he will wake up and he will not know what happened to him, and tomorrow or the next day or the next day a new romance will enter my life and my temper will get me into trouble and if I'm patient or maybe if I'm just lucky, someday my baby brother will come back to me.

TRIAL

"I'm so sorry, really," the man said to Sam on his way out of the single-person restroom, head ducked in apparent shame. Sam stole a quick glance at him before entering the john. Long, dark, wavy hair; the bushy in-between of beard and stubble covering chin and cheeks; flowy, bohemian-patterned pants and wannabe-pirate shirt—all typical of those crusty French Quarter hipsters who relieved themselves in the busy cafe's restroom without paying for so much as an apple on the way out. Sam sighed and let the heavy door of the restroom shut behind him, fully expecting that the apologetic young man had left a real stinker in the toilet without flushing, or clogged it completely, or both. Sam had brought his laptop into the bathroom for safekeeping and gently placed it on the floor beside the door. Finally, he took three wary steps across the black-and-white tiling, breath held in trepidation.

But the toilet bowl was empty! Sam inhaled cautiously, first through his mouth, then through his nose. The comforting smell of lavender-scented cleaning solution and old, rusty pipes filled his nostrils. He sighed with relief. He pulled down his trousers and sat. What Sam loved most about single-person, gender-neutral restrooms was that he could urinate sitting down in peace. More than that, he didn't have to relieve himself in the vicinity of heterosexual men who invariably shot him dirty looks, seeming automatically to peg him as a queer and no doubt suspecting him of peeking over the urinal divider at their flaccid cocks in spite of the fact that he was *already married* (and would never do such a thing even if he weren't).

Sam was no lover of urinals, neither their forced proximity nor, more to the point, the pressure they placed on him to expedite the process of relieving his bladder. Anyway, a colleague of his over in the political science department had recently persuaded him that urinals were ableist and transphobic, so when Sam, a cisgender gay man, sat down to urinate, he liked to believe he was committing a small act of resistance toward the patriarchy, even though taking his time on the toilet was something he enjoyed doing anyway. As with everything in his life, Sam preferred to take his time. To luxuriate. To ponder in peace, without his fellow bathroom users finding fault with his masculinity, or the possibility that someone might take the stall next to him, defecating noisily and with vocalized satisfaction. Or, even worse, attempting to make conversation, as had once happened to him!

Contemplating his current exegesis on the different species of birds in Chaucer's "Parliament of Fowls," which made up the third chapter of his dissertation, he let his eyes wander.

That's when they settled on the tip of a long, thick black tendril snaking down the exposed-brick wall in the corner by the door. He followed its vine-like path, face pinching in disgust. More disturbing than the slimy, serpentine shape, however, was his realization that it was no snake or vine at all but was, in fact, the tentacle of what looked to be an oversized octopus of a dark, gunmetal gray, holding fast to the ceiling just above the door with its suction cups. The wrinkly bulge of its head, striated with dark red veins, pulsed with a slow rhythm that suggested a strong, calm heartbeat. Its blank, pupilless white eyes seemed aimed directly at Sam with a stare that saw both into the depths of him and directly past him as if he were not there at all. It filled the space between door and ceiling like a black hole with its web of tentacles spread across the walls and the mirror above the sink.

Through the jolting flutter of his heartbeat, Sam's first absurd thought was to thank the stars he'd witnessed this terror while already poised over the toilet, lest he have to worry about ruining his good corduroys at the sight of the eldritch horror. Then, he squeezed his eyes shut, opened them, and slapped himself once, hard, in the face. When the pain confirmed that this was no dream, he ran through his family's mental health history and concluded that this tentacular nightmare of a creature was no dream or hallucination or product of late-onset schizophrenia. This was Sam's way: to take stock of every possibility, accept things no matter how disadvantageous, and move forward with the most rational course of action. It was the reason he was such a successful academic and such a nightmare at parties, on vacation, or at any activity selected in the inefficient spirit of whimsy or adventure. Except basketball. He loved to play basketball.

He took stock. This menacing creature hung above the only exit from the restroom. It hadn't plopped atop his head and strangled him on the way in, which either meant the creature had a slow response time, was harmless (unlikely), or was intelligent and wanted something from him that it couldn't obtain by attacking him immediately. Sam knew that this restroom was a dead zone for cellular service, not because he participated in the vulgar, somehow socially acceptable activity of using his cell phone on the toilet, but because he did occasionally check the time on his phone while urinating—afterward, of course, he always wiped his phone down with waterless cleaning wipes, designed specifically for cell phones, which he carried in his knapsack.

This left three options: make a rush for the door (the biggest risk involving the most unknowns), scream for help, or (if the creature was sentient) try to surmise what it wanted.

He opened his mouth to scream.

That's when he heard a gentle baritone voice, which seemed to surround him rather than come from one particular source. "If you scream, no one will come," it said, so calm it sounded almost bored.

Sam screamed anyway, releasing the pent-up terror he'd been trying to think himself out of. If he could have hovered out of his body in that moment and seen himself—face red, pants at his ankles, veins bulging from his straining throat—he'd have been humiliated at the counterproductive display.

But he could not help it. His reason had never failed him so utterly before.

Unfortunately, no polite tap at the door or gentle *Everything okay in there?* answered his pleas. Then, abruptly, sound ceased to leave his lips. Strain as he did, mouth wide open, nothing came out, as though he'd abruptly contracted all-encompassing laryngitis.

The smooth voice sounded around him once more: "There, now if you've gotten that out of your system, we can talk things over like two reasonable beings, shall we? I'll let you speak, with the understanding that if you scream again, there will be consequences. I told you no one would hear you, and my hearing is quite sensitive."

Though the grotesque octopus had no mouth that Sam could see, he knew for certain that it was the source of the sound, that none of this was imagined, and that it was making a promise, not a threat. He decided he had better do what it said, as calmly and rationally as he could. He could make up for the first impression by dazzling the monster with his levelheadedness and superior intellect from here forward.

"Are you going to eat me?" he whimpered instead, disgusted with himself. It was as if some pathetic wimp had taken over his voice.

"I should think not!" said the calm baritone, a hint of amused disdain coloring its timbre. "It would present some logistical issues in terms of the size of my current corporeal form, and besides, I don't imagine I should really enjoy the taste! Anyway, I don't experience hunger, as it were. I assumed this body out of convenience, as this is how the young devotee imagined me when, right before you entered, he invited me to this plane of existence. You'll have to excuse his lack of originality. I had nothing to do with it, but I am bound by it." The creature emitted something like a sigh.

Sam pieced it together—the apologetic young boheme, head hung in shame. Lord Almighty! Leave it to the twenty-something hipsters of the French Quarter to summon some esoteric, Lovecraftian monstrosity and leave someone else with the fallout! The worst part? Sam had no doubt that the "young devotee" who saddled him with this demonic octopus had left without so much as purchasing a scone! Indignant, he nearly asked the monster what in the hell it wanted. But his restraint had returned, at least to some degree. Asking what the creature wanted implied Sam had something he'd be willing to give. A dangerous thing to suggest.

Instead, he said, cautiously, "Well, if you're not going to eat me, I'll just wash up and get back to my writing, then. Working on my dissertation. You understand. Lovely to meet you!"

He got up and pulled his pants up while he said this, buttoning them with shaking hands. He even had the wherewithal to lower the toilet seat. But when he stepped toward the door, two tentacles whipped toward him and wrapped themselves tightly around his arms and chest, squeezing the air from his lungs while forcing him onto the toilet. Then, the tentacles released him and receded to the far wall.

All this happened so quickly that Sam had no time to struggle nor to scream, nor even to feel fear before the tentacles released him and slapped wetly against the exposed brick across the small room, where they rested, quivering slightly like softened linguini in a bubbling pot. Only then did Sam's breath begin to quicken, his heart to pound, and his ears to ring, just as the rush of adrenaline can come in the moments *after* one narrowly dodges an oncoming bus, not during or before. At least he'd lowered the lid of the toilet seat, preventing him from splashing in toilet water, and at least he'd gotten his pants back on. In other words, he hadn't lost *every* shred of dignity he had. Small mercies.

"I only said I wasn't going to eat you," the creature told him. "I did not say that you could leave. Learn to ask me the right questions. Directly."

Sam hugged himself to keep from trembling visibly. "Are you going to hurt me?" he finally asked. Then, considering what had just been demanded of him, he asked, "Are you going to kill me?"

"Not necessarily," the creature said.

Sam swallowed back tears, hating himself for how afraid he was. Fifteen years ago he'd decided he wasn't going to be afraid anymore, that if he planned for every eventuality, he would have nothing to fear. He'd saved up money from a summer job scooping ice cream for two years before he came out to his parents at age fourteen, fully prepared to make his own way in the world if his parents kicked him out of the house. Luckily, they hadn't, although his coming out did forever ruin his relationship with his already distant father (a small price to pay, he'd decided pragmatically even then). After coming out to his classmates at his small Jesuit school in Corpus Christi, he'd endured the expected first beating from one of his peers in stoic silence and only told his friends later that he'd expected worse. People had left him alone after that.

His senior year, he'd even taken his boyfriend from another school to prom; he and his best friend, who was a lesbian, had filled out the prom paperwork required for students bringing dates from outside of the school, using each other's partners' information. Then they'd walked into the ballroom hand in hand with their own partners, resplendent in rented tuxes and ballroom gowns. Sam's husband Marcos was not the young man Sam had taken to prom and then, after enough pulls from the flask in the inner pocket of his coat, taken to the hotel room he'd reserved weeks in advance. No, as far as Sam was concerned, the concepts of the "high school sweetheart" and, particularly, the "one true love" were for a subset of deluded heterosexuals who'd been conditioned by mass media Rom-Coms from which, due to lack of representation, gay people had been spared. But bringing another boy to the prom remained a proud achievement for him. By then, he'd already enrolled himself in boxing classes, and nobody dared come near him. He'd been generally regarded as brave by his classmates, but he'd simply learned to prepare for the worst and, above all, never to grovel.

But he'd never planned on being held hostage by a sentient, oversized cephalopod. It had literally silenced his screams, which implied it had the power to do much more, and it had shown fierce, effortless strength with just two of its tentacles. There was no telling what it would be able to do to him if he did not cooperate. So, in spite of all he stood for, he said, "What do I have to do for you to let me go unharmed?"

"Simple," said the monster. "All you have to do is prove to me that you deserve to continue living!"

No jury of his peers. No lawyer. No clear set of legal codes or criteria of intrinsic value to contemplate. Only this tentacular abomination: his judge, jury, and, should he fail, his executioner. A single, many-armed court. Sam didn't even have a notebook with which to organize his thoughts (he'd left his backpack, with nothing worth stealing in it, out at his little round iron table just inside the entrance to the café). Lord knew he wasn't about to risk reaching for his laptop, which lay on the floor below the calm, pulsing octopus demon that would determine his fate.

"May I ask why you're doing this?" Sam asked, in hopes that learning more about this creature might offer him some insight into what it was looking for. If nothing else, it would buy him some time.

"You may ask," said the creature with the smugness of a middle school English teacher.

"Why are you doing this?" Sam said after a pause, trying hard not to roll his eyes at this piece of pedantry given the stress of his delicate position.

"Because I must, of course! When I'm brought to your plane of existence, whether by accident or on purpose, I require the energy generated by one sacrifice in order to return home. I do not take the killing lightly although—make no mistake—I do enjoy it. Thus, I place each human I encounter on a little ad hoc trial, usually starting with the one foolish enough to summon me in the first place! I must admit I've come to enjoy this process. I find it most enlightening to learn about the individuals of your curious race."

Though offering Sam no obvious hint on how to survive, the creature's answer comforted him somewhat. Surely Sam would have an easier time proving his worth than the wannabe pirate bohemian who came before him. But where to begin? Conscious again of the monster's earlier warning to ask the right questions, he decided to seek clarification before he began.

"Will I be judged based on human criteria of being worthy of living, or is there some set of criteria specific to your . . . species I should be meeting?"

"The time for questions has passed!" said his inquisitor, the first hint of real irritation creeping into its smooth baritone voice. "You will be judged both for your arguments themselves and for the criteria you select as important. You will plead your case, and I will ask you any questions I deem necessary. Understood?"

"Understood."

"Well?"

The creature wasn't even going to give him time to plan his case? He began, desperately: "Well, first of all, I do not deserve to be executed. I have committed no major crimes and I've always done my best to live a life that causes no harm toward others. I've never killed anyone, which is usually the only action deemed worthy of execution in our society." He didn't add "as long as you're white," as he normally would in the spirit of social justice, because such a caveat might overcomplicate his argument. He continued, "I've never raped anyone, or stolen anything except a candy bar, once, when I was a kid, and one time in college I took a leftover slice of my roommate's pizza from the fridge without asking permission, but I did it because we usually shared that type of thing anyway, we just also typically asked . . ." Sam realized he was in danger of losing track entirely. "I'm a generally honest person. I don't typically lie, unless the truth would really hurt a person's feelings. I don't even exaggerate to make a story more interesting. So, you see, there's no reason for you to kill me, since I haven't done anything to deserve it!"

Sam stopped, a bit irritated with himself for how trite the argument sounded. But wasn't that the point? The average, generic person did not deserve to die. One could argue nobody did. But Sam was surely less deserving of death than a murderer or a serial rapist. Surely.

"Interesting," the creature said after a pause. "But so far you've only proven what you haven't done to deserve death. Why should you live?"

"Because everyone born into the world has the right to life," he blurted. "And liberty, and . . ." But he couldn't even finish that empty, platitudinal trash.

"And you believe this to be true? This is how your world works?"

"Not really," Sam admitted. "It doesn't work out that way for everyone."

"Then tell me again: why should you live?"

"There are people who would miss me if I were gone," he said, feeling lame, but he actually did believe this, and anyway it was too late to stop, lest he test the creature's patience again. With no opportunity to plan things out, he could not expect from himself the kind of nuance and eloquence he was accustomed to presenting in an academic context. "My death would cause grief and pain to other people."

"Interesting. Who?"

"My two sisters. They'd be crushed. And my . . ." He paused at mentioning his parents, to at least one of whom he knew he, the only son, had been a severe disappointment, both in his homosexuality and his choice to pursue a career in academia instead of a career in law, *in spite of every opportunity his parents worked so hard to hand to him* (a reminder his father never failed to deliver). "My mother would be pretty unhappy, I think. And my husband, well, he wouldn't know what to do without me. He wouldn't know how to live."

"Husband!" cried the creature, delighted. "I am pleased to hear that, since my last visit to this plane of existence, your species has finally learned to procreate among both sexes! Most efficient. You know, each time I come here, though it's not my purpose, I do enjoy learning as much as I can about your intriguing species. Tell me, how many offspring have you planned to produce with this husband?"

Sam grimaced, glancing at the changing station with its large blue teddy bear sticker, covered in indecipherable graffiti, some black, some red, some faded with the evidence of an attempt to scrub it away. The possibility of having a baby to care for had always horrified him. Not to mention giving birth, were such a thing possible for a man. Now, here, this creature touted it as a triumph!

"Not exactly. I mean, none, I mean . . ." Which question to respond to? He said simply, "We're not going to have children.

We can't."

"No?" said the creature in a dull, disapproving voice. "What's the purpose of a union without procreation?"

For the first time since encountering this strange judge, Sam responded in anger, scooting to the edge of the toilet and slipping into armchair rhetoric he'd joked about a hundred times without realizing, until now, that he actually believed it. "In a world where overpopulation is leading to the decline of our planet, the ideal of procreation as the end goal of companionship is becoming more and more destructive! The way I see it? An increase in queer coupling is evolution's response to overpopulation. Without the ability to reproduce, my partner and I can focus on supporting each other, being good stewards of the environment, caring for our fellow human beings, making the world better, and most importantly, choosing not to contribute to the ruin of the planet by creating greater demand for its ever-scarcer natural resources! Sure, we can adopt, or we can do in vitro, but we'd never do in-vitro because we've made the commitment not to contribute to the excess of waste and the strain on natural resources that humanity's rate of reproduction has created! Didn't your little acolyte tell you anything about climate change?" He did not add, *You disgusting wannabe Lovecraft villain,* and he felt proud of his restraint.

A silence followed, during which Sam supposed the creature weighed his responses. In the meantime, he busied himself using his newly recovered fortitude to dream up a plan in the highly likely event that the creature, with its blank eyes and flaccid, pulsating head, did not find his responses satisfactory. He had his keys in his pocket, which he could use to slice into the inky flesh of any tentacle that lashed out to constrict him, or jab into those endlessly judging eyes. For some reason, he had the sense that some of its incorporeal power, beyond its physical strength, lay in that milky gaze that seemed to probe him to his core. The wooden end of the plunger to his left could also be used to stab the creature through those hateful eyes, or to turn the lever-style handle of the door.

Sam's left hand twitched in anticipation of snagging the plunger at just the right moment. He recognized that using its wooden end as a bludgeon would likely require him to grasp its rubber end, which had no doubt come into contact with true horrors of human waste in that restroom, but he swallowed back his aversion. This was life or death. Finally, the creature spoke.

"Are you arguing that you and your husband do these things? That you're good stewards of the environment, that you make the world a better place, and so on?" said the creature in that placid baritone, as though Sam hadn't had an outburst.

"Sure, my husband and I absolutely do what we can to lower our carbon footprint—eating mostly vegetarian, sharing a car . . . hybrid, by the way. I could go on and on, but why can't we leave my husband out of this? Aren't we arguing about me?" Sam demanded.

"Ah, but you argued that the value of same-sex partnership lies in your ability to support each other in these endeavors. Thus . . ."

"And to be happy," Sam amended, and in his renewed fervor he *nearly* launched into another tirade about how heterosexual couples, even those with medical conditions that prevented them from having offspring, never had to justify the utility or value of their union—how, in fact, American society demanded that gay people and racial minorities justify their utility, the force of their love, and yes, their right to exist as they were in the world, in subtle and not-so-subtle ways on a daily basis, while everyone else was automatically granted the right to lead ordinary, unremarkable lives, and that he was sick of it, just fucking tired, and maybe this freaky space demon should wrap its clammy arms around his throat and get it over with right now if its judgments were going to be as arbitrary and awful as Sam's own patriarchal shitstorm of a human race, to whom Sam would be expected to justify himself continually, quietly but fiercely, the second he emerged from this restroom, anyway.

But the creature's tentacles quivered ever so slightly again, and Sam's desire to survive trumped the existential dread the creature had unearthed. So he held back.

"Well?" the creature said. "Do you support someone who makes the world a better place? Are you both happy, then, as well?"

"Yes," Sam said, intending to leave it at that, but the can of worms had been opened. Before he could stop himself, he launched into a confession:

He told the creature how, after five years of marriage on top of a three-year relationship, Sam—in the midmorning stage of his thirties, with the occasional white hair amid his dark curls, with the skin at his midsection beginning to loosen, perceptible only to him, over the diligently maintained muscles of his abdomen and obliques—secretly wondered whether he'd wasted his most attractive, virile years settling down with a man seventeen years his senior. Marcos. Marcos was a man he'd met at the right time, who'd been interesting enough and, most importantly, reliable enough to fall in love with. Marcos, the young at heart, who in spite of the age gap had made so much sense to old-souled Sam in his early twenties.

Marcos, the warm. Marcos, the political artist. Sam, the academic, the analyst of the arts. Marcos, whose sex drive had not waned the slightest over the years while Sam's own had. Sam, who'd receded further into his studies and had become so sensitive to the New Orleans humidity when trying to sleep that he could hardly tolerate Marcos's warm, sleepy embrace even with the air conditioner on full blast. Marcos who occasionally forgot to take the keys out of the ignition of the car they shared, leaving it available for anyone to drive off with, but who could repair the transmission on that same car with a surgeon's precision because he'd once seen his mechanic father do it. Marcos, who led slam poetry workshops for teenagers and became anxious when he didn't hear back from Sam within an hour of sending him a message.

All this Sam told the creature, unable to help himself, unable to stop himself from smiling fondly, and then, firmly believing it, he repeated his opening sentiment: "Yes. The world is better because my husband is in it."

"And this is in part because of the support your partnership provides?"

"Absolutely," said Sam without hesitation, and then he forgot himself and chuckled. "He wouldn't know which way was up without me, some days."

"Fine, a perfectly acceptable answer. And I can tell by your conviction that you truly believe what you're saying, this time. Let's spend no more time on it. You *are* the one on trial, after all, and not him. So what about you? In what way is the world a better place because of you specifically? You've failed to explain that thus far. You've told me why you don't deserve death and why certain people would suffer as a result of your absence. In other words, you've defined your life only by its negation. This is your last chance to prove your worth, to tell me what it is you're doing that's worth continuing to do."

And what was Sam doing? The creature had, at last, landed on the real problem. Sam was obtaining a doctorate, spending most of his time studying obscure, often unfinished dream visions by a long-dead poet, in an iteration of English nobody had spoken for centuries! Other than the old adage, "The life so short, the craft so long to learn," what contribution had Chaucer's dream visions really made to humanity? What further contribution could studying that work make, other than to satisfy Sam's own thirst to know and to interpret, as well as that of other academics like him?

Sam taught basic writing classes far below his level of expertise to a bunch of trust fund babies at one of those ivory-tower universities in the nice part of town, fully protected from the heart of the city, its crime, the harsh living conditions of its continually displaced inhabitants, the police violence, the food deserts in the poorest parts of town, all of it. He lived in New Orleans, a city he believed would be fully underwater in the next couple of generations, while he did what he could to stop it, which was not nearly enough. Beyond what he'd mentioned, he drove his discarded glass to the recycling plant, attended the occasional rally, called the occasional senator (not nearly as often as he let people think he did), and encouraged his students to email him all their assignments so they didn't waste the paper. Why, hadn't he forgotten to ask for his iced coffee *without a straw* just thirty minutes ago? But the existence of so many societal ills overwhelmed him. Where could he even start making a plan to contribute when there were so many causes? How to decide which ones were the most pressing, the most important? Environmentalism was simply the easiest, given his situation. He was in graduate school. Who had time for activism when they were getting their PhD?

And as for happiness, no matter how he convinced himself that he lived an objectively fulfilling, satisfactory life, he still felt strangely moved at the sight of small towns off obscure highway exits, the kind of towns in the long stretches between cities that didn't even have fast food or gas signs. He had escape fantasies about pulling over one day, on impulse, and driving through their streets, maybe stopping at one of their tiny cafes, spending a few nights in the scratchy sheets of a seedy motel in the hopes, perhaps, that some strange adventure awaited him, one that required him to act on pure instinct. Some spur-of-the-moment affair or mysterious town secret that, by coincidence, required his highly specialized expertise to solve—some forgotten Middle English text nobody else could read, or some series of riddles, perhaps, that only a highly specialized literary brain could solve. And sure, if he occasionally experienced homophobic harassment in a city like New Orleans, the surrounding towns might offer more of a challenge in that regard, but he'd so seamlessly be able to prove his value in such circumstances that it wouldn't even matter to the small-towners around him; perhaps they'd learn a thing or two about acceptance; perhaps he'd be a positive queer influence on some closeted gay teen who finally felt empowered to be who he was. All the while, he'd relish the thrill of being unknown to the people around him and having his whereabouts unknown by the people who knew him. Of escaping his highly systematized life, if only for a little while. Of finally acting on impulse, even if it meant fleeing to a mundane, obscure locale and doing little of value to the world at large.

"I'm a teacher," he began, in the same tone of voice he'd listed the rights to which all human beings are supposedly entitled. "I foster empathy for the world around us with my students by . . . by . . ."

But Sam was overcome—by not only the conviction that playing this monster's game was a losing battle, but also the realization that his long-coveted opportunity to act on instinct was now, and finally, the gut feeling that his harsh judge, with its piercing eyes and pulsing red veins, was unlikely to find the conglomeration of his arguments satisfactory enough to let him live anyway. It was too much. He found himself unable to play its game any longer. In a swift, decisive motion, Sam hefted the heavy ceramic cover off the toilet's tank behind him and hurled it at the creature—a move he had not considered. Sam was an above-average basketball player, at least in his academic social sphere. It was always a secret point of pride for him to be a tall, lean-muscled fairy dribbling circles around his heterosexual colleagues. At any rate, he had good aim, and he made his mark.

The rectangle of ceramic hit dead in the center of the creature's wrinkled, saggy bulb of a head. As those long tentacles went momentarily rigid and squirted black liquid every which way, the tank cover split into two pieces, one of which clattered to the floor and further shattered, the other of which smashed directly atop Sam's computer by the door. The creature, flailing about, fell to the floor with a squelching sound immediately after. Sam took advantage of its disoriented attempts to right itself by grasping the plunger's mercifully clean rubber cup. He rushed at the writhing gray and black mass, its tentacles convulsing with grotesque violence in the air around it. Even as the tentacles slithered up his legs, squeezing painfully as they worked their way to his torso, Sam jabbed the plunger's wooden handle at the creature, employing the same frightened brutality with which he took a shoe to a palmetto bug while Marcos cowered elsewhere in whatever room of the house he'd spied the offender. Sam aimed for the eyes and, after a few narrow misses, he got the wooden handle clean through one of those white targets. The vise-like grip of the tentacles, now up to his waist, slackened ever so slightly. Ink and slime splattered over Sam, the walls, the already dirty mirror. Sam pulled the wooden tip of the plunger out, and it was covered in the same syrupy red as if the creature had been human. Simultaneously sickened and encouraged, Sam went for the other eye, and this time he hit on the first try. The creature went completely limp, some of its tentacles falling to the floor with a moist plopping sound, some wrapped vaguely around his ankles, impotent.

Sam felt saliva fill his mouth and bile rise in his throat. He managed to disentangle himself from the tentacles, step over the creature's head—only glimpsing for a moment the two soupy holes of red, white, black, and gray—and make it to the trash can by the door, which he leaned over and heaved into, losing his lunch, along with half his iced coffee and the triple chocolate cookie he'd eaten with it.

When he finally inhaled a ragged breath through his acid-filled mouth, he heard that unmistakable baritone all around him.

"There, now if you've gotten that out of your system, I'd like to give you my verdict."

Sam straightened and looked wildly around. The creature still lay limp and mangled at his feet, amid the rubble of shattered ceramic and the pool of red that gathered around it.

"I'd like to congratulate you, first and foremost, on finally throwing caution to the wind and choosing instead to act on—" was all it got out. Sam snatched up his laptop, grabbed the door handle, and burst through the door where a middle-aged white woman must have been waiting for god knew how long. Of course, she couldn't have heard him screaming. The creature had made sure of that, and it would make sure nobody could hear her either.

"I really, really wouldn't go in there if I were you," Sam said breathlessly. Then, as he brushed past her with his head down, he added, "I'm so, so sorry. It wasn't me. I swear."

He knew she wouldn't believe him, especially after he'd been in there for as long as he had. He didn't care.

Sitting in his Prius, Sam allowed himself to sob with the weight of his impossible experience. He cried heavily, efficiently, and quickly for a couple of minutes, forehead against the steering wheel. Then, he sat up, shook his head vigorously, and started the car. Life-or-death encounter with an interdimensional octopus monster or no, that brief moment of bliss when the air conditioner pierced through the humid heat was enough to restore his composure.

He puzzled over his verdict. If that had been his trial, he might reasonably expect parole. Clearly his inquisitor could have stopped him from killing it—had not, in fact, even truly died in spite of its mangled appearance, unless Sam's fit of violence had finally pushed him over the edge into complete delusion and he'd truly imagined the creature's voice at the very end. Was he being congratulated on his violence? He would not have expected violence to be a virtue even for this sacrifice-hungry entity, nor did he believe that he'd revealed some hidden valor in spontaneously attacking the creature. He'd only acted in such haste to save his own skin. But perhaps that was it. Perhaps it was his willingness to do something he would not have expected himself to do that had saved him. How he wished, driving away from the café he knew he could never return to, he'd had the nerve to stay for the creature's verdict! And yet he was afraid he wouldn't have liked what conclusion it came to about him.

Sam kept glancing in his rearview mirror on his way to the freeway, half expecting those white eyes to stare at him from the back seat. He smelled vaguely of low tide, recognizing with a shudder that he'd need to scrub the car clean of the slime that covered him but seized with the fear that perhaps the smell meant his judge and jury lay in wait in the trunk. Under the imagined watch of that strange being whose body he'd destroyed but whose voice had remained, he drove right past the exit he normally took to get to his home in Mid-City, reasoning at first that he was going to the only Apple store for miles around to get a quote on fixing his dented laptop—of course, he'd have to wipe down the ink and slime before taking it in. When he skipped that exit, too, he finally took out his phone and surprised himself by sending a text to his husband (ordinarily, on principle, texting and driving was not something he did, but today had been no ordinary day): "I won't be home tonight. Nothing you need to worry about. Sorry I can't explain. I love you."

Then he rolled down his window and tossed his phone out into the whooshing air, driving and driving past the airport, past the outskirts of the city, driving without thinking until the sun disappeared and the highway lights spread sparser and sparser, until it became clear to him that if he didn't stop at the next town, he'd be driving all night.

BOREALIS

On the morning it all started, it took Lisa Marie four tries to get out of bed. Each time her alarm went off, she awoke for a few hazy seconds, struggled to lift a hand leaden with the weight of invisible chains, and silenced the soft but persistent tinkling that had awoken her. Each time, as the greedy hands of sleep pulled her back down into oblivion, she wondered with a brief panic if she had accidentally hit "STOP" instead of "SNOOZE." But each time she wondered this, she was powerless to check. The fourth and final time she opened her eyes, she lolled her head over and saw that it was 11:14 a.m., and the horror of that was enough to thrust her into full wakefulness, albeit in a thick haze as if submerged in syrup.

Still, she lay inert for twenty minutes more. Her dilemma was this: despite the fact that it was the middle of June, she felt unbelievably cold, and not even the promise of coffee—would her parents have left any for her in the pot downstairs?—was enough to propel her from the warmth of her goose-down comforter. Only when the unbearable pressure in her bladder from ten hours of sleep demanded she tend to it, lest it burst, did she slip languidly from her bed and pad across the room to her bathroom.

As she went about her morning business, her slow, sleepy thoughts enveloped her with dread. It wasn't like her to oversleep, let alone to be so incapable of waking. She had felt this way once before, the first and last time she had taken nighttime cold relief medicine when she was eleven years old. She'd hated the helpless feeling of it, like she'd been subjected to a witch's spell, like anything could happen to her and she'd be powerless to stop it. Though her heart had pounded and her breath had come short with the beginnings of what she hadn't understood then was a panic attack, her body had betrayed her over and over, succumbing to stupor. No, if anything, Lisa Marie was a light sleeper and an early riser, sipping the occasional weak chamomile—the only sedative her sensitive body could handle—when she needed a full night's sleep. Fortunately, she had nowhere to be today. She didn't start college for two months yet, and it was a Saturday. Still, it unnerved her.

As she ran the warm water of her pale pink sink over her cold hands in hopes that the blood would return to them, she scanned her memory of the previous day for any possible cause of her oversleeping. Of course. Luke. The Old Well at Chapel Hill, beneath the grand little Grecian dome in the center of the semicircle of brick. Her boyfriend on one knee before her. The ring. The brief flash of humiliation as the random passersby paused to steal not-so-subtle glances at the spectacle. The numb articulation of the word "yes." Luke, her boyfriend—no, fiancé—rising to his feet to embrace her. Her family and his awaiting them in the grove with a picnic. And Lisa Marie, all the while too worried about whether or not she was displaying the appropriate amount of surprise and joy to experience either of the feelings at all.

That was it, she decided, shutting off the faucet although the water had failed to warm her. Yesterday had simply been a big day for Lisa Marie. The most important of her life so far, she supposed. Or so she'd been told. Surely after such an overwhelming day, she'd needed the rest.

But she was not convinced. She padded down the curving staircase into the high-ceilinged foyer, the same staircase she'd descended two years ago in a princess-worthy gown of white and pink tulle adorned with fabric roses, on her sixteenth birthday. The same day Luke asked her to be his girlfriend—a gesture of romantic gallantry that Lisa Marie would secretly hold against him as being selfishly timed on *her* special day, no matter how much she wanted him to ask her out. No, the reason the "big day" explanation of yesterday's engagement failed to comfort her was because, if she was honest with herself, the events of the previous day hadn't released the flood of emotions she'd expected. Replaying them in her mind now, she could still conjure little more than a sense of relief that she was finally to be married—and a vague, inexplicable anxiety over that same fact.

It wasn't that she didn't want to be married to Luke, or that she hadn't seen it coming. She'd turned down acceptances to Georgetown University (her father's alma mater) and Dartmouth (her mother's) so she and Luke could both attend UNC Chapel Hill—the most prestigious school to which *he'd* been admitted. She'd told nobody but her mother about these acceptances, including Luke, who had himself been confident about his chances of Ivy League acceptance and had been extremely touchy on the subject, blaming everything from affirmative action to his parents' choice to send him to Catholic school instead of a prestigious prep school which, he assured her, would have cost the same amount of money. Lisa Marie had gone to the same Catholic school, but at the behest of her mother, she was not about to rub it in "poor Luke's" face that she'd gotten into more than one of his dream schools. In short, she'd planned her future around it.

The issue was not marrying Luke. Lisa Marie was pretty sure she loved him and knew that, more importantly, he was a great match for her and came from a great family. It was just that her entire life, her mother had encouraged her to dream about marrying, and building a family, and all the steps along the way. But Lisa Marie didn't feel as if she'd done anything to earn her relationship with and then engagement to the handsome, wealthy Luke aside from, perhaps, taking some care to maintain her stunning—if conventional—beauty and making sure to be clever enough to charm him without ever letting on that she had the upper hand where cleverness was concerned. She'd simply learned it was something she ought to want and allowed it to happen when it did.

"Mornin', Rip Van Winkle," her father said, sitting at the marble kitchen island and evidently waiting for Lisa Marie's mother, who bustled about at the stove behind him, preparing lunch. "Or should I say afternoon?"

"Hi, Daddy." She smiled sheepishly. Her father's gentle Southern lilt never ceased to charm her, in spite of—or perhaps because of—the fact that he didn't come by it honestly.

Both of her parents were born and raised in the Northeast, having simply taken to the wealthy North Carolina gentility like naturals before Lisa Marie was born. They even lived in a plantation-style home. When Lisa Marie had first learned about slavery in school, she'd told her mother, horrified, about the kinds of things that had happened on planation properties like theirs, to which her mother had replied, "Oh, baby, don't be silly. This house was never *that* sort of plantation, or any sort of plantation at all! It's just made in that style." Still, Lisa Marie was plagued for months by nightmares and was convinced, on the two occasions she awoke with the pressure of sleep paralysis on her chest, that she could see the ghosts of slave children in the corners of her bedroom and the shadows of the half-opened closet door. When she related the dream to her mother, her mother had simply stroked her cheek and replied, "Honey, ghosts are a trick of the devil to make us believe in something other than heaven and hell." This had neither made sense to nor comforted her, but she never brought it up again.

"You must have been awfully tired after all that excitement yesterday!" her mother remarked from the stove, back turned.

"You stay up too late looking at flower arrangements for your wedding?" her father said. "You are your mother's daughter, after all."

"No," Lisa Marie said distractedly. "I mean, I don't know. I don't know what's come over me."

In spite of her late morning, she couldn't shake off her sleepiness all day. That night, she went to bed before midnight and set her alarm for 8 a.m., sure she'd wake up refreshed.

The next morning she woke up a mere hour earlier than the morning before, in spite of having gone to bed at least two hours prior than the previous night. And the morning after that, she awoke again after eleven. She didn't understand it. It wasn't as if she was tossing about all night, anxiously contemplating her future as a college student or, as her father suggested, a wife. If anything, she fell asleep earlier and earlier, and the late afternoon began to feel like the evening. The early afternoon was the only time she could get anything done: registering for classes, selecting dorms (she and Luke would *not* be sharing a dormitory until after they were married in the spring, thank you very much), and so on. And every morning it was the same desperate attempt to awaken, until Lisa Marie stopped fighting it and her mother had to drag her out of bed.

Doctors were visited. Tests were run. No medical explanations were found. They ruled out sleep apnea, narcolepsy, heart disease, thyroid dysfunction. Psychiatrists, of course, were out of the question. Lisa Marie, her parents reasoned, had no cause for unhappiness or psychological unrest. She had a happy life and everything she wanted. Anyway, they agreed, psychology was a *soft* science. Who, they wondered, would trust a doctor who prescribed pills for *that* sort of thing, the sort of thing that prayer and a good sit-down with a pastor could fix?

It was around the time that Lisa Marie was only capable of wakefulness for between one and three hours a day, and only then with barely more coherence than a somnambulist, that her parents decided it was time to call in the aunt.

Her mother's only sister lived far up north, estranged from the family. She wasn't a wicked or sinister figure in any way, not the sort of fairytale aunt whom her relatives feared would hex their children at a baptism. Rather, her eccentric habits and desire for seclusion caused Lisa Marie's mother to relate less and less to her as they grew older, inviting her to fewer and fewer holiday gatherings with their many brothers. Anyway, she seldom showed up to the family events she was invited to and came capriciously to those she wasn't, so what was the point of reaching out? How she knew enough to show up uninvited to any gatherings was beyond anyone's guess—she had no confidant among them. The family at large had begun to view the aunt as a "wild card," who came and went as she pleased and who, despite being two years the senior of Lisa Marie's mother, never showed any interest (horror of horrors) in marriage.

They suspected her to be some sort of pagan and, if they were frank, probably a lesbian. The first time she'd set foot in their house for a party celebrating Lisa Marie's christening, she'd stopped in the foyer, grabbed Lisa Marie's mother by the wrist, and told her that Lisa Marie should never, ever learn to sew. Then, she'd fallen into a swoon, which she later explained, upon waking up on the red velvet chaise in the living room, was the result of the "intense, overwhelming spiritual energy in the house." Lisa Marie's mother laughed it off and changed the subject, mortified already in front of the fashionable friends into whose social circle she'd spent the last several years clawing her way and had finally *made it, dammit.* Still, without ever telling her why, Lisa Marie's parents had never let the girl touch spindle, spool, needle, or thread. Now, the family never contacted the aunt except to solicit her strange homeopathic remedies, which always seemed to work when all else failed.

This time, the aunt called first. Just as Lisa Marie's mother reached for the landline to make contact, it rang.

"I've been living in a cabin in northern Maine," said the aunt in lieu of greeting, the moment Lisa Marie's mother picked up the phone. "On a clear night, you can see the aurora borealis. I'm certain that what your daughter simply needs is rest in the cool, clean air."

"Nice to hear from you, too," said Lisa Marie's mother. How her sister knew these sorts of things, Lisa Marie's mother preferred not to ask. "But the air here is plenty clean."

"As close as you are to Raleigh?" the aunt replied, gently. "Not like it used to be. Let her come stay with me for a while. Have I ever been wrong?"

"Please, tell me," said Lisa Marie's mother, her voice finally breaking. She stood in the kitchen, the evening sky a pale purple through the window, her husband leaning against the counter nearby with his arms crossed. "What's wrong with her? Is she dying?"

"Dying? Nonsense, my dear. She's only eighteen. She's just never learned what she has to live for, not really."

Before Lisa Marie's mother could ask what this mysterious (and vaguely insulting) diagnosis meant, the aunt said, "I'll be down there in two days, maybe three, to pick her up. I'm driving."

"Is that, I mean can you afford to do that? To leave your . . . business like that," Lisa Marie's mother began uneasily, knowing her sister, unlike herself, was not a woman of means. But she already knew what the reply would be.

"I can afford to do anything I please." And the aunt hung up.

When the aunt entered the house this time, her dark hair pulled back in an elaborate knotwork of braids and her pale, gray-blue caftan managing to look both pristine and extremely comfortable for travel, she neither fainted nor delivered a prophecy.

Staggering at the threshold only briefly (the air was still thick with the trauma of house ghosts), the aunt offered a tight smile in lieu of greeting and strode past Lisa Marie's mother, who wore a white sundress that, to the aunt, seemed remarkably constricting to her sister's already thin midsection, especially given this time of year. The aunt's sole thought was, *She looks well considering the air quality in this part of the country.*

Lisa Marie's mother, taken aback by the aunt's lack of greeting, took in the aunt's appearance, from the flutter of fabric to the utter lack of makeup to the intricate braids, and cursed her older sister, inwardly, for looking so much younger than she. As the aunt floated up the stairs like a wandering cloud, Lisa Marie's mother considered the foyer's huge, ornate mirror: her own trim waist, her impeccably bleached hair kept in a sensible but exciting bob (it looked almost as convincing as Lisa Marie's rose-gold locks, full as her own hair had been at that age), and the smoothly applied blush contour she was sure didn't quite hide what she felt like she had become, with her only child on the precipice of college fallen prey to a mysterious sleeping sickness: a hag. She looked at the staircase her sister had ascended. *I'm sure she thinks she looks just fine without makeup, but she'd look much prettier with a little foundation and a little something for those thin lips,* thought Lisa Marie's mother, smoothing her wrinkle-free dress across her midsection. And then, savagely, *She wouldn't look half as good as I do if she had children, and we both know she's too old for that now.*

When Lisa Marie and the aunt came downstairs, murmuring conspiratorially to one another like intimate friends, Lisa Marie's mother felt a stab of jealousy. Lisa Marie hadn't arisen since the day the aunt had called except to drift across the bedroom floor to relieve herself, no matter what Lisa Marie's mother had tried. And she'd tried it all: drenching her with a pail of water (which led to Lisa Marie's mother having to change the girl's drenched nightgown with the help of her uncomfortable husband), grabbing her by the shoulders and shaking her with the strength of a gale-force wind (which left her feeling like one of those *Evangelical* parents who hadn't heard that the whole "spare the rod, spoil the child" adage was out of fashion), and even calling dear, sweet Luke over for daily visitations (supervised, of course). Nothing had worked. And yet here Lisa Marie came, in her nightgown of rose-tinted silk, the liveliest she'd been in weeks. Granted, her eyes were half closed, and even when not speaking, her mouth remained half open as if in a perpetual state of yawning, but Lisa Marie's mother hadn't gotten so much as a peep out of her in what felt, at this point, like a lifetime.

The pair fell silent when their feet hit the floor of the foyer, and Lisa Marie stopped to allow her mother to embrace her while murmuring, "My baby, my baby!" and staining the girl's face with the ghosts of lipstick.

Lisa Marie's arms hung limply at her sides. She gazed straight ahead without changing her expression and returned the affection with a dull, "Goodbye, mother."

The aunt took the purple duffel bag from her sister's shaking hands. It was marked "Princess" in white cursive letters, with a gold, glittery crown over the "i." Then, the aunt led Lisa Marie out the door and across the parking lot to a dark blue station wagon, with a trunk so long it could have been a hearse and a vanity plate that read, "VVIITCH." The aunt opened the back hatch, and Lisa Marie crawled into a many-colored nest of pillows and puffy blankets. Lisa Marie did not look back, not even once, at her mother who stood forlorn in the doorway with tears more of enraged envy than a genuine sense of loss.

—~—~—

For most of the two-day journey, the aunt left Lisa Marie in peace, playing her favorite Loreena McKennitt CDs and humming softly to herself. Occasionally, she talked Lisa Marie through the rest stops, accompanying her to the restroom and feeding her by hand before they continued on the road. At the very first rest stop, she drew the dark curtains she'd installed in her station wagon and insisted Lisa Marie change out of her skimpy nightgown (*What was her mother thinking?* she thought but didn't have the heart to say). In the absence of any practical garments in Lisa Marie's duffel bag full of other silk nightgowns and heinously uncomfortable-looking bras, the aunt eventually coaxed Lisa Marie into shimmying into one of her own caftans over the nightgown. It was a touch too long for the girl, but it would draw less attention than the silk. The aunt announced the crossing of each state line to Lisa Marie in a cheerful singsong: *We're in Virginia! We're in Delaware, dear, but not for long! You know, New Jersey is prettier than people give it credit for, but you wouldn't know that zooming through the turnpike like so.* Lisa Marie seldom responded.

Only once did she sit up, staring wide-eyed at the Delaware river as they crossed its majestic bridge into New Jersey, and confess, "I've never been allowed to leave North Carolina, except to tour colleges."

"My, well look at you now!" replied the aunt. "You're growing worldlier by the minute."

Lisa Marie took in the glittering river dotted with sailboats and said, "The gateway between the Age of Pisces and the Age of Aquarius is on the other side of many rivers slicked with gasoline and the collective realization that this is not the legacy we want to leave for our children."

The aunt flashed an astonished glance in the rearview mirror, but Lisa Marie simply frowned dreamily, fell back into her nest of soft fabrics, and went back to sleep.

Finally, they passed through the sparsely populated Main Street of Limestone, Maine, where the aunt worked as an apothecary. It was close enough to the border of Canada that she could acquire certain pharmaceutical substances not quite legal in the United States. The border patrol turned a blind eye, she explained to Lisa Marie (who would remember this information dimly later in her life without recalling where she'd learned it), for they depended on the aunt for certain sedative tinctures and dream enhancers they could find nowhere else. They drove past the industrial park, past the perverse, igloo-like hovels in the road, which, covered over with grass and weeds, used to house nuclear weapons.

"Cold War," remarked the aunt disdainfully.

"The atom bomb won't bring about the demise your parents feared," Lisa Marie assured the aunt with the same clarity as before, this time without so much as sitting up. "It will be something else. Something slower."

The aunt felt her arms prickle with gooseflesh but said nothing. The roads grew narrower, and the foliage grew thicker, and eventually they turned off onto a bumpy dirt road that the casual passerby would easily miss. Leaves and thin branches thwacked against the station wagon, but the aunt, unconcerned, drove on. Lisa Marie neither moved nor made a single peep.

Finally, in the sharp golden light and long shadows of the late afternoon, they arrived.

To the casual observer, the aunt's house might have looked like it couldn't decide whether it wanted to be a shabby wooded cottage or a Victorian Gothic mansion. Covered in wooden slats that were weathered and stained almost to the point of looking abandoned, the house was three stories high with a small, boxy perimeter and a single, rounded tower protruding from its center that extended two full stories above the third floor. The roof of the tower was black and as pointed as a witch's hat. Vines of many-colored roses clambered up the two purple-painted columns of the front porch and spread like pastel cobwebs up and across the walls of the house: lilac, orange, purple, and even a few pale green blossoms.

Roses were the one thing Lisa Marie's mother and the aunt had in common, although the mother preferred them store-bought and wrapped in plastic, whereas the aunt never plucked them from the beloved garden growing on the wall unless the vines sagged with a labored heaviness.

To the aunt, who stepped out of the car and inhaled the crisp, mossy air and the sweet smell of her darling roses, it was merely home. And it would be to Lisa Marie, too. The aunt extended a hand to help her out of the trunk, and Lisa Marie drifted past her, through the unlocked front door, past the front room, up the first two flights of stairs, and then, finally, up the winding staircase to the top of the little tower, climbing into the four-poster bed and collapsing back to sleep without pulling down the covers.

Lisa Marie did all of this without the aunt having to lead her or to tell her where she'd be sleeping.

Several times during Lisa Marie's long slumber, the aunt came to her bedside and gently roused her into a state of hypnagogia to feed her, give her water, bathe her with sponges, take her blood (something the aunt did with all her patients), help her to relieve herself, and yes, consult with her. The two conversed. Sometimes, the aunt asked her to recall her dreams, which, years and years later, Lisa Marie would describe as being overall pleasant, if at times strange, but she would be unable to recall them in their entirety. Sometimes, the aunt asked her specific questions related to the movement of the planets, the future of the ever-rising seas, or even matters of her own life, her apothecary business, and so on. In a soft voice, she guided Lisa Marie through the process of sitting up, opening her mouth, chewing whatever soft food was at the tip of the fork, and swallowing—slipping in the occasional, *Darling, what* are *we to do until Mars stations direct again?* Occasionally, the aunt paused her duties as nurse to scrawl one of Lisa Marie's semi-coherent responses into her notebook. *The illusion of strife in Aries' rotation rests on our tacit acceptance of masculine aggression,* the aunt scribbled in her brown leather notebook with its single carved eye, and then she'd quickly scoop up another bite of mashed peas, lest Lisa Marie slump forward into the deeper pools of sleep. *The pipeline will burst no matter what they say, just like a man who promises to pull out before he ejects.* Years later, Lisa Marie would remember only her aunt's soft voice floating through the pastel landscape of her dreams like murmurs from the other side of a wall, but she would remember none of the words either spoke. Nor would she recognize many of the dreams recorded in the aunt's journal, although she would always respond sharply, if asked, that she *never* dreamed of her wedding day.

Other nights, when the sky was clear and the aurora borealis shimmered across the sky like alien curtains or the glowing folds of an oyster, Lisa Marie squirmed from her blankets, crawled to the edge of the bed, and sat before the window. The aunt would find her there with her eyes wide and her face aglow with green, violet, and pink. The two would sit there together in silence, hand in hand, until the aunt's own eyes drooped and she was forced to retire to her own room downstairs. These moments Lisa Marie would remember years later with startling clarity, although she would never be able to say for sure whether she was truly awake.

Months passed. Lisa Marie's mother, having access to all

of Lisa Marie's passwords at UNC Chapel Hill as well as all other requisite personal information, deferred her daughter's enrollment until fall the following year, figuring that when Lisa Marie recovered, she could focus on more important matters—such as planning her wedding. She signed documents from the school in Lisa Marie's name, forging her daughter's signature without consent, and even answered phone calls on her behalf, softening her voice and raising it in pitch so as to sound like the young, currently comatose woman. Intermittently, she called the aunt to check on her daughter's progress, and though the patient's condition hadn't changed, the aunt always assured Lisa Marie's mother that Lisa Marie was, indeed, on the path to recovery.

Lisa Marie's mother grew extremely close to Luke in this time. It started with the wedding planning. Though Lisa Marie's mother professed frequently and with much emphasis that she "just hated" to rob her daughter of the joy of planning her own wedding, she understood that, aside from the secret joy she took in seizing control over this illustrious occasion, the show must go on. Her husband, of course, couldn't care less about what happened at the wedding or who was invited, provided that the bottom line, as he joked, did not require that they take out a second mortgage.

Thus, Lisa Marie's mother began regular luncheons with Luke, reasoning that they were the two souls who knew Lisa Marie best and cared for her more than anyone else in the world. It was always her treat, of course, anywhere from country clubs to the burger joint at the edge of campus. "I know you 'broke college students' can always use a free meal," Lisa Marie's mother would say, winking when Luke feigned his obligatory objection to her paying the check. He never countered that, far from being a "broke college student," he had an enormous trust fund that he'd hardly have to touch as a result of receiving in-state tuition and an athletic scholarship for swimming. Lisa Marie's mother already knew this. Anyway, she thought it essential to keep an eye on Luke. During their weekly and sometimes twice-weekly lunches, she spent a little bit of time discussing the color palettes, guest lists, recommended hotel accommodations for out-of-town friends and family, and so on, but mostly she asked him endless questions about how he was adjusting to college life, what his studies were like, and what sort of *exciting new friends* he was making. These questions bordered on probing, and if he ever mentioned any young women in his extended social circle, she'd force herself not to narrow her eyes and answer, in a light voice, *Really? And what's this miss so-and-so like?* His answers were always polite, and they lacked the certain darting-about eyes or dreamy, barely repressed smiles of a burgeoning crush that Lisa Marie's mother watched for like a hawk. She was satisfied that he was staying out of trouble.

She came to more of Luke's swim meets than his own parents did, hand-delivered little care packages to his dormitory, and offered to proofread his papers (so she could call him at arbitrary times, unannounced, with her feedback). From what she could tell, Luke kept himself incredibly busy with swim practice (which, due to the odd hours it required, was prohibitive for many kinds of social activity and necessitated that he spend most of his time with other boys his age), threw himself into his studies (Lisa Marie's mother happened to know that he still hadn't forgiven the Ivy Leagues for not accepting him, and he'd vowed to make them sorry by being ten times more successful than their students would ever be), and actively involved himself in Campus Christian Fellowship (a boy after her own heart, *bless him!*). The truth was, Lisa Marie's mother had been to college and knew the wealth of temptations it offered in the realms of substance use, liberalism, and the opposite sex. She figured that if he couldn't enjoy the constant companionship of Lisa Marie, he should at least enjoy the constant reminder that he had pledged himself to her, in the form of her ever-loving mother, and not to some hussy stealing glances at him during late-night prayer circles.

Come December, however, Lisa Marie's mother grew impatient. It was enough that Lisa Marie, for the first time in her life, had spent Thanksgiving away from the family. The aunt had offered to drive her down, but Lisa Marie's mother could not have her daughter slumping into a plate of mashed potatoes in front of both fashionable family friends and, for the first time, the family of the future son-in-law himself. It put Lisa Marie's mother in an awkward position, having to choose between no bride-to-be at all or the drooling, somnolent mess that was the bride-to-be in her current state, but ultimately she and Luke had decided it was for the best not to *disturb her rehabilitation*. Neither said "lest she embarrass us," but such was the sort of winking, nudging, twinkling-eyed nonverbal communication the two fast friends had developed.

By early December, the nearing of the end of Luke's first semester, Lisa Marie's mother had hoped that her daughter could at *least* be bothered to wake up long enough to secure some kind of definitive winter break plan with her future husband. But alas, Lisa Marie's mother would, as always, have to take matters into her own hands.

"Luke is spending his first week of break skiing in Vermont with his family," Lisa Marie's mother said to the aunt over the phone. "I was hoping he might spend Christmas with you and Lisa Marie, maybe stay there through the New Year."

"Impossible," said the aunt, the light of the aurora borealis dancing across the dark wood of her kitchen. "This time of year, the roads are just murder. Freezing rain, snow, what have you."

Strictly speaking, this wasn't entirely true. The snow and freezing rain didn't start until early January, at least never more than a light dusting that melted within the day. But the aunt couldn't see what bringing Lisa Marie's fiancée would accomplish.

"Anyway, no man has ever entered this house," mused the aunt, as if talking to herself. "It doesn't take kindly to men." On the rare occasion the aunt took a male lover, she did so in the open air, under the stars, and though they might talk into the late hours of the night under blankets sipping hot cocoa spiked with spiced rum, she never let him past the wicker loveseat on the porch. There was no reason for a man to enter this house, let alone one that the aunt had never met and couldn't trust not to knock over any of the delicate arrangements of bones, crystals, feathers, candles, or savory pies left for various ancestors and spirits of the air on her altars. Anyway, Lisa Marie had never asked about Luke, had never expressed any sleeping or half-waking interest in discussing her fiancée or the impending wedding. And the aunt, needing to be sure, had asked. Lisa Marie expressed nothing more than a pleasant ambivalence.

"When do you think she'll be ready?" the mother said.

"Soon enough," said the aunt. "The coming of spring is a rebirth for us all."

"But the wedding is in April!"

"Yes," said the aunt, and hung up.

Late in February, Lisa Marie's mother called again. "I've scheduled fittings for her all through the first two weeks of March," she said. "I *hope* you've at least made sure she's kept her figure, Miranda." It was late morning on a Sunday. She'd skipped church with her husband, complaining of a headache which, strictly speaking, was not untrue considering the *headache* that was planning a wedding with an absentee bride (this she'd giggle to Luke in the next fifteen minutes or so, when he came over for finger sandwiches to hear the results of the phone call).

"If anything, she's lost weight," the aunt assured Lisa Marie's mother. "But she's been able to eat a bit more lately, which I take as a good sign."

"Mm," said Lisa Marie's mother. "Maybe hold off on that until the wedding's over. The camera adds ten pounds, as they say. I expect her back here by next week."

"She's not ready!" hissed the aunt. "Everything we've done, everything we've worked for! Do you want your daughter to be asleep for the rest of her life?"

"I want," said Lisa Marie's mother through gritted teeth, "to fit her for a dress and marry her off to this eligible, handsome, and dare I say *supremely* patient young man before he, pardon the pun, *wakes up from this nightmare* and realizes he's wasting his time!"

"I can send you her measurements, but I can't make any other promises."

"If you don't send her on the next plane to RDU, I'll come and get her myself."

"I'd like to see you try," said the aunt. "What with the roads being the way they are." And this time, she wasn't lying. Through her kitchen window, she watched fat snowflakes land like whispers on the snowdrifts that had collected at the edge of the evergreen trees.

To the end of her days, Lisa Marie's mother would start this story off with a bitter laugh as the time she kidnapped her own daughter. But the aunt had left her no choice. The wedding was a mere three and a half weeks away, and though the bridal shops had shown her some promising prospects with the measurements the aunt had given as promised, it would have been absurd to decide on one without seeing it first on Lisa Marie, let alone sending it to a tailor for some final alterations. As it was, she was promising exorbitant amounts of money for the last-minute rush. Her husband, bless him, had suggested they have Lisa

Marie's mother's wedding dress simply altered to fit, and Lisa Marie's mother had vetoed this idea. Aside from finding the quaint idea tacky and unfashionable, Lisa Marie, though she had not an ounce of fat on her, had inherited something of her father's swimmer's shoulders, not to mention his height. This fact, Lisa Marie's mother had presented with the secret glee of someone who knows that, at the same age, she was smaller than her own daughter.

She and Luke—sweet, princely Luke, ready to rescue his princess!—drove mostly in silence up the coast, taking turns at the wheel so they could drive through the night. No time could be wasted, they had decided at first. They would need a day or two of reconnaissance, and Luke wanted to spend *some* of his spring break with his fiancé outside of a vehicle. Lisa Marie's mother approved of this desire—was in fact relieved that after all this he still wanted anything to do with Lisa Marie—though of course a small part of her was wistful at the thought that the *tête-à-tête* the two shared would no doubt dissolve, or at least be diminished, at the bride's return. Things between the two of them would never be the same. The weather, along with the flora on the side of the highway, grew increasingly bleaker the further north they traveled. Gone were the whispers of near-spring flowers, gone was the occasional warm breeze. The drive north reminded Lisa Marie's mother of exactly the reasons she'd never live anywhere but North Carolina for the rest of her days, where she could still experience the seasons, but where winter didn't linger like an unwelcome houseguest who hasn't taken the hint. She couldn't believe how much snow lingered on the ground past New York City, the quantity increasing to blankets of white crystal, and then to full snowbanks. Horrific.

Though Lisa Marie's mother had entertained secrets of finding a rustic-but-just-right sort of bed-and-breakfast, when no such option presented itself the two checked into the Best Western in Limestone. "Two beds," she said primly to the uninterested young man at the front desk. When she was sure the clerk wasn't looking, she cast a wicked grin at Luke who, to his credit, did not seem to wonder why they couldn't simply book separate rooms at such a shabby establishment.

In Limestone, they staked out the aunt's apothecary, a tiny storefront in an unremarkable shopping center where no hours were posted, in order to get a good sense of her schedule. It proved to be erratic. She never worked full days, and the times she came in ranged from early morning to the middle of the afternoon (the two would roll clandestinely past to see her dark blue station wagon with its disgraceful vanity plate, "VVIITCH," already in the small parking lot). The pair of perfect sleuths agreed that they needed at least a full workweek to establish a pattern, and an additional day or two the following week to test their theory. Luke had never missed classes before; surely his professors would forgive the impeccably behaved pupil this once! They leaned into their roles marvelously, even stopping the next town over for high-collared trench coats and thick sunglasses (at the mother-in-law-to-be's expense, of course). The outside observer might have suggested they were extending their stay unnecessarily. Indeed, Lisa Marie's father asserted as much by telephone on the fourth day, but Lisa Marie's mother brushed him off:

"Oh, darling, this is precisely why Luke was just the one for this trip and not you," she said, the cord of the beige hotel phone wrapped around her pinky finger. She winked at Luke, who entered the room wrapped in a towel, the bathroom exhaling a cloud of steam behind him.

She made no effort to hide the appraising gaze she gave the V of sinewy muscle that plunged toward his pelvis as she continued on the phone with her husband: "You don't have a drop of creativity in your blood, and no sense of adventure whatsoever. We've waited this long to get our daughter back. Why not a few extra days?"

With no discernible rhythm in the aunt's work schedule emerging by the ninth day, Lisa Marie's mother and Luke agreed that they must simply act the moment they saw her car arrive in the parking lot. Surely the aunt would be there for no less than half an hour, and if she caught them in the act of trespassing, what would she do? Lisa Marie was not her daughter. They were not the ones kidnapping. Lisa Marie's mother repeated this mantra to herself on the day, noon, they drove out past the Aroostook National Wildlife Refuge to spirit Lisa Marie away: *We are not kidnapping her. This is a rescue.*

Far from being thieves in the night, Lisa Marie's mother and Luke drove past snowbanks glittering in the midday sun, along with pine trees whose splendor, Lisa Marie's mother thought, was rather dulled by the dusting of snow still veiling the green. At least the snow beside the ever-narrowing bumpy road, unlike the snow beside the Maine highways, was *clean.*

Lisa Marie's mother began to understand what the aunt meant when she turned onto the narrow, barely visible pathway to the aunt's house. Finding it had been tricky. At Lisa Marie's mother's expense, Luke had rented a jeep on the second day to tail the aunt considering that his future mother-in-law's gunmetal gray Rolls-Royce Phantom would have aroused suspicion. On the sixth day, she decided she'd rather be discovered in her Rolls-Royce than caught driving around in such a hideous specimen. Now, Lisa Marie's mother found herself wishing they'd kept the dreadful rental. An abundance of bumps on the icy, unpaved road forced Lisa Marie's mother to slow the vehicle to a crawl. Branches of spruce and pine and fir brushed against the hood of the car, and then swatted at it, and then full-on battered it, as though the forest lived and could sense the intruders. The swaying and thwacking branches dropped fistfuls of snow and ice so that it seemed fists pounded against the roof. Lisa Marie's mother began to worry that the windshield would shatter or that the car would skitter out of her control. In spite of their snail's pace, her grip on the steering wheel whitened her knuckles to the same hue as the snow outside.

When they finally broke through to the clearing where the aunt's house sat, Lisa Marie's mother shivered at the ghastly sight in spite of the Rolls-Royce's spectacular heating system. The first-floor windows were high up enough that Luke had to scale the wall like a cat burglar, clutching onto the rose vines, which pricked his half-numb hands through their gloves and which, despite the snow piled high every which way, were somehow brilliantly, eerily in bloom.

When Luke—poor Luke, dear, brave Luke—got to the window, something strange happened, which Lisa Marie's mother might describe as the house *shuddering*, if only she had the nerve to share this ludicrous detail aloud. The side of the house seemed to ripple for half a second, like a horse twitching its leg to shake off a mosquito, and Luke went tumbling into the rosebushes. She ran to him just as he was pushing himself unsteadily to his feet. He took a wobbling step toward the wall again, but Lisa Marie's mother reached through the thorny vines to stop him. Her sister's nonsensical words from months before floated back to her: *Anyway, no man has ever entered this house. It doesn't take kindly to them.*

It was impossible. Nonetheless, Lisa Marie's mother said, "Don't. I'll go. Wait for me on the porch, and I'll let you in." And so she scaled the wall easily enough, silently thanking her Ripped Abs Aerobics™ and Beach Body Barre™ instructors and wondering if Luke, even in his dazed state, looked back at her lithe form as he went to the front of the house. She barely minded the thorns that dug into her ankles as she climbed, though she did note that hers and Luke's blood would be all over the house. But what could be done? It was not as if the aunt could call the police on her for *rescuing*, not *kidnapping*, her own goddamned daughter.

The window slid open easily for Lisa Marie's mother, and

the house did not buck her off as it had Luke, although she did have to tear through a layer of plastic wrap the aunt had presumably installed over the window to save money through the winter. Blood from her thorn-eaten hands slicked the torn up plastic, and gleaming in the afternoon sun, she thought, the red liquid looked innocent, almost fake. She let Luke in through the front door, pulling him into the gloom before the house could devise some other plan to throw him out.

Without having to search the shadowy house, the two understood where Lisa Marie must be, and they ascended the stairs to find their darling girl as comatose as she'd ever been (little did her mother know, she had been up and about for nearly twelve hours each day keeping books for her aunt and studying the local herbs), her fair hair a feathery halo around her. Unlike when the aunt came to pick her up months before, Lisa Marie's mother had to carry her down the stairs, and more of her blood streaked the sheets. Her bag of silken nightgowns, marked "Princess," sat by the door in the room in such a mess of dust and cobwebs Lisa Marie's mother made the executive, albeit irate, decision to leave it behind. Anyway, the house gave her the creeps, all the shelves of bones and *things* in jars and old-looking books, the cloying smell of incense soaked into the very walls. She couldn't wait to get out.

When they finally heaved her into the back seat of the car, sitting her up and placing a pillow between her lolling head and the window, Luke got the good look at Lisa Marie he'd missed out on in the haste indoors. Yes, she was as beautiful as he could remember. The cheekbones were sharper, perhaps, and the plaid-flannel nightgown she'd been dressed in hid her delicate curves. But her skin was clearer than ever, and her hair looked like it had been brushed for hours every night, and Luke declared then and there that he'd never been more in love with her. He leapt into the back seat with her and covered her face with kisses, murmuring about how much he missed her and how happy he was to see her and how, asleep or awake, he couldn't wait to spend the rest of his life with her. Lisa Marie did not so much as stir.

Lisa Marie's mother watched this with a curious mix of tenderness and disgust before she hissed, "Buckle her up, you dope! And hurry!" To her surprise, after he obeyed and strapped Lisa Marie's seatbelt, he strapped himself in the back there as well. As if Lisa Marie's mother were a damned chauffeur. No matter. There wasn't time. Who knew when the aunt would be back?

The Rolls-Royce Phantom bumped through the woods, with as much difficulty as before, if not more. Halfway to the main road, Lisa Marie's mother remembered once more about hers and Luke's blood all over the house with a sinking feeling, but even if the road were wide enough to turn back, she knew it was too late to do something about the evidence. But anyway, evidence for what? What would the aunt do? Call the police? *She* had been the one holding Lisa Marie hostage.

All the way home, unless it was his turn to drive, Luke stayed in the back with Lisa Marie, murmuring to her or falling asleep on her shoulder. Lisa Marie woke up only once, in Delaware, in a fit of screaming and thrashing and groaning that didn't stop for a whole fifteen minutes. Luke wrapped his arms around her to keep her from grasping at the door handle or doing something else that might harm either of them until finally, having evidently tired herself out, she didn't awaken until the day of their wedding—at least not in their presence.

Still, he and Lisa Marie's mother agreed that using Luke's extra long-sleeved shirts to bind her at the ankles and wrists would be the wisest course of action, lest Lisa Marie do something truly batty, like open the door on the freeway. And if they should be pulled over, Lisa Marie's mother would simply tell the police officers that her daughter was a danger to herself and others.

It was darling Luke's idea. Lisa Marie's mother thought the two made a great team.

When the aunt returned that evening to the open window, bloody plastic wrap, and empty tower, she let out a shriek so fearsome that every rose, though they had survived the deadliest frost, withered and died on the vine. But she did not get in her car and barrel down the expressway after them. No. Rather, she squeezed her sister's blood from the mangled plastic wrap into a tiny vial, and then she went outside and scraped Luke's frozen blood from the outside wall into another vial. She had three important advantages: the patience of a Venus flytrap, a wedding invitation, and a curious detail she noticed the moment she entered the house. She had the blood of a pregnant woman as well as that of the one who must (the aunt needed no psychic assistance to know) have impregnated her.

See, blood speaks to those who know how to listen, whether with laboratory equipment or a sense of smell as sharp as the aunt's. When she'd entered the house, she'd smelled her niece's absence and the blood of her sister and Luke immediately, and she knew what they meant. But when she'd entered the kitchen to blend herself a calming herbal brew, she smelled something else that gave her pause: that low-tide tinge to the coppery smell of her sister's blood, a smell that belonged only to women who were expecting a baby. How curious.

Over the next three-and-a-half weeks leading to the wedding, she made some calls. It has been noted before that certain officers at the border depended on the aunt for various pharmaceuticals she smuggled from Canada. What she did not mention to her niece at the time was that some of these officers came to occupy Very Important Positions in the government. Through a combination of genuinely fond feelings toward the aunt and the years they'd accepted bribes in the form of illegal substances from her, some of these Very Important People felt they owed her something. Or, at least, they wouldn't refuse her if she called in a favor. Not that the aunt ever blackmailed anyone. She didn't need to.

One such person was a man who worked for the Department of Health and Human Services. "Do you know how difficult it is to track that sort of thing before it happens?" he objected over the phone. "They send that sort of thing our way *after* the deed is done. I'd have to call every abortion clinic in the state! And maybe in the surrounding, the way these things go. Can't it wait until she has the—"

"Sorry, no. If it helps, I have strong reason to believe she'll make the appointment in about a week, when she finds out she's pregnant. It can't wait. It's extremely time sensitive," said the aunt, examining her fingernails. Then, before hanging up, she added, "Thank you. So much."

Using information embedded in the bridegroom's blood, the aunt prepared an herbal tincture, of a shadowy sort of herbalism as yet undiscovered by modern science but passed down for generations. In short, the aunt understood how to create the sort of mixture that, based on an understanding of how allergens affect the blood (so complex the casual observer might think it mystical), could be consumed by two people and cause the one's throat to close, but not the other's. All this the aunt understood. She also believed she understood, by this point, her niece's feelings about the marriage, but she could not be sure. She could offer nothing more than a way out, a sword for someone to fall on. In a regular shipping box, she covered the smaller box containing the secret present in rose-gold wrapping paper with a white bow and a note that said, in looping script, *For the bride's eyes only.*

—∞—∞—∞—

Almost as shocking to the wedding guests and Lisa Marie's mother as the aunt's black dress and her sweeping black cape of unmistakable mourning was the fact that the "devil-worshipping heathen of a woman" didn't stop or stagger in the doorway of the iconically beautiful, if almost rustically simple, All Saints Chapel. The old All Saints Chapel, its outside not far off from a child's line drawing of a house and its inside a dream of dark wood and colored glass, fell silent as the aunt's high heels echoed on the hardwood floors for a few steps before she stopped at the door, where Lisa Marie's mother—wearing a dress of creamy beige, with hand-beaded flowers and chiffon at the bodice, a gathered cinch at the midriff, and a sweeping train— greeted each guest with a kiss on the cheek.

Rather than submitting to a kiss on the cheek, the aunt extended a pale hand to her sister and said, icily, "My blessings to the bride."

"And the groom?" said Lisa Marie's mother with a tight smile, still holding the aunt's hand. On the day of her baby daughter's wedding, Lisa Marie's mother decided, in the wide magnanimity of her heart, not to add, *Nobody asked for your blessings, you despicable hag.*

"I don't waste my blessings on the damned," the aunt said quietly, pulling her hand away and taking her seat in the last row on the left behind the rest of the bride's family, who avoided her gaze.

The ceremony proceeded without a hitch, and when Lisa Marie floated down the aisle as elegantly as one might in a frilly nightmare of a mermaid gown no one but her mother could have selected, jaw set with intense focus behind the veil, the casual observer might not know that this was the most awake she'd been since that fateful day she overslept. And not a single misty eye could hope to catch the dark gleam of the capsule between the bride's teeth that she bit into before drinking her half of the ceremonial rose wine, that mixture of white and red that was supposed to symbolize the blending of two lives, handed to her reverently by her father-in-law-to-be. Who but Lisa Marie (and one other) could know that a thimbleful of backwash made especially for Luke passed through the bride's lips into the wine before she handed it to her mother?

Lisa Marie's mother then handed the wine over to the ill-fated groom, and all would remember that the mother was the last one to touch the glass. They would also remember Lisa Marie's radiant smile and the tears gleaming in her eyes, threatening to spill. *It was the happiest she looked all day,* some would recall. *Poor thing, if only she'd known.*

Yes, if only.

It was somewhere in the old priest's waxing about the bitterness, and joy, and sorrow, and love shared between them in drinking from that glass, for all the rest of their days on this Earth, and in the next should they meet again in the Kingdom of Heaven, et cetera, that Luke began to wheeze, and then to cough, and then collapsed to the ground making no sound at all. *My poor daughter,* Lisa Marie's father would say later, in court, as his wife sniffed and swiped away a tear nobody else could see. *This was supposed to be the happiest day of her life. She's the one that has to live with this!*

Among the honored guests was Raleigh's chief of police (Lisa Marie's father had made a generous donation to the force at the now-annual Blue Lives Matter Ball), who had the situation under control immediately. Paramedics were called, but before they arrived, Luke's family doctor had already pronounced him dead in front of the whole congregation.

"If I had to guess," the doctor said to no one in particular, though everyone in the chapel leaned in to listen intently, "I'd say it looks something like anaphylactic shock. Or, and this is going to sound crazy, it's too strange a case to say, but maybe he's been . . ."

"Poisoned," a clear voice said from the other side of the room, and the crowd erupted in murmurs when they turned to the other end of the aisle, where the aunt stood.

"Well, yes," said the family doctor, who had thick brown hair on the sides of his head but was bald as an egg on top. "That is what I was going to say, but it's just too strange. Who would do such a thing?"

"The woman who was carrying his child, perhaps," the aunt mused, stepping forward.

Everyone looked at Lisa Marie, who hadn't moved from her spot at the altar and did look, they all thought, like her tears were genuine.

This time, the chief of police spoke up. "Now, ma'am, that's just not right, throwing around accusations like that. The young lady is clearly distraught." He put his hand on Lisa Marie's shoulder.

"No, officer, not her. Her mother. My sister." It took ample self-control for the aunt to keep from grinning at a room full of stuffy Christians performing their shock at the idea. Before the mother in question—who hovered near her daughter with the most outraged look of all—could speak, the aunt continued, "She called me before she had the abortion."

At this, the congregation erupted. And who could blame them? It was all so shocking, so raw, so dramatic to watch a groom fall dead before saying his vows. And now, here it came that an upstanding Christian woman in their community had murdered her poor, unborn child? People began to shout, and only a few were in the *how dare she make such a hideous claim* camp; most had all they needed to throw the first stone.

"Enough!" bellowed the police chief, who was admittedly less impressive without a weapon, but nonetheless the crowd calmed. “I can’t arrest someone based on these claims—”

“But that Jezebel killed her own unborn child!” someone shouted, adding nothing about Luke.

“—but if we gather enough evidence,” continued the chief, “I may need you to testify in court, ma’am. Are you willing?”

“Perfectly,” said the aunt. “I can give you the time, date, and location of the procedure.” And here, she told a little white lie: “My sister asked me to call in the appointment for her so her husband wouldn’t find out.”

Lisa Marie’s mother, who’d stayed uncharacteristically silent through all of this—no doubt exercising her Fifth Amendment right—looked nervously at the crowd, who still seemed out for blood. She muttered something quietly to the police chief, who nodded and escorted her out of the building.

With a promising suspect apprehended, the police let the excited crowd go without further questioning. They’d dealt with enough. And what was more, the priest offered to perform funeral rites free of any additional charge, having been spared the remaining duties of the wedding ceremony. The wedding became something of an impromptu wake for poor Luke, and even Lisa Marie felt sorry for the young man who had essentially been collateral damage in her great flight for freedom and personal empowerment. *But then again,* as Lisa Marie vaguely recalled her aunt once saying, while they looked up at the aurora borealis, *how many women, not to mention witches, have been collateral in the power-grabbing whims of men over the years?* The wedding feast and the exorbitant fees for an open bar had not been for naught, and anyway, when the alcohol has flowed for long enough, who can tell the difference between the sloshing tears shed at a wedding and at a funeral?

Throughout the entire thing, the bride was nowhere to be

found. Everyone assumed someone else was with her, consoling her and making sure she was no danger to herself. Nobody asked. She was most likely weeping somewhere, everyone reasoned, or even (though only those closest to her particular situation could guess it) sleeping.

But no, Lisa Marie was neither weeping nor sleeping. In fact, as she barreled up the interstate in a certain dark blue station wagon with a vanity plate that read "VVIITCH," she felt more awake than ever. And she'd stay that way, as much as was normal for any healthy adult, for the rest of her days. At last, she'd been given a reason. And who would blame her for absconding, rather than remaining to live with her baby-murdering (and groom-murdering, though family friends would emphasize the former over the latter) mother?

Her aunt snoozed in the passenger's seat beside her. Up north, the snow melted, and the roses needed rehabilitating, and the patients needed treating with mysterious tinctures, and herbal research needed completing after Lisa Marie finished the studies she'd picked up, of her own accord, during the later stages of what she would lovingly refer to for years to come as her chrysalis phase. And there were Ivy League schools to reapply to. So she drove and drove, toward the quiet hills, toward the trees that stayed green through the most impossible frosts, toward the many-colored curtain in the clear night sky.

A THEORY ON LAMPPOSTS

Lily fell backward when the tree she was resting against disappeared into thin air. She rubbed her shoulder and squinted as she searched for a new spot in the park to escape the harsh sunlight. But one by one the trees in the park were disappearing, and in each of their places grew a lamppost, shining brightly despite the sunny day. The replacement of shade with more light—unreasonably bright light that was harsh and painful to look at—particularly irritated Lily, who had left her sunglasses at home and who was to meet with a boy on the other side of the park in only seventeen minutes, according to her watch.

Lining the street, instead of lampposts, enormous maple trees leaned in toward the road, rustling in the wind as if gossiping about the cars beneath them. Sitting beneath a tree on the side of the road, thought Lily, did not make for a superb first date. She wondered how she would look when she met him here beneath the lamppost where her tree used to be, face scrunched up from the surplus of light around her, and felt embarrassed. Should she call him and tell him not to come? Should she tell him that she was feeling sick?

But no, surely he would see her at school the next day in perfectly good health and assume she had stood him up. Lily sighed. Boys, she understood, were stupid. This particular boy, Jason Horowitz, had been positively fixated on her but, as Lily's friends had learned from Jason's friends, terrified to talk to her. Her, of all people! Just short of asking him out herself, Lily had walked up to Jason while he was in the middle of a conversation with two boys on the baseball team and one boy on the lacrosse team. Jason didn't play sports anymore himself, though he excelled in PE and generally got very good grades in school. She'd set her hand lightly on his shoulder and asked if he would walk her to English, staring directly into his small brown eyes with her wide hazel gaze. His three friends had left immediately. And here they were, about to meet on a Saturday afternoon in a shadeless park in exactly three minutes and thirty-seven seconds.

Lily hated to be kept waiting, so she was most delighted when Jason arrived twenty-six seconds early.

"Hey," he said. His hair was dark brown, and he was muscular.

"Hi," said Lily. "Let's get ice cream. This light is killing me."

The creamery was dimly lit and where lights should have been small oak trees grew upside-down out of the ceiling, fully mature like bonsai trees. Lily ordered a scoop of bubblegum-flavored ice cream in a cup, no toppings. Jason ordered cookies 'n cream, also in a cup but with hot fudge and Oreo cookie crumbs on top, which baffled Lily as the cookies in the ice cream were also Oreos, but she said nothing.

They sat down. Jason kept squinting up at the trees on the ceiling with alarm, but they didn't bother Lily. It was summer, so the leaves didn't fall into the ice cream. The creamery still smelled strongly of fresh waffle cones, not of an ancient, mildewy forest. They felt familiar to her, the trees, and she liked to see them occupying the space where the lights usually were.

Lily wished Jason would pay more attention to their date and not the stupid trees.

"I hate bubblegum ice cream," she declared, spooning a bite daintily into her mouth.

"Then why get it?" said Jason.

"I like the idea of eating it."

"You like pink?"

"No, stupid," she said, not unkindly. "I like the idea of eating ice cream that tastes bad, not for the sake of pleasure, but for the sake of eating ice cream."

"Oh," he said.

"It's that ice cream is a dessert," she explained. "So its sole purpose is pleasure. When you choose a disgusting flavor, like bubblegum, you're giving yourself over to the idea of pleasure, but you're not experiencing the pleasure itself."

"So you don't like pink?"

"No more than green or maroon. And I don't play with dolls. Jesus Christ, Jason. I'm not a little girl. Do you pick things that are blue because you like the color blue, because they painted your nursery blue when you were a boy?"

"No."

"Let me ask you something. And be honest with me. Do you like pink? Even a little?"

"Yes."

"Very good."

Their minutes turned to hours, and their hours turned to years. Lily published several books. Her first book, *A Theory on Lampposts,* was an international literary triumph, translated into French, Russian, Spanish, German, Hebrew, Portuguese, Catalan, Arabic, Mandarin, and Japanese. She had six children by Jason Horowitz, two pairs of twins bookended by a girl (the oldest) and a boy (the youngest). She was editor in chief for *The Paris Review.* The tree hanging from the ceiling in her office was a cherry blossom. There was a lamppost at her window.

Everything was equally efficient, what with the trees and the lampposts switching. This is what Lily had posited in her first book. A lamp in the corner, on a table, hanging from the wall—a lamp where a plant should be, in other words—gave light just as well to a room, and a tree hanging from the ceiling was as aesthetically pleasing as a potted tree next to the living room couch. The shadows cast were all different, she had written, but everything worked perfectly once you adjusted your eyes to the light. The reading public went wild over interpreting the polarizing meaning of the text, with most concluding that it was some sort of metaphor for the reversal of various societal roles and others dismissing such a role reversal as relying far too strictly on a binary its spirit seemed to oppose.

When asked, Lily herself would only demur, "I'm so glad that my work has inspired so many interpretations, and I truly believe that my theories and their meaning no longer belong to me once I've put them out into the world. All I ever set out to say is that with lampposts and trees moving the way they are, and so keen to switch over behind our backs just as soon as we think we've replaced them, why go back to the way things were when the world so clearly wants to move in a different direction? Consider, for example, the state of . . ." And the interview would melt into a sea of qualifiers and counterarguments until it was clear only Lily was still following the thread but that everyone listening felt they were on the verge of arriving at something brilliant and important. With such widespread interest from both serious scholars and armchair philosophers, some hailed Lily for resurrecting public interest in contemporary philosophy, and though Lily vehemently protested such claims, anyone noting her blush could tell they pleased her.

Jason made periodic visits to her so she could breastfeed the babies in her office. They had both thought it best for the babies to be breastfed by their own mother. Plus, Lily welcomed the break from her work and the opportunity to make small talk, or large talk, with her husband. He was a good listener. He would stand there in the springtime as her cherry blossom tree above dusted the office with pink-tinted petals and listen as she told him about her favorite submissions for the upcoming issue, about the weather on her way to work, about whether he thought Jupiter was really as big as they said it was. When he left, he made no attempt to brush off the pink cherry blossom petals that covered him.

The lamppost at her window drank in the sunlight idly, and Lily never changed her last name.

AND THEN AGAIN TO THE NEXT

Famagusta, 1974 CE

I knew the city would fall when he stood on the veranda staring out at the Mediterranean in the half-red of sunset, black-and-white striped trunks squeezing the meat of his lower back, his thighs. I tried to muster the enthusiasm I'd had for that form two years ago, tried to resurrect the flutter in my stomach at that spray of hair between his shoulder blades, at the hard divide between his too-tan hamstrings and the pale, smooth caramel of the skin above, shielded from the sun by the thin, tight fabric of his bathing suit. *What's the point of working in a tourist town,* he'd purred once, stretched across the recliner on the veranda, *when you can't let yourself be a tourist every now and again.*

I watched him standing by that same recliner now, his back tense, and I tried to conjure up those old feelings. But they wouldn't come. Because no matter how irresistibly beautiful he was, he'd feel my eyes on him from the other side of the sliding door, turn, pad toward me across the tiled floor of the living room, and straddle me on the merlot-colored couch—too eager, too earnest, too obviously anxious I wasn't in the mood. And he'd be right: I wouldn't be in the mood, not because he *wasn't* desirable, not because I *didn't* want him, but because he was so sure that I didn't, so sure that he'd ceased to be desirable to me. And I'd fail to perform, and then he'd be right, I wouldn't want him, not like that. And he'd sulk, and the sky would go purple, and then black, and maybe he'd be there in the morning, but probably not. Maybe neither of us would.

I'd lived enough lives to know when the tide had changed. I only ever met him in doomed cities. It was always the third year when I found it hardest to love him. Somewhere between the waning of the second year's halo of bliss and the constant weighing of whether the differences were worth working through. Sometimes we made it through the third year and sometimes the city would fall first, and sometimes we'd break up, only to seek each other out like contrite wanderers in the dark of the desert who realized they could not, in fact, give up on water. Only for the world to end before we could patch things back together.

In Famagusta, that year, it was the air strikes.

Pompeii, 75 CE

He tossed his head back in my direction from halfway across the bustling macellum, arm curled around the basket of figs and onions at his hip. He waited for me to catch up to him before he acknowledged me. Later that night, feeding me one of those very figs, he'd tell me with a smug smile that he'd let me follow him for some time just to see how long I would. I'd blink twice, stunned, and stammer out a denial. Truthfully? I hadn't known I'd been following until he pointed it out to me.

That day, as we walked across the macellum, Hercules' hill loomed through the distant haze. When I was just a boy, the demigod had indicated displeasure with our humble city by rattling the earth between his hands like a child angry with its toys, until columns collapsed and houses cracked and mothers and brothers and cousins and fathers were dragged, lifeless, from the rubble. Last year, a single belch of smoke had risen from the mountaintop, accompanied by a hiccup of a tremor, like a warning. But the day I met my soon-to-be lover, as I took the basket from his hands and balanced it on my head, I imagined Hercules, and all the gods, smiling peacefully upon us from atop the heavenly hill.

He caught the basket as it slid from my head, laughing. This was only the second life where I remember meeting him, so of course I had no idea what was to come. I thought I'd been given a second chance.

Bab edh-Dhra, 2353 BCE

When the fishing boat bobbed in from the Dead Sea that morning, when he set foot on the salty shore that glittered in the already burning sun, I knew what he had done. In the way his shuffling feet scuffed salt aside to reveal the sand beneath, in the way he stared down at his sandals to avoid my gaze although I knew he saw me there, in the way that he emerged from the boat first, and then lion-haired Laban emerged last, behind the rest of the crew, as though I wouldn't see, wouldn't remember the two had been in close quarters together, surrounded by the smell of salt and working men all these weeks as they traveled from our end of the Dead Sea all the way to the River Jordan and back—in all these ways, I knew. He could hide nothing from me.

In each lifetime I meet him, some things about him are different, like his name, and some are unmistakable. This time a street magician, that time a museum docent, another time a fisherman, another time a carriage driver. This life his hair brown, tightly curled. That life his hair short, coppery, wisp-thin. But always that flair for the dramatic. Always that crooked smile. Always that tendency to talk in his sleep, from full conversations with me he won't remember in the morning to incoherent gibberish to the muttering of the words "I love you" each time

I slip from our bed, and again each time I return. Always our instant, irresistible draw, our accelerated intimacy, our sheepish admission that *it feels like we've done this before.* Always my secret hurt that he can't remember how many times we already have.

Always his jealousy.

That day at the shore of the Dead Sea, before the fire from the sky, before the glowing, fair-haired strangers in the square at whose feet I watched my lover throw himself into the desperate lust of a man deserted, before self-righteous Lot used that divine prescience to spirit only his own family away while leaving the rest of us to the flames, before all that, I learned this for the last time: it is always the most jealous man, the most certain you'll cheat, who takes another's bed behind your back. In the next life, I would see the signs early on, and I would know how to stop it. But in this life, I threw him out of my house with a divine wrath of my own.

Alexandria, 365 CE

He filled the hall with his music to the contentment of my honored guests, his long fingers flitting across the strings of the lyre, his delicate voice bouncing from marble wall to marble wall. Glint in his eye, exultant grin tugging up the corners of his mouth. In my house, he played with more confidence than I'd seen in him at any amphitheater, perhaps because of the secret knowledge that, no matter how distinguished my guests, none were more distinguished than he.

Yes, perhaps as penance for his past infidelity and as reward for my patience, The Fates decreed in this life that I was master of a house, and he my courtesan. A musician to whom I'd offered a higher bounty than his previous patron. Within my home, where I ran things as I pleased, he was much more than a courtesan, but he did have an exceptional gift for music in that life, and largely because of him, my house had a reputation for its illustrious feasts.

Of course, there were fewer and fewer feasts like mine where the old gods were celebrated alongside the pleasures of the flesh, since Theodosius had unleashed his tidal wave of Christianity. With the rise of that religion, the empire as a whole had taken a downward turn, but we were still a Christian empire in name only. That punitive new religion's strict sense of moral superiority would take years yet to gain any real foothold. We'd seen other gods rise to prominence, other rulers fall to decadence. Many of my friends still thought we'd outlive Christianity, and though I knew better, I had my parties, and I maintained my house as I pleased, and he shared my bed and commanded the household as though he too were its master.

I had my own concubines, and to his surprise I allowed him his. It was part of my plan in that lifetime to see if taking away the possibility of infidelity would strengthen our bond, show him that, while others could come and go, we would always come back to one another at the end of the day. In each life I tried something different. In this life, as was customary for someone of my stature, I had a veritable harem to choose from, and so I made no attempt to keep *him* for myself alone. It was only fair.

But therein lay the problem between us in all our time in Alexandria: it was always what I allowed. Though I kept no slaves—how could you, when you've lived to see their liberation in another lifetime?—everything we did together he accepted with the desperate gratitude of a plebeian toward the "master" with whom he'd found favor. He'd do anything I asked him to, but I was sure he did it more out of a sense of duty than the unconditional love I pined for. He loved me, make no mistake, but never as an equal. And so, though we both had independence, and in that lifetime his jealousy was perhaps mitigated, it was largely because, I believe, he never felt he had any *right* to be jealous.

It was hellish. I came the closest I'd ever come to telling him of our past lives, of our intertwined futures, but afraid the spell would break and I'd lose the seemingly infinite opportunities I'd been given from gods-knew-where to get things just right, I cut myself short at the last possible moment. I was almost relieved when one of the servants interrupted our midday lovemaking to tell us, in a breathless panic, how the gods had pulled the sea out toward the horizon like a rug, leaving fishing boats alongside horrific sea creatures in the sand and slime.

Ys, 434 CE

"You want to know what your problem is?" I said in the dark of the tavern as I helped him up from the puddle of beer and broken glass and blood—his blood, and that of the three men he'd picked a fight with because they'd been "looking at me funny." Even fairy-made cities of cedar and gold and crystal, walled off impossibly from the sea, had their bar fights.

I groaned as I hefted him up, dazed as he was, so much dead weight. He was rather heavy in that lifetime, rather hairy, and his strength lent his usual theatricality a certain brutishness that grated on me while making me, in spite of myself, weak with lust. This wasn't the first time he'd stuck up for me when I wasn't sure I needed help. We made a strange pair in that life, he a burly blacksmith, I a waifish druid in a city where being a druid had begun to fall out of favor. It wasn't the kind of prejudice you might think. No, that was a simpler era, where fairies consorted publicly with humankind, and two men could walk freely through the streets without fear of violence or harassment. It was my being a druid that made people cast wary glances at one another or move to another table if I sat too near, not my being with a man. Still, having a reason to protect me gave him a wonderful confidence in that lifetime. I think it was good for him.

On his own two feet at last, he swayed briefly before plucking an abandoned goblet of mead from a nearby wooden table, taking a swig, and belching.

I continued, "Your problem is that you'll do anything to get my attention, but you've already got it."

"And *your* problem," he replied with a good-natured smile, mead sloshing from a new goblet as he gestured toward me, "is that you think you know me better than I know myself."

I opened my mouth to protest, as was my habit with him, but the words wouldn't come. What could I say? I'd been his lover across life after life he'd apparently forgotten. Of course I knew him better than he knew himself.

Didn't I?

The bell tolled in Ys for the last time, that same bell whose ghost people would hear on a calm day for years to come. He finished his drink.

Osaka, 2083 CE

The elevator sunk two hundred thirteen floors, and my stomach pitched in spite of its smoothness, its silence. Perhaps he was following, sinking down in an elevator seven stories behind mine, praying he'd catch me before I drove away. Something told me that he wasn't. We'd paid for the full hour of counseling. Surely he was getting the last twenty-five minutes' worth of our money to process what had just happened.

When I got home, I ran my hands under the chemically cooled water in the bathroom sink, splashing it on my sunburned face (I was having to replace the UV-blocking resin on the windshield with greater and greater frequency, in those days). I mumbled over and over into the mirror as I did so. We would weather this. We always weathered it. We would, we would, we would.

Take every moment as it comes was one mantra I'd written on the bathroom mirror with the AR mapping only my contact lenses could pick up. *Remember the mistakes of the past while leaving room for a future you can't imagine* was another. And then, of course, the old proverb, *Fall seven times, stand up eight.* Mantras: the recommendation of my therapist. Ours. Ancestors only knew what *he* had mapped on the mirror that I'd never see. Ancestors. A funny set of spirits to believe in when you've lived a hundred lives, but Shintoism had survived here when everything else had fallen prey to the cynicism of a world slowly dying, and perhaps there was something to be said about that. How many of us were our own ancestors without even knowing it? I certainly couldn't have been my own. I'd tried to be with women a handful of times in past lives, and unsurprisingly, a baby had never taken. I'd even *been* a woman a couple times, but never been able to conceive.

But I'd done it. I'd told him. Stupid, stupid, stupid. I'd told him. Why had I thought he'd believe me? By this stage of the anthropocene, enough research had been conducted to create the vocabulary to talk about reincarnation, about past life regression, with some statistical certainty. I'd been flipping through a book about it in the white, round-edged waiting room of our therapist's office. I'd insinuated enough to our therapist about how I knew things about our relationship, our past, our future, that I'd been *reasonably* certain she knew what I'd been hinting at.

So I blurted it during our session. They'd both blinked, slowly, and she'd asked for clarification. I'd given it, in painstaking detail, as if to children. I'd explained all our lives together with the confidence of someone who's had an accumulation of centuries to analyze what was happening to us. I ignored the slow widening of their eyes, jaws clenching and then slackening, brows furrowing and then unfurrowing. At their reactions, I simply thought I'd overwhelmed their one-lifetime minds with too much information, or perhaps they were experiencing their own awakenings. When I finished, he sank into his plush chair and stared at me blankly. Even lifetimes later, I can't forget the words, spoken more to himself than to me: *I should've gotten help for us sooner.* I remember that day as the first, in any lifetime, that I had any doubt about the truth of my condition.

I don't know what to say. I had to do something. It was our fifth year together in that life. Things between us were permafrost-thin.

The cool chemicals of the sink usually worked wonders on the swelling around the eyes, but not this time. Salty heat ran down my face, and I couldn't stop it, and I kept repeating, *Fall seven times, stand up eight.* But I'd tried to stand, really stand, once and for all. Stupid! I shouldn't have. There were some things no one could know. Some secrets you carried to the grave, and then again to the next.

When I heard the front door to our apartment whoosh open, then close, I shut the door behind me, but he came in anyway—something he'd never done in any lifetime, violate my privacy—and beyond the mantras written on the mirror I spied his face: stony and unreadable, I thought, that of a man who had decided his husband was crazy and would subdue him until he was taken away.

He placed his hand tentatively on my shoulder, like a child reaching out to pet a capybara for the first time (they existed only in petting zoos by then), and said, "If you know it's going to end up like—"

"I never know exactly how anything's going to—"

"Please. Just let me finish. If you know it's going to end up like this—something *like* this, why do you come back to it every time?"

I straightened from my slouch, pushing with both arms, and turned to look at him directly, not through the mirror.

"Do you even have to ask?" It wasn't as if I had a choice,

as if I hadn't invested eons in our love, as if I could wake up in another life and see that crooked smile as I walked down the street and keep on walking. And then, afraid of the answer, I asked, "Wouldn't you?"

He looked down at the tiled floor for a murderously long moment before he closed the gap between us and said, "I think I would."

Something awakened in me at the uncertainty in his voice, and I kissed him, desperately, needing him. It was the first time in months I'd been the one to initiate intimacy between us. All my lives, I'd been so sure things were inevitable between us, so sure that even if I lost him, he'd be back again in another life, and he wouldn't be able to resist me. The idea that we had a choice, that *he* had a choice . . . For the first time I was relieved of the burden of holding all the power.

I won't say I realized just then what a complete ass I'd been, that I understood in that precise moment why he was so insecure: I'd been engaging with him each life as if our relationship was doomed from the start. And I won't say it wasn't. Doomed, that is.

The duration of that life can only be described, though I hate to use the term, as a slow burn. It wasn't the wool-pulled-from-over-the-eyes, suddenly-everything-made-sense sort of life I might have imagined. No. Too much damage had already been done, too many gaps that, no matter how well we thought we understood each other from that point on, were too late to bridge. But we held on, along with the other millions who had more important things to worry about than a revelation in couples' therapy. We held on after the onslaught of hurricanes that forced the unyielding tungsten barricades to yield, after the unbreakable dams broke, after the sea came in with tsunamis of nuclear waste and oil and all the other poisons we'd poured into it. We even held on as the ocean claimed anyone brave enough to try to leave the safety of the skyscrapers, while the rest of us simply starved.

In past lives, I'd been eaten alive by the guilt that, if I'd just said something sooner, if I'd just told him I knew we were destined to meet in doomed cities, we could've fled, but I'd been paralyzed by the fear he wouldn't believe me or the fear that we'd leave the city only to be claimed by another disaster, that no matter what I did it would always find us.

In this life, at least, I was assuaged of the guilt. Even if I'd said something sooner, we both knew there was nowhere else in the world to go.

San Francisco, 1906 CE

I wasn't rich enough for one of the earthquake cottages in Franklin Square, so at first I drifted west to Presidio, where I floated like a specter for weeks searching for him among the tents, unnervingly crisp, arranged in neat rows by government agents. Then there were the Golden Gate Park shanties, which were rather rudimentary by comparison, rather dodgy, rather less safe. But at least the walls were made of wood, not canvas. He was nowhere to be found there either. Meanwhile they pulled out body after body after body from the debris and the ashes. I scoured the papers until finally I saw his name among the dozens of others.

I didn't know what to do. It had been an exceptionally blissful two years that lifetime, then a moderately rocky third, followed by a solid fourth, and before the earthquake hit I was sure that, finally, we'd gotten it right. I wasn't hiding our reincarnated history from him anymore. In each lifetime, I'd promised that after the last, I would come clean as soon as I was sure he would listen.

Hours after I found out he was dead, fingers of fog crept through the narrow margin beneath the door to my shack, and

I hung myself from the low ceiling with what must have been two inches of space between my toes and the floor. I was eager to start over, to get this life over with and start the next one so I could see him again. Well, wouldn't you know, the rope was too short and the chair I jumped from was too low to snap my neck, so for some time I flailed there, gasping and sputtering and choking, certain I'd made an awful mistake. As I jerked about, I heard the roof begin to creak, all tin and two-by-fours. I wiggled my weight around all the more ardently, thinking, *All right, if I make enough of a ruckus, perhaps the roof will collapse, and I can forget I ever dreamed of this suicide nonsense and move on with whatever crummy life I have left in California.*

And then it did, the roof collapsed, but that did nothing to help me forget about *this suicide nonsense*. Rather, I looked up in time to see a razor-sharp edge of tin rush toward me. Then nothing.

Let me tell you, that was the last time I'd make that mistake. It took me three lonely lifetimes to see him again, tragically long lives uninterrupted by premature catastrophe.

Famagusta, 1569 CE

A common misconception is that reincarnation happens linearly. You die one year, you are reborn in that same year. Not so. I have come to rest in one life only to be reborn a millennium and a half earlier.

When you've lived the lives I have, déjà vu chafes you like the ghost of an uninvited guest. There's something awful about realizing you've lived in a city before, at its end. Living a stolen life in a place you know, centuries later, will meet its demise. Knowing its distant future and, therefore, knowing the future of this life—if Famagusta is fated to fall four centuries from now, you won't meet him for the fourth life in a row. You come to understand this when you realize where you are, and that you were born here before, in a future in which the city fell. And you're tired, yes. Tired in a way few could hope to understand the word.

And then, walking along the beach nostalgic for a past you'll live hundreds of years later, a past where sweaty bodies lie prone in the sand to bake in the afternoon sun, you see a man kicking rocks at the edge of the sea, and he looks back, smiling his crooked smile, and you realize some cities are destined to fall more than once.

THE OAK I KNEW

"Why do the birds go on singing?
Why do the stars glow above?
Don't they know it's the end of the world?
It ended when I lost your love."
—Skeeter Davis
Music and lyrics by Kent and Dee

You could say a hurricane took him from me, although that wouldn't quite be right. Oak: shaggy and slender and short, my pint-sized Jesus, as I liked to call him. I didn't exactly lose him to the hurricane alone. Not that he was mine to lose. This is not a love story. At least, not the kind you think.

Morning, the day before the storm, I sat across the fire from Oak at the edge of the forest behind our house, while he bent over the flames to make breakfast for our half of The Compound. The sky? That ominous clear that could only precede one thing. Even the greenish morning haze, one of the ghosts of our ancestors' excesses, had burned away early in the swell of the November sun. The weather was fine, if muggy, but we knew the next night, we'd be huddled in our houses, felled trees clanging against The Shell, the metal half-dome we erected for every major storm. Uncle M had never been wrong about the weather.

I attempted to entertain Oak: "You know, they used to name

each hurricane that hit the shore, and even some that never made landfall." With too few humans left on Earth to form any real sense of collective history, my role at The Compound was to research what society had been like before The Great Thaw, so we could learn from their discoveries and mistakes.

"Like human names?" Oak said, a dubious smile spreading his short-cropped beard to the boundaries of his thin face. He cracked an egg as big as his head into the cast-iron pan on a grate above licking flames. Ostriches were one of the few birds that had survived The Great Thaw and were capable of laying edible eggs, thanks to facilities called "zoos" which had displayed living animals for our ancestors' entertainment. Each ostrich egg fed ten. After my careful research about ostrich care, we'd determined they were worth breeding since we had a hundred adults at The Compound and about half as many children.

"Yeah, human names."

"If we started naming hurricanes, we'd run out by the end of the y—"

A screen door slammed nearby. We both glanced at the nearest house to see Uncle M striding toward us. Uncle M: sexagenarian, lover of our ancestors' gadgets, secret-but-not-so-secret holder of the belief that society's acceptance of queers like me had led to The Great Thaw, the scores of hurricanes each year, the tornadoes tearing across continents bearing flaming trash and molten plastic, the hilly coasts turned to clusters of tiny islands. Of all the things to have survived The Great Thaw, the occasional belief in this particular version of a god had never made sense to me. They'd gotten their Armageddon, but it hadn't turned out remotely the way they'd said it would. Wasn't that proof enough? But no, one of the first books I'd had to salvage had been a Bible—quite a feat to find such a work with all its tiny letters unmarred by water damage—and a handful of those who had lived before The Great Flood gathered every seven days to look at it, had even begun to indoctrinate some of the children. I guess everyone needed *something* to cling to.

Oak flipped the enormous egg, then waved cheerfully at Uncle M with a faded, pinkish-red oven mitt. My closest friend had a way of defusing negative moods with that wide, friendly smile of his.

I half-raised my hand in greeting. Uncle M didn't deserve the energy required for a full wave. We were all about conservation at The Compound.

"Storm's coming. How you boys faring," he said, flatly, not seeking a reply.

"Oh, you know," said Oak. Flashing me a sidelong smile, he launched into a painstakingly detailed account of the day so far, from the friskiness of the ostriches in their pen at dawn to his ideas about the naming of hurricanes. Our private game: how far could Oak, beloved workhorse of The Compound, stretch Uncle M's patience? He'd just begun to explain his thoughts on the morning haze when Uncle M finally cut him off.

"I have a favor to ask of you," he said. "Confidential."

"Of me?" I said, winking at Oak. We all knew he wouldn't act this polite if he needed something from *me.*

I saw Uncle M's eyebrows, orange with traces of white, pinch as he considered some emasculating reply. But he wasn't stupid enough to insult me in front of Oak if he needed a favor.

"Actually," he said, hands folded over his crotch in false meekness. "This is a job for Oak. It might be a bit too . . ." he grasped for words, but it was too late.

"Manly for me? Too technical? Too . . . heterosexual?"

"I wasn't going to say that."

"Don't worry," I said, voice dripping with honey. "You can mutter it to me later, when Oak's not around. I'll leave you two alone."

I blew a kiss at Uncle M and stalked across the grass, making eye contact with Oak and pantomiming masturbation with three flicks of the wrist. This broke his neutral mask long enough for a snort of laughter.

If anyone should find what I've made of my journals and accuse me of oversensitivity, know that Uncle M had been, at the time, launching quiet warfare on the utility of my work. Never mind that I always got my share of chores done before I set out. Never mind that he owed so many of his gadget-tinkering skills to engineering books I'd acquired. Never mind that The Compound wouldn't know half of what we knew about weather, nutrition, agriculture, even the politics of collective living, without my research. Never mind the incredible peril I risked in traveling to The Archipelago, the hilly coastal metropolis turned into a string of little islands rife with toxic waste and turf wars among The Great Thaw's survivors. Never mind the physical demands of these trips to often-flooded libraries: diving through pools full of plastic that might wrap around your legs and drag you into the depths, climbing over the rubble of fallen buildings like a mountaineer.

No, to Uncle M, books were for the idle. He'd drop hints of this to our cohabitants here and there, manipulate the chore charts to make it more difficult for me to get out to The Archipelago unless he needed a particular engineering book or some religious text, in the name of "pulling my weight."

From the corner of my eye, I saw Uncle M move toward him, his gut bulging behind his light blue shirt, gesturing with rehearsed precision. Oak, a head shorter than him and bone-thin, stared at Uncle M without moving, save for running his fingers through his long mane of brown hair, like he did whenever he was biting his tongue. And he bit his tongue often enough.

That evening, when it came time to erect The Shell, I positioned myself near Oak to coax the contents of the whole "confidential" conversation out.

The Shell, a dome of aluminum and steel, consisted of six massive curved trapezoids, which we attached to foundations that surrounded the outskirts of The Compound, the short ends of the trapezoids pointing outward like a lotus flower (another living beauty now found only in moldy picture books). By a system of pulleys, we pulled the short ends to the top of six beams in the center of The Compound, and on top we fastened the seventh piece to cover the opening. Several people on ladders stood at the top of the beams to fasten all the pieces in place. The Shell was lined with tiny holes so we could breathe, and because The Compound sat atop a hill, flooding was not a concern. I'd discovered its blueprints, invented by our ancestors too late to make a difference. A team of us at The Compound salvaged the materials we needed from the suburbs of The Archipelago to create it. It was quick to erect and nearly impenetrable. Though not perfect by any means, The Compound was safe. Safer than any life I could envision since The Great Thaw.

I stood next to Oak as we hoisted up one of the curved trapezoids.

"So, M has this machine that harnesses lightning and stores it as electrical power," Oak said. It took very little coaxing. "It's a sort of lightweight tower."

"Okay," I said. Electrical power. A fickle thing with an unquenchable thirst for resources—one of the main excesses that helped bring about The Great Thaw. So, of course, Uncle M had what they used to call a *hard-on* for it. "And?"

Oak kept pulling his rope without looking at me. "He wants me to try it out."

"What's the problem? What are you not telling me?"

While we waited for the next command to pull, I rested my thumb against his knuckle in assurance. Before you jump to conclusions, no. We were simply comfortable with each other. Sure, I'd done an awful lot to convince myself he wasn't my "type," all twig-thin and lean muscle, but mostly Oak didn't swing that way, as far as I knew. I'd never detected any interest from him, toward me or any other man in The Compound.

We heaved. The tip of our trapezoid reached the top of the two beams, and we held fast while men on ladders latched our part of The Shell into place. Above, plump clouds tinted with purple and orange sailed by at an alarming pace, as if to outrun the coming storm.

Oak sighed. "The tower has to be set up offshore. Something about how lightning hits the water and spreads, and how it's more likely to strike the tower with nothing else around."

"What? But you'd have to leave—"

"Before dawn, if I'm going to make it to any kind of shelter. I'm supposed to wait out the storm in The Archipelago. Apparently the tower collapses, and it's light enough for me to drag down the hill by myself. Some sophisticated thing from before The Great Thaw."

Above, a metallic clang told us our portion of The Shell was secure. My hands burned when I released the rope. For a moment, my fingers wouldn't unfurl, as if I'd been holding so tightly, for so long, that I'd forgotten how to let go.

"You're not going, are you? I mean, he can't make you do something like that without a vote."

"Well, he said he'd hold an emergency vote tonight if I didn't agree. There's no point. The elders are on his side." The elders—our snarky name for Uncle M's generation, who held a silent majority when it came to major decision-making at The Compound.

From the sound of Oak's voice, I guessed he hadn't put up much of a fight, as was his way. Well, that was why he had me.

I spied Uncle M through the space between two houses, by the animal pens at the edge of The Shell, his hands on his hips, apparently "supervising." I marched toward him, ignoring Oak's cry of "Wait!" behind me. I knew he wouldn't follow.

"What the fuck is this all about?" I said in mock friendliness when I was close enough.

Uncle M swung around toward me, all feigned obliviousness, as if I hadn't caught him glance twice at me approaching and look performatively away before I could meet his eye. "Oh, we're just bringing the oxen—"

"Not that. Walk with me."

"I'm a little busy," he said, flicking his eyes nervously around for some excuse. "Shouldn't you be—?"

"Shouldn't you?" I snapped.

We walked. That was the thing about underhanded people like him: when pressed directly, they caved.

"What you're asking Oak to do is suicide." I was good at pressing. Not so much at subtlety.

"Don't be dramatic," he said. "I'm sure you can survive the night without him."

I ignored the gibe. "Why him? Why not one of *you?* Anyone else? Me?" That last word hung for a moment, a silent dare. I hadn't quite formed the thought, but something told me this was about something beyond electrical power.

"He's the only one with the strength and technical know-how—"

"I've read all the same books—"

He talked over me. "—to pull it off. Nobody from my generation would last out—"

"Let me go instead."

This actually managed to stop him, both from talking and from walking.

I continued, "Any mechanical stuff you and Oak know came from books I found."

"It's more than just curling up by the fire with a book in your hand. You—"

"I've been to The Archipelago more than anyone here. If anyone knew where to find shelter—"

"Then you can give Oak some pointers. Look, it's too late.

I'd have to clear it with everyone in The Compound—"

"Like you did with Oak? Or are you pretending he volunteered?"

"Don't be stupid, Carl," he finally growled. And there it was. You play dumb long enough with cowards like Uncle M, it's amazing how direct they suddenly become. "One of you had to go, and unfortunately, we don't have another archivist. There are those here who value what you do too much, Lord knows why."

"Wait, what?" This time, I wasn't playing dumb.

"Believe me, I wish it could be you. At least Oak tries to hide *whatever it is* going on between you two, and he's a hard worker. But a few of the others said we have plenty of hands," he sighed, and then said pointedly, "and *we* can always make more hands." By "the others," of course, I assumed Uncle M meant those of his generation, the silent majority, but I couldn't be sure of anything at this point.

"I don't understand," I said, which was to say I didn't want to understand. "We're not even . . ." And anyway, so what if we were? There was no law against it at The Compound, last I'd checked. The first law of The Compound was to value survival above all else which meant, tacitly, valuing human life in every form. All my life I'd believed this. All my life I'd believed it kept me safe, kept us all safe, to value each other in this way.

As if he heard my thoughts, he said simply, "The survival of our species depends on its ability to reproduce."

I stared at him, awestruck.

He continued, in his normal, mockingly reasonable voice: "Now, there are *children* in The Compound who look up to you both, for whatever reason . . ."

I heard nothing else he said. I saw torches in my periphery as others lit the evening work. I heard distant laughter and the pounding of my own blood. And I surprised both of us by punching Uncle M in the face.

I'll admit, I had no idea what I was doing. I'd been aiming

for his nose, but I must have nicked just next to his eye, because only half my fist throbbed with pain. As he reeled back, caught off-guard, I wondered, *Am I supposed to hit him again?* But punching had hurt more than I'd expected, so I settled for a kick to his crotch, except I missed and kicked his hip instead. Still, he went toppling over with a satisfying grunt.

Others were quickly upon me, those people with torches, dragging me away before I could get another word in.

We didn't have prison at The Compound. In the rare occasion of major wrongdoing, you were taken back to your home where your housemates had to keep watch outside the house for three days. Beyond your own forced isolation, four other people slept outside during that time, suffering worse than you did, angry as hell by the end of it. It was extremely efficient punishment, shame. In the past, our ancestors had held one another captive for years, sometimes lifetimes. They even killed their own for certain transgressions. The idea of murder had been drilled into our heads as unfathomable, here at The Compound where survival was god and loss was luxury. And I had believed it—all my life I had believed that The Compound valued life above all else.

Yet here went our elders, sneakily sending Oak to die, to set an example that *certain* behaviors would not be tolerated. Evidently, the possibility of romance between two men was more of a threat to the survival of The Compound than some cloak-and-dagger execution by way of a mission doomed to fail, more of a threat to survival than the precedent such an execution entailed. How could anyone begin to make that distinction? To say that the net good a person could do for their community would be nullified by the harm they'd caused—or in this case, *the harm their example would cause?* Was it so likely that all the children in our community would see two grown men together and decide to forgo reproduction when they themselves grew up? I didn't think so. Before I had the refuge of books to teach me there was nothing unnatural about what I desired, I'd developed my attraction with nothing but examples to the contrary. And Oak? Well, now I wondered if I'd ever be able to ask him.

Thus, I spent the following days alone, holed up in a house large enough for six roommates, like the lonely ghost wandering the halls of the haunted mansion in those gothic novels I snuck back from The Archipelago for Oak sometimes. Except the houses in The Compound were a single story, so there were no grand spiral staircases for me to sail up and down, no great halls through which my otherworldly moans could echo. The worst part was that I couldn't give Oak "some pointers," as Uncle M had put it. I couldn't even draw out a map, clue him in on spots in the Archipelago with the most shelter. I was cut off. I couldn't even say goodbye to him before he went out on an errand that might end his life, let alone hedge his bets for survival. Leaving the safety of The Shell during a hurricane. It was criminal!

The first night, I yearned for him in a way I didn't know I could yearn. I obsessed over the thought that if only *Oak* had socked Uncle M in the face, something he would never do, they'd have had no choice but to confine him for the hurricane. Then, if Oak survived, which it seemed like nobody expected, what would be next? Would we have to move into separate houses? Avoid each other? Because we were *a threat to survival?* My mind turned and turned all night, over the knowledge that my friend was essentially being punished because of my sexuality. That sexuality had become punishable at all.

The next morning, I awoke to a loud clang and perfect blackness. The Shell had been sealed. I imagined Oak out at sea by now, staring out over the filthy water toward coming storm clouds, wind whipping around him.

I bumped around the house, feeling along the walls and

knocking crotch-first into furniture, until I found last night's dinner ration left for me just inside the front door: cold porridge accompanied by a reasonably fresh hunk of bread. I'd like to say that the food turned to ash in my mouth from missing Oak, that with Oak gone, maybe never to return, I couldn't scare up an appetite. But I ate it on the spot, right there, on my knees. I was starving, and it was good even cold.

Out there, I could hear the crackling of morning fires, the outbursts of laughter, the voices of my cohabitants. Who else was behind this? Who else had betrayed Oak so thoroughly?

And another, admittedly selfish question had begun to nag me: Who else had seen something I hadn't in Oak's behavior toward me? And were they right? Was there something between us?

I got up, stumbled through the dark to Oak's room and found his guitar, a ratty thing I'd found for him at The Archipelago. I sat there on the floor of his bedroom, twanging out shaky chords, surrounded by the smell of him. I could hardly manage the basics he'd taught me, less so in the dark. But when all you've got to do is think, thinking is the last thing you want to do. I imagined he was there with me, patiently correcting the placement of my fingers with his own, as he'd done so often before, a gesture so simple and sincere that I'd never thought anything of it. But it was too hard. I was just no good at the guitar. I never had been.

I began to cry, softly, at first with the frustration of trying to force music out of the unyielding instrument. In the thick shadows of the empty house, a lifelong friendship of tiny intimacies, maddening in their ambiguity, unfolded before me. One of my earliest memories: child-Oak reaching a slender hand out to help me, and only me, across a filmy stream of red-tinted water in the forest before we ran to catch up with the other orphan children of The Compound. Sunsets after long days of tilling as teenagers, after I'd grown far taller and bigger-boned than he. I would carry him on my back from the modest fields at the edges of The Compound, his sharp cheekbone pressed against the back of my neck and the warm, slow breath of his half sleep itching at my sunburned shoulders. And so on. As with Oak's unsuccessful attempts to teach me music, I'd ignored the light tug in my abdomen every time, never daring to name it even before I knew it had a name.

I set his guitar aside. I ate. I napped. I longed. And yes, I wept more than I'd care to admit. I stopped trying to keep track of time until I heard the first crack of thunder and figured it must be evening. The first arms of the storm were swinging by us.

I slept in Oak's bed, enveloping myself in his blankets and the comforting smell of his dried sweat. At times I half dreamed he lay there with me; at times, awake, I pictured him setting up inane machines in the tormented sea, and in those moments I tried to force myself back beneath the tide of dreaming. If Uncle M had been right about him, if there had been something between us I'd simply not allowed myself to see . . . it was too much to bear.

Does dwelling on that last possibility—that I might be losing the only shot at love and intimacy I might ever have *on top of* losing my best friend, *on top of* losing any faith I had in the community that was supposedly keeping me safe—while my friend might still have been out there, while I might still have a shot at helping him, seem a little selfish to you? Well, then you're not the only one. Even as I pitied myself I chided myself for not thinking happier thoughts about my gentle friend, as if the least I could do while trapped in here was picture calm shores for Oak, imagine his safety, his long fingers gripping his canoe as he dragged it uphill in triumph. But each time I pictured those long fingers I couldn't help but see them entwined in mine, and the cycle would repeat.

The final day and a half of my confinement was the worst. When The Shell came down, afternoon sunlight streaming through the windows, I still had no way of knowing whether Oak was all right. The Compound strictly prohibited communication with anyone in confinement except in emergencies. Although I wanted to believe Oak would find some way to tell me he'd made it home safe, I knew it would have been unwise to risk any more on our behalf. So came the maddening pendulum: hope that he'd survived, certainty that he hadn't. He was Schrödinger's cat: both alive and not, both in love with me and not. Only I was the one in the box. Believe me—I burned for him by then. I'd really talked myself into being in love with Oak, now that he was gone.

I did know, since nobody came to fetch me, that the hurricane had done no meaningful damage to our community—or at least to our property. Our ancestors had designed The Shell's technology well, even though they'd discovered their need for such protection far too late to make any real difference in the fate they'd set in motion.

That morning, I felt more charity toward their timing than ever before.

When I was allowed to leave on the evening of my third day, none of my housemates guarded the front door, not even stand there with their arms crossed to guilt me for their having to stand outside day and night. Everyone sat in a circle at the center of The Compound. A Circle, where everyone in The Compound old enough to make a decision gathered. I scanned the Circle for Oak, not finding him. I joined the Circle myself, squeezing in between two women. I fought tears. He wasn't here. He hadn't returned.

None other than Uncle M walked around the inside of the ring of rapt faces, waffling: ". . . definitely unfortunate, but he insisted on being the one to go. We haven't heard from him since he left us before the storm. So we can only assume he didn't make it."

There was only one person he could've been talking about. My face burned. It was a sham! It was a sham, and everyone played along, nodded gravely like they actually believed him. The elders wouldn't be so bold as to come out and say, "We made an example of him." But they had. Uncle M had told me they had, and in the shadows, regardless of what he was saying out in the open, this wriggling bottom-feeder, "Uncle" to us all, would make it known what had really happened and why.

I watched the proceedings of the Circle numbly, watched the illusion of "collectivism" for what it was: a play performed by its own writers, its own directors, who could barely be bothered to deliver their lines with any real conviction. Except nobody, not even the elders who had set it in motion, seemed to see it as such.

"But here's the thing, friends," Uncle M continued in his brief and insincere eulogy. Friends! Without a trace of irony. "The tower could still be out there. The weather's fair, friends. And if my calculations are right—and they haven't failed us yet, have they, friends?—if my calculations are right, let's not let the last act of this treasured member of our community be in vain! With the amount of electricity that device should harness, there's no telling what we could build! How much progress we could make!"

"Hear, hear!" someone actually shouted. Others followed, and not just the elders. My god, he was really getting away with this. Were they really going to trample over the body of our hardest worker, our sacrificial lamb, to take advantage of the stupid machine he'd been manipulated into dying for? I'd never seen Uncle M so eloquent before, so capable of seizing a moment and saying all the right things, out in the open in front of everyone. He must have had help. He hadn't written this script alone.

"It won't take much," he said, arms spread. "Just one or two—"

"I'll go," I shouted, rising amid the scandalized murmurs of the crowd. The homosexual had emerged from his chrysalis to stir things up again.

Uncle M opened his mouth as if to protest, but I continued, "Who else knows the coast as well as I do? And The Archipelago? If Oak's still out there, lost or unconscious or worse . . ." I paused for effect, sweeping my gaze over the circle, dodging Uncle M's eyes. "Who'd know better where to look?"

I'd like to say there was thunderous applause, but even if anyone had clapped, it would have been a hundred people in the open air on a windy day. Triumph looked more like many thoughtful glances, then a vote by a show of hands in which even most of the elders consented. "Makes sense," someone said, and I wasn't sure whether this person was hoping I, too, would fail, or if they recognized that although they weren't talking about it, Oak had been sent on his fool's errand because of his friendship with me. Either way, I was grateful. Others nodded along. I was to leave at dawn.

Afterward, hardly anyone spoke to me, especially not the men. I didn't blame them after what had happened to Oak because of me. I took my dinner by one of the fires, sitting alone on damp grass, watching people I'd known my whole life talk around me as if I were a ghost. If there's no one to notice we're here, what are we if not ghosts? I'd spent my life believing the people around me were all that could keep me safe, doing everything I could to keep them safe, too. To value our survival above all else. It didn't feel like "ours" anymore. I went to bed early.

Sunrise. I made my way downhill in the hazy green of the morning pollution, walking toward the coast without fanfare or farewell. I dragged a canoe full of enough food for a couple of days but little else—only Uncle M's drawing of the lightweight disk attached to its retractable tower and, of course, my notebooks. I of all people understood the importance of cataloguing experiences. As an archivist, I hoped at least in some small way I could contribute to the understanding of future generations, not only through the books I took notes on, but by journaling furiously, when I could find a free moment, about the things that happened to me. There are reasons to keep writing, even when the world has fallen apart. There was no telling who would stumble across something, be helped by it, like how the farmers who kept records of their goings-on never could have known they'd help keep the human race alive long after their own demise.

Anyway, I like to write. I think I'm pretty good at it.

It didn't take a genius to get to the coast from The Compound. The line of trees to my left ensured that I was going in a straight line. I thought pityingly of Oak, dragging a supposedly "light" metal contraption along with his canoe, a death march with two crosses to bear, one metal, one plastic. Dragging the canoe was awkward enough, and after the hurricane, an abundance of errant branches and tree trunks blocked my way. Even the mild November sun pounded into my back an hour in, the kind of sun we did our best to shield ourselves from. According to science texts I'd read and from the word of our elders, the sun burned more fiercely, cancerously, than in our ancestors' day. Other dangers lurked in this peaceful, post-storm landscape. Gale force winds could whip around me at any moment, flinging the worst of the debris at my unprotected head. Though we seldom worried about dangerous wildlife—so little remained that there was little statistical possibility of running into any large beasts—the kinds of creatures that survive an apocalypse as thorough as The Great Thaw are accustomed to extreme conditions to begin with. Scorpions and Gila monsters who suddenly find their desert domains expanding might spill over into even the grassiest of hills. All these and more we risked when we left The Compound, and I was no less vulnerable to them even after frequent visits to The Archipelago. But small, slender Oak would have been ever more vulnerable than I.

As I scanned the debris for anything that crawled, bit, or stung, a different existential threat occupied my thoughts. Supposing Uncle M's battery contraption was still intact, did I destroy it for revenge? Or did I bring it home safely, winning back the favor of the folks at The Compound? Did I return to the only safe place I'd ever known? Pull back the curtain, shine a light on the strings wrapped around the wrinkled fingers of our elders (I think that's how puppets work—I've only ever read about them)? I had to hope that others would listen, that enough of us with open eyes could set things right, to value the human life in front of us before its propagation.

And then there was the absurd hope that Oak was still alive, lost somewhere in The Archipelago. What then? We couldn't exactly walk back arm in arm and hope we'd seen the end of it. And no, I wasn't in denial. I'd accepted that he was dead the moment he'd said he was leaving. Still, I had hope.

I made it to the coast by the afternoon. Putrid water lapped the grass. The line of trees at my left continued into the sea, each tree sinking further beneath the waves until their shaggy tops poked through the oily surface of the ocean, through the plastic and paper and filth our ancestors had left us with. I'd read of beaches, even seen photographs of them: strips of land at the edge of the water covered in rocks and shells that the rolling waves had pulverized into a fine grain. Our ancestors used to lie seminude at the water's edge getting skin cancer so the sun would change the shade of their skin. Surveying the grassy slope interrupted by stinking grayish water, where bottles bobbed atop the sea foam—the beaches of old were all underwater, by then—I smiled at the thought that anyone would spend their time around this enormous toxic trash receptacle.

The biggest danger of rowing to The Archipelago was hardly what you'd expect of a massive climate apocalypse. As far as we knew, no hideously mutated, violent beasts of leviathan-like proportions had risen from the ashes of civilization, waiting to drag its stragglers to the depths. Capsizing, however, was a very real concern, and it was the reason sending Oak out during a hurricane was so obviously a death sentence. Capsizing most likely meant you and your paddle would be tangled in one of the endless webs of plastic waste, unable to grab hold of your vessel in time to right it as the current snatched it away. Also, the creatures our ancestors had named jellyfish—which were neither fish nor made of any kind of gelatin—were one of a handful of living beings we knew about that had truly thrived in the warming of the seas. These graceful, delicate creatures sometimes drifted through the webs of plastic in equally flimsy swarms, and a critical mass of them merely brushing up against you, depending on its species, could cause anything from excruciating pain to paralysis to cardiac arrest. No matter how many times I'd rowed this path, my blood still spiked each time a larger wave rolled beneath me.

Uncle M had instructed Oak to row the battery tower out about two miles offshore, halfway between the edge of the trees and The Archipelago. Once I got my canoe over the mounds of junk metal, tangled plastic bags bearing words like "HappyMart" and "THANK YOU!"—*Thank you for bringing civilization closer to its inevitable destruction!*—it was a straight shot. The farther out I went, the less trash floated about, but it was always with me, like a shadow. Plastic waste: unlike the ghosts in the old storybooks, this ghost of our ancestors wouldn't go away, no matter how much we atoned for their past transgressions.

The tower wasn't there. I paddled about halfway to the Archipelago. No net-like tower of lightweight metal, expanded like an accordion, swayed in the waves. Behind me: the rolling hills of the coast rose on the horizon. Ahead of me: The Archipelago's spires pierced the air. Around me: nothing but the trash. I hadn't really prepared for the possibility of turning up completely empty-handed. A number of things could've happened. Uncle M could've undershot the length of the anchor's chain. The storm's winds could've been too strong for it. Or, of course, the storm could've beat Oak to the coast. Would he have gone for it anyway, resigning himself to his fate, capsizing in the white-capped waves while he towed the collapsed tower on its floating disk behind him? I wasn't ready to consider that just yet.

I paddled toward The Archipelago, where I'd start by looking for the tower on the shorelines—and maybe, by way of finding that, Oak. The tower would be a start. I couldn't exactly ask around, *Hey, have you seen this man whose features bear a striking resemblance to whitewashed images of the Christ?* Not that many around here would've seen a painting of our ancestors' "savior" or known what they were looking at if they had. They'd think me some sort of postapocalypse preacher, and anyway, they'd probably frisk me for supplies. How to describe the people of The Archipelago? They were, well . . . conditions were tougher out there. I'd once had to surrender the books I'd found to a woman bearing a machete, who demanded them for kindling. Kindling! Can you imagine? I knew better than others at The Compound, who painted this picture of the dwellers of this decayed city as savages, as cannibals, even. But really, they were brutal pragmatists.

What used to be a city of tall hills now rose from the trash-riddled sea, like the mottled spine of a great beast who'd drowned beneath the waves or perhaps slept, waiting to rise. The central islands provided the highest ground and, therefore, the best shelter. I navigated through narrow channels flanked on either side by broken-down houses on hills, built so close together they looked squished. Little flitting shapes wove through the beams of porches and in the shadows behind broken windows: cats, the only creatures native to the city to survive The Great Thaw, who no doubt had licked the bones of every human corpse clean years ago. One of the little islands featured homes burned utterly to their foundations, with a single house inexplicably standing.

Back then, cities were like fortresses to protect against the untamable wilderness. Now, compared to the placid plains that surrounded The Compound, The Archipelago was the real wilderness.

I searched with little plan. The problem was that Oak didn't know The Archipelago like I did. I could search the most logical hideouts, the buildings with the strongest foundations or the little buildings sheltered from the wind in the shadow of larger ones, but Oak wouldn't know what to look for, especially if he'd come here in the desperation of escaping an ever-intensifying hurricane. I spent most of the day searching the concrete shores for a washed-up canoe. And yes, for a body. I found neither.

By dusk, in need of a morale boost and a place to sleep, I reached one of my favorite little islands. High on a hill, through overgrown woods, was a space called a "botanical garden," where our ancestors planted all sorts of crazy exotic vegetation and built pathways so they could wander around, feeling connected to the natural world that they slowly destroyed. It was here, leaving my canoe in some bushes and climbing up the hill beneath the cover of thick trees and quickly falling darkness, that I stumbled upon them.

I watched from the shadows of the trees as a group of twenty-ish people huddled around someone I couldn't quite make out in the dark from behind. They stood before a structure, unmistakable against the last reds in the sky: a short tower with a web-like network of thin metal bars that matched Uncle M's sketch, attached at its base to a disk of rubber and metal. About an arm's length in diameter. Sleek enough for a single person to drag down a hill.

I saw a huge blue spark, accompanied by a thunder-like crackle, cause the pile of logs to go up in flames immediately, illuminating everything. The gasping faces, the cable running from the disk and tower to the flames, and Oak, amid the amazed faces of the crowd in the light of the fire. He rose from the ground, brushing dirt from his knees.

It wasn't prudence, at first, that kept me from springing from the bushes, bounding across the lawn, and throwing myself at him. I was paralyzed. Here was the friend I'd convinced myself was both dead and the posthumous love of my life. Looking at him now, I realized neither was true. I felt happy to see him, but I didn't feel the urge to gallop toward him, our mouths colliding in a lifetime of unrealized passion as I'd fantasized about in my three days of solitude. In fact, I wasn't so sure about kissing him, now. What would his breath smell like after three days away from the peppermint water of The Compound? My eyes filled with tears of . . . what was it? Relief that all was as it should be between us? Or was it disappointment that I didn't feel that burning ache for him that I'd felt when I'd slept alone in his bed, played his guitar in the dark, imagined his touch against mine? Then, there was the question of these strangers; in addition to Oak's audience, others milled about, talking, rolling out mats, carrying themselves with none of the aggression or guardedness of others I'd seen around here at The Archipelago. Still, outside of The Compound, one could never be too certain.

But then again, if the past two days had taught me anything, it was that I couldn't be too certain of anything *inside* of The Compound, either.

I waited until night fully fell, keeping my eyes on Oak all the time, until I crept out into the open field straight toward him, like I belonged. I passed unnoticed. I'd had plenty of practice as a ghost in the last few days.

He stood by the fire talking with two men, their backs to

me, and here is where I took the risk, stepping fully into the fire's ring of light and calling his name. All three figures turned to me, the fire at their backs obscuring their faces in the shadow. And just as the two men's posture went defensive, legs back in unison like leopards preparing to spring, Oak leapt at me instead, his arms wrapping around my neck and his legs wrapping around my waist in a harmless embrace. I staggered back in the grass with the weight of his affection, but I didn't fall. The weight of his slender body was familiar. He'd never been able to tackle me.

"I didn't know how," he said into my ear in a low voice, "but I hoped you'd find me." He assured the others that I was a friend. He led me by the hand to the edge of the fire he'd sparked and sat in the grass with me. I'll admit his touch confused me, because it felt good and right, but also foreign. It was nothing like the powerful electricity I'd expect to feel if I were in love with someone. Then again, how would I know? It was, well . . . it was something. His touch made me nervous in a way it never had before.

He touched my elbow, and shoulder, and even my knee as he described sleeping under the stars in the company of these kind people, who'd found him at the shore curled around the base of the tower. It was a sort of ceasefire zone, where people came and went and shared their skills, scattering to personal hiding places about The Archipelago when storms came. It sounded nice, if a bit disorganized, notably less secure than The Compound. Finally, he came out with it:

"I feel wanted here. Needed. Like I have a lot to give."

I opened my mouth to protest, that he was *needed* at The Compound, and then I remembered what they did to him because of me. *We can always make more hands,* Uncle M had said. Then, I almost said that *I* wanted him, but truly I was confused. I'd convinced myself that I did want him, romantically, and then I'd seen him from the trees and decided I didn't, but then, here, in the firelight, with his fingertips brushing my knuckle, I didn't understand what I wanted. Still, I knew that I needed him.

So I said nothing. And he said nothing. And we looked at one another. And the fire popped and cracked.

"If you want to go back tomorrow," he said carefully, "you can take the tower. It's not good for much besides starting fires, without anything to power up."

"If?" I repeated, not knowing what else to say. It was the first time I'd considered that as a serious option. Leave the safety of The Compound? For what? All my life, I'd been taught even pride and principle were laid down at the altar of the god of survival. On the other hand, how safe was it, really, for people like me, if Oak could be sent out to die after some secret agreement made in the shadows around the illuminated pages of a book some elders considered holy?

He pointed his smile toward the ground. "They might have a lot to learn from us here. Both of us."

God, if only he'd just say it. I got bold. One of us had to. "Is that what *you* want?"

He surprised me by reaching his hands forward and taking mine. "What I want is for you to stay here with us for a couple nights in the open air, under the stars. And then, we'll see what you want. What we both want. Unless you're in a big hurry to get back."

"Are you really going to stay here?"

"At least for a little while."

"What if they turn out to be just as bad as the folks at The Compound? Or worse?"

"Then we'll go somewhere else." He caught himself. "Or I will."

"Are you saying we'd be better off as nomads? The weather being what it is?"

"I'm not saying anything. Just that I might want to try. And maybe you might, too."

Oh, Oak. Believe it or not, this was him trying to be direct.

I looked at our fingers interlaced, looked at his face, the Oak I knew, never one to confront something head-on. The Oak I knew, whose gestures of affection right now would get us *both* sent on a fool's errand of certain death back at The Compound. The Oak I knew, alive and well. The Oak I knew, but different. Freer. As if who he'd been at The Compound had been a mere ghost of his whole self. And he was still a mystery to me, Oak was. After my eternal three days of confinement poring over it, I'd expected everything to become clear if I found him alive. But I still had no idea whether he really had feelings for me, whether I even had feelings for him. I had no idea what parts of myself I'd have to better conceal for the safety of The Compound, let alone what parts of myself might come to light away from it. Would I like what I became? I didn't know. Couldn't. Nor did I know that anyone at The Compound would listen to me if I told them what had really happened, what had always been happening under our noses, who had been calling the shots in the name of our god of survival, our demigod of safety, our supposedly sacred reverence for human life.

A hurricane had robbed me of that certainty, and a hurricane really did take Oak from me, too, in a way—it took the Oak I knew and replaced him with someone strange but not unfamiliar.

But what I did know? I knew that at The Compound, we'd tried the return to something like society as it once was, and we'd seen what else had returned with it. I knew what it felt like in my belly to have Oak's hand in mine, that here whatever I decided I felt about Oak himself, I liked the thrill of *this* feeling well enough to want it more. So I decided, well, I thought I could spare a couple nights here with him under the stars. At the very least.

THE AGE OF OCEANUS

Everyone would remember where they were the day the first river goddess died.

The viral video came from Mexico, spreading first across the internet and then across the news, as such things go. It was the slightest bit grainy, caught at the early stages of dusk with what must have been a cellular phone. Chalchiuhtlicue, a goddess long since presumed dead along with most of the Aztec tradition, dragged herself onto the muddy bank of the Rio Grande, jade skirt slicked with oil and winged headdress tangled with plastic six-pack rings that captured other plastic jetsam of a species driving itself, and its world, to extinction. Chalchiuhtlicue managed to stand, stagger a hunched step, and lift her face to the camera with her mouth open in a silent plea before she fell face-first in the mud.

All this came accompanied, of course, with cries of surprise in the crisp sibilance of Northern Mexican Spanish, *"Mira, mira, que es eso?"* According to sources, this was not the only sighting of Chalchiuhtlicue in the last decade. Other locals reported having seen the wide-hipped *diosa,* in varying states of filth. A drilling technician's wife even reported a midnight sighting of Chalchiuhtlicue in which the goddess opened her mouth, allegedly with a look of desperate warning on her face, when heaps of stinking fish poured, dead, from her mouth.

It was not the first sighting, but it was the only one with clear footage, decisively clearer than any clips of UFOs or Yetis or Nessies or *chupacabras* or ghosts or any other wonders of cryptozoology, conspiracy, myth, or religion. However, it would be the last sighting of the living goddess, Chalchiuhtlicue: for there she lay, face down in a heap of oil and trash and mud, and there she would remain.

In the weeks following the death of Chalchiuhtlicue, videos and photographs and reported sightings of other dying river goddesses poured into news stations. Images of increasing quality emerged as something of a sport developed, like tornado chasing or whale watching, wherein professional videographers and hobby photographers camped out along the world's most significant and polluted rivers in the hope of capturing the perfect shot. Ganga making one last ride past Rishikesh, the lotus in her hand wilted, her crocodile steed coughing up what could only be described as human sewage, Ganga herself shivering with the cold of death in spite of the mid-October heat. The hag Peg Powler rising from the River Tees in Dinsdale Park at sunset, water steaming against her skin that bulged with what looked like the embers of coal beneath it, her green hair slashing out like serpents and wrapping around nearby children in an attempt to drag them with her into death as their parents tugged and tugged (leading viewers to wonder what kind of person would stand by and film this), until her hair finally flopped to the ground like limp spaghetti as the burning coals inside her glowed brighter, the steam around her thickened, and finally she plopped into the water and floated away, burnt like a pork roast left in for too long. Still shots of Oba lying akimbo atop the dam at the Ogbomoso reservoir. And the sightings kept coming.

News pundits debated the veracity of the videos; politicians largely ignored them; conspiracy theories developed; cults formed; scientists shook their heads, for even if they could come up with some explanation for what seemed like another worldwide natural disaster, the ever-changing climate had proven time and again that nobody with enough power would listen.

Still, one thing was certain: everybody remembered where they were when they saw Chalchiuhtlicue die, and even those who would deny what they saw felt a clenching somewhere between their heart and their belly, a voice deep down telling them that the time to reverse the tides of the changing world had passed. In its place, a new age—one of learning to survive in a dying world or choosing to die with it—had begun.

ACKNOWLEDGMENTS

The body of work that comprises *Tea Leaves* spans approximately a decade of life, as well as a lifetime before that of preparation and failed projects. I imagine that many first collections are like this one was for me: not only the work itself, but the process of becoming who I am as a writer and wading through many, many stories and rehashings of those stories to get there. Thus, I owe this particular collection not only to the people who helped me make these stories better, but to the people who helped me pave a pathway to being an author writ large and who encouraged me to be better when my stories were barely better than gimmicks.

While I'm grateful to my whole family, my mother is one of nine children, so I'll mention a few key figures who had a hand in my development as an artist and thus the path to this specific book. My parents, Sue and Don Budenz, are of course to blame for bringing me into the world in the first place, but it is their relentless work ethic and desire to make a good life for their kids that allowed me to nourish my creativity and try to make something lasting of it. When my mother gave me my first creative writing journal, she said, "Do something meaningful with it." It is because of my parents that I understand the importance of living a meaningful life rather than an easy one. I owe them everything for that just as much as I owe them for the tough love they gave me about the life of an artist—*that's fine, but find something to do that will make a living in the meantime.*

I'm grateful to them, and to my eternal twin Alex who inspires me daily and who hasn't missed a play, a chapbook release, or a show if she can help it. I truly feel that since birth, Alex has believed in me and my potential even when it felt no one else would, and having such a strong bond has saved my life more times than I can count. My grandfather, Neal Kay, also encouraged my creative pursuits from an early age—he still sends me the odd vintage rhyming dictionary or diagram of the circle of fifths every now and again. My Uncle Josh helped me see what a creative career could look like. He taught me photomanipulation and synth composition when I was a preteen, and together with my Aunt Aimee and Aunt Julie he is probably the reason I have any decent taste in film or music.

Numerous friends and colleagues have contributed to the success of the stories in this collection, providing encouragement to persist and keen editorial eyes. Leanne Gossels and Emily Bihl are two of my earliest supporters and writer pals. Leanne in particular was the first to point out value in my work as well as to let me know when I was full of shit. "I can just tell that *you* don't even buy it," she once told me about an ending I'd totally phoned in when we were undergrads. She was always right. I have many colleagues to thank from my MFA program, but especially my yearly Dream Team writing group: Isabelle Barany (our fearless leader), Marissa Bleiler, and Christopher Romaguera. It is rare to find a group of writers so relentlessly driven to understand what a story is trying to be and help it to *be that* as best as it can. If any of the stories in this collection don't suck, those three are probably responsible. I'd be remiss not to mention Ty Baniewicz, whose dear friendship and brilliant mind have provided endless hours of inspiration—from dreamy talks about the writing life to heated late-night debates over what school of writing gets to claim Flannery O'Connor. These friends and colleagues pushed me to revise the hell out of these stories, to think critically about what I wanted to put into the world, and to stop moping around and push past rejection.

I am grateful to several mentors along the way, starting with some key players in the University of New Orleans Creative Writing Workshop. I am especially grateful to Joanna Leake for understanding and believing in my work, to Barb Johnson for calling me on my bullshit, and to M.O. Walsh (a.k.a. Neal) for the baptism by fire. Sorry, Neal—I kept the one about the croutons in. I would be remiss not to mention Richard Goodman, too, whose nonfiction workshop may not have had direct bearing on these stories but whose depth of kindness, compassion, and love came at a crucial time in my writing career and whose environmental writing "field trip" quite literally changed my life. Because of Richard, I see the artist's role in the fight against environmental destruction as clearly as I see the activist's, and I strive to carry on both mantles where I can. I'd like to acknowledge Jessica Anya Blau, Joe Martin, and Eric Puchner, as well, the first undergraduate professors who made me believe a career in writing and the arts was possible for me.

Thanks to my editor, Michael Nava, who took a chance on this debut short story collection by a bona fide weirdo and who offered thoughtful, incisive, and diplomatic feedback along the way. To dave ring, whose *Broken Metropolis* anthology was one of the first projects that made me feel like a "real" writer, and Michael Tager, another editor and friend whose indefatigable ability to connect writers with one another or with opportunities has been invaluable in the early stages of my artistic career. I've worked with many editors of journals and anthologies over the years, but these three have provided me with transformative opportunities. I'm grateful for that.

Thank you to anyone who has ever read my work and told

me it was worth something (or told me exactly why it wasn't). There are countless others—friends and frenemies and former lovers—to whom I owe plenty of inspiration and perhaps an apology. If you read this collection and suspect you might see pieces of yourself in here, don't ask me about it. I'll never tell.

ABOUT THE AUTHOR

Jacob Budenz is a Baltimore-based writer, actor, director, musician, and performance artist with an MFA in Creative Writing from The University of New Orleans and a BA in Writing Seminars and Spanish from Johns Hopkins University. As a resident actor with the Baltimore Annex Theater from 2012-2017, Jacob was involved in several acclaimed productions, including his original adaptation of *The Master and Margarita* which appeared on *Baltimore City Paper's* Top Ten Staged Productions of 2016. His poetry chapbook, *Pastel Witcheries,* debuted in 2018 with Seven Kitchens Press, and an extended edition called *Spellwork for the Modern Pastel Witch* was one of the winners of the Hard to Swallow Chapbook Contest at Birds Piled Loosely Press.

Among other things, Jacob Budenz's work focuses heavily on dreams, storytelling, the occult, mysticism, queerness, the grotesque, and the unfamiliar. His work in all mediums seeks to empower audiences and move them to experience dramatic catharsis, while exploring the lives of society's outliers. He has performed all over Baltimore, as well as New York, Pennsylvania, DC, New Orleans, and Spain. His writing has been published in presses such as Assaracus and Polychrome Ink, and his work has been commissioned or recognized by organizations such as *The Writer's Digest,* The Baltimore Museum of Art, and Spark Creative Anthologies.

Amble Press, an imprint of Bywater Books, publishes fiction and narrative nonfiction by LGBTQ writers, with a primary, though not exclusive, focus on LGBTQ writers of color. For more information on our titles, authors, and mission, please visit our website.

www.amblepressbooks.com

www.ingramcontent.com/pod-product-compliance
Lightning Source LLC
Chambersburg PA
CBHW020123120726
47903CB00007B/2083

* 9 7 8 1 6 1 2 9 4 2 7 5 9 *